GROWING UP
PUERTO RICAN

ALSO FROM WILLIAM MORROW

Growing Up Asian American
Growing Up Chicana / Chicano
Growing Up Jewish
Growing Up Native American

GROWING UP PUERTO RICAN

An Anthology

Edited and with an Introduction by
JOY L. DE JESÚS

Foreword by
ED VEGA

WILLIAM MORROW AND COMPANY, INC.
NEW YORK

A list of permissions, constituting a continuation of the copyright page, appears
on pages 231–233.

Library of Congress Cataloging-in-Publication Data

Growing up Puerto Rican : an anthology / edited and with an
    introduction by Joy L. De Jesús ; foreword by Ed Vega.
        p.   cm.
    ISBN 0-688-13740-7
    1. American literature—Puerto Rican authors.   2. Puerto Ricans—
United States—Literary collections.   3. Puerto Rican children—
Literary collections.   4. Puerto Rican youth—Literary collections.
I. De Jesús, Joy.
PS508.P84G76   1997
813—dc21   96-36885
                                                              CIP

Printed in the United States of America

First Edition

1   2   3   4   5   6   7   8   9   10

FOREWORD

GROWING UP IN ANY ENVIRONMENT INVOLVES CONTRADICTIONS, paradoxes, and a certain amount of confusion before one steps fully into adulthood. However, any subject about Puerto Rico and its relation to the United States is even more complex. Facile interpretations, stock answers, and chauvinistic posturing do not serve the subject well. The purity and honesty of the fiction writer, however, imbued with a need to place things in their proper context, gives us a crystal-clear view into the soul of a culture.

This anthology is not a canon of Puerto Rican literature. Rather, it is intended to offer insights into the island and the diasporic aspects of our culture in a variety of social settings. Without pretense, *Growing Up Puerto Rican* presents the more literary writings of Puerto Rico. At the same time, it introduces some newer Puerto Rican authors and writers whose work has not been widely published. Alba Ambert, Julio Marzán, Yvonne V. Sapia, Aurora Levins Morales, and Rodney Morales, for example, have not yet had the national and international exposure they deserve for their fiction.

The writers in this anthology, each in his or her own style, use the magnifying lens of their personal experience to amplify the problems that beset the passage from childhood to adulthood, from innocence to sophistication, from sociopolitical naïveté to critical analysis of the complex environment and culture that has shaped them.

Growing up in the U.S. as a member of an ethnic group, especially if one is Puerto Rican, places the individual within the biggest contradiction, that of personal identity. Does one remain part of the family, the peer group, and the ethnic configuration of one's culture? Or does one venture into the larger United States society to become an American, a misnomer to be sure since the United States is only one sociopolitical entity within the hemisphere that is North and South America and includes citizens of over thirty countries, all with the right to call themselves Americans?

There are two cultural and political issues that incense many of our people who identify themselves as Puerto Ricans. One is the juxtaposition of island to mainland. For people who consider Puerto Rico a colony of the U.S. and cherish the idea of eventual independence for our homeland, the term *mainland* is a capitulation of sovereignty, for it means we are part of the United States when in effect we are a separate culture and nation, notwithstanding the political and economic hegemony that the United States has exercised over the island and its people since 1898 when Puerto Rico was annexed after the Spanish-American War.

The other term that reeks of the need for the United States to homogenize its people is the term "people of color." Growing up in Puerto Rico I was always aware of my father's dignity, character, and kindness and my mother's quiet strength, gentleness, and fierce determination to see her family triumph. Not until I came to the United States at age thirteen did I come to realize that my mother was considered white and that my father, because of his African features, was considered black. Where did this place me? The answer became very simple and perhaps therein lies one of the great strengths of Puerto Rican culture in the United States. I simply became even more Puerto Rican. The rejection of many Puerto Ricans by the greater society because of color becomes both a hurt and a shield. Rather than having to choose, like hundreds of thousands of others with African heritage, we identify, above all else, with the culture of our nation, Puerto Rico. For an island thirty-five by one hundred miles, Puerto Rico should be a cultural dwarf. But our culture has a rich musical heritage with well over a hundred forms of classical, folk, and popular interpretations; a history of fine art that boasts classical, impressionist, and abstract expressionists; and a tradition of literature, unequaled by a place so small, that highlights poetry, the short story, the literary essay, the novel, and drama dating back several centuries. Cultural pride is a significant part of the Puerto Rican identity.

When I was growing up in Puerto Rico until age thirteen and had the great good fortune to have parents who were involved in the arts and politics, our dining room table was ablaze with discussion on the many issues of our island's society and its relationship to the United States. For the first ten years of my life I heard about the Ponce Massacre almost weekly. The event took place in 1937 when I was a year old and my mother and father—a graduate of the University of Puerto Rico and the Baptist Seminary—were living in the town of Ponce while my father exercised pastorship of a rural community. That I grew up a Protestant speaks volumes about the intrusion of United States culture into a formerly Catholic country. My father, an avowed socialist and follower of Pedro Albizu Campos, was eager to join the demonstrations, but my mother opposed his joining the march, much as she opposed his becoming a chaplain in the United States Army during World War II, each time pointing to the contradictions of his acts. The 65th Regiment, composed solely of Puerto Ricans, fought gallantly in both World War II and the Korean War. To date it is the most decorated regiment in the history of the United States.

For those of us for whom the historical event of the Ponce Massacre has become embedded in our psyches as a metaphor for the relationship between the United States and Puerto Rico, reading Ana Lydia Vega's "Liliane's Sunday" places one into the politically fraught time once again. Nearly fifty years after the Ponce Massacre, Abraham Rodríguez, Jr., born and raised in the Bronx, undoubtedly one of the best of the third generation of Puerto Rican writers whose work is in English, crafts the beautiful and touching "Boy Without a Flag" about the ambiguity of being Puerto Rican but living away from the Island.

My great-grandfather, Cesareo Martínez, was an abolitionist. An integral part of the Lares Revolt, he opposed the United States when its forces landed in the port of Guanica in 1898. During the revolt to liberate Puerto Rico from Spain in 1863, his task was to ride into farms and estates and, with gun in hand, liberate the slaves in the hopes that they would join the revolution. In many ways, this explains why my father, a person of obvious African heritage, was loved so dearly in my maternal grandmother's home. Cesareo Martínez's granddaughter, my mother, was instructed in the English language all through her primary and high school years, but knew little English, a testament to the will to resist the efforts of colonization, not an unusual occurrence among most of the women of her generation. Upon coming to the United States, however, she quickly learned the language and became a fluent speaker and writer. In 1950, one year after her arrival, she entered a contest sponsored by Alexander's Department Store and won an eight-inch television set with a magnifying glass. We were the only family in our Bronx Irish neighborhood with a TV set.

It is important to place the stories in this anthology into a historical context in order to understand some of the writers' concerns. During the nineteenth century Puerto Ricans struggled to free themselves from Spanish rule and its strangling economic policies. On September 23, 1868, a citizens' militia in the central mountains of Puerto Rico seized power from the Spaniards in the now famous Grito de Lares uprising and declared the Republic of Puerto Rico. While the efforts were thwarted by stronger military might, the event fixed in the psyche of the nation a rallying point for its need to become free of Spanish rule. The struggle was carried on for the next thirty years, culminating with the November 20, 1897, granting by Spain of a Charter of Autonomy to Puerto Rico. The charter was a prelude to the independence Puerto Rico would ultimately have achieved.

With the Spanish-American War and the defeat of Spain at the hands of the United States, Puerto Rico became a possession of the United States. While the independence of Cuba from Spain was accepted by the United States, Puerto Rico, a more strategically situated island, was absorbed into United States control. The United States immediately set about the colonization of the island, changing its name to Porto Rico, a name that was not to change again to Puerto Rico until 1932. English became the mandatory language and for years citizens struggled with the contradiction of carrying out all its daily life in the Spanish language and being instructed in English.

It is no surprise then that out of historical necessity, the literature of

Puerto Rico exists in two languages. While other ethnic groups in the United States have been assimilated linguistically and write primarily in English, nearly all of the writers in this anthology are bilingual. Befitting the duality of expression, we present six of the writers here in translation from the Spanish, the language in which they write. The writers who appear in translation, particularly those of the seventies generation, speak English, and Pedro Juan Soto, who belongs to the fifties generation, was raised in part in the United States. Unlike other ethnic groups who have reinvented themselves in the United States, Puerto Ricans, despite the fact that some speak Spanish while others communicate in English, have a rich tradition of letters uniting them. From its origins as a separate Creole literature with the publications of "El Gíbaro" by Manuel Alonso in 1849 until the publication of Rosario Ferré's *The House in the Lagoon* in 1995, there is a century and a half of Puerto Rican literature, first in Spanish and then in English.

The translation of Puerto Rican writers from Spanish to English presents another look into the political aspect of our relationship to the United States. It is significant that during Operation Bootstrap, the United States' attempt to help the Puerto Rican economy, there was an effort to translate the writers from the fifties, most of whom are men. The United State, having accomplished its goal of subjecting Puerto Rico to a seeming acceptance of Anglo culture and alleged democracy, then allowed the women writers to come to light and has been translating their work into English since the seventies.

Thus Magali García Ramis, Rosario Ferré, and Ana Lydia Vega are included in this anthology. While the women have their male counterparts from the seventies, the only ones thus far translated are Luis Rafael Sánchez, whose highly acclaimed *Macho Camacho's Beat* was translated several years back, and the late Manuel Ramos Otero, a significant literary figure who lived in the United States, wrote passionately in Spanish about the gay experience, and returned to Puerto Rico to die, the victim of AIDS. He leaves behind a rich legacy of writing. Unfortunately, what could have been included in this anthology as it pertains to growing up has yet to be translated. The same is true of Sánchez and his body of work. There are a number of other male writers from that generation who could easily be translated, their work being of equal quality to the women's. The work of Edgardo Rodriguez Juliá comes to mind as one of high literary value.

This anthology creates as broad a spectrum of writing as possible, but finding pieces about growing up Puerto Rican that had been previously published in English, the criteria in selecting the stories, was challenging. What is it about growing up Puerto Rican in the United States that has caused such a minuscule literary output? I am defining as literary that which uses crafted and poetic language as its impetus. The Puerto Rican immigrants to both Hawaii and the continental United States were for the most part illiterate peasants from the highlands of Puerto Rico or poorly educated black and racially mixed people from the coast and urban centers, factors that undoubtedly influenced their decisions to eschew becoming writers. In contrast, the writers who remained in Puerto Rico and write in Spanish and who are presented in translation to English are almost always college graduates with a sound grounding in the values of the middle and upper classes of Puerto Rico. The ability and desire to write literature requires time to read and study and the leisure to craft the language, two commodities not readily afforded a struggling class grounded in poverty.

My own history as a writer is a curious one. Raised in a literary household where poets were in and out of our home, I went into a linguistic silence from thirteen until I began writing again at about age twenty-two. Other than academic work in college, I wrote fiction secretly until I finally published my first short story at age forty-one. I have steadfastly refused to write immigrant testimonial books in the hopes of elevating our experience to the level of inventiveness required for a literature. In this anthology we can see a trajectory from the testimonial to the purely fictional.

Because of the political situation of Puerto Ricans in the United States, and because of cultural prejudice against our ethnic group, there has been a stand on the part of our community to view any Puerto Rican writing in English as sacred. Little self-reflection has taken place and very seldom is critical analysis the order of the day. In the past, criticism has been in the hands of sociologists whose main agenda is sociopolitical. The particular slant of defensiveness in the face of perceived or real attacks on our people has caused publishers to look at the writing one-dimensionally and not to expect more literary coherence on the part of Puerto Rican writers. In the past decade, two critics and professors of literature, Margarite Fernández Olmos and Lizabeth Paravisini-Gebert, have brought their substantial critical skills to an examination of our literature in English. Their work serves as an example for greater critical literary analysis and as a call for more literary Puerto Rican writing.

Of all the groups in the United States, Puerto Ricans present the greatest problem in terms of being categorized as ethnic citizens of the United States. The vogue is to say Asian American, African American, and so on. It is a concession to diversity, an all-inclusiveness and constitutional absorption into the United States. The term Puerto Rican–American is not only linguistically clumsy, but one fraught with confusion. Puerto Ricans became citizens of the United States on February 20, 1917, and do not go through the naturalization process. Because of the proximity to the United States, Puerto Ricans growing up in New York, for example, travel back and forth to the Island and live in both cultures with as much ease as we go from Spanish to English.

In this anthology the bridge between the two existences, languages, and cultures is the novelist and short story writer Pedro Juan Soto, who wrote "The Champ." Soto was born on the Island, lived in New York, and returned to the Island to stay.

But what unifies these writers more than anything is the experience of being Puerto Rican regardless of where one resides. Whether we are reading Jesús Colón's "Kipling and I" about the struggles of a young man in the thirties and forties in New York City or Rodney Morales's "Ship of Dreams," in which Puerto Rican culture appears peripherally as an obsessive influence in a young Japanese boy's curiosity about Puerto Rican music and a Puerto Rican girl, we see the influence of our culture. Colón was not only a pioneer of the migration from Puerto Rico to the United States, but also the father of our literature in English. Morales, on the other hand, is the product of a little-known piece of the Puerto Rican diaspora to Hawaii that resulted when, in the 1890s, the United States passed anti-Asian exclusionary laws. By 1900 the Hawaii Sugar Growers Association was feeling the dearth of cheap labor and went to the new United States colony. In one of the darkest and best kept secrets of the colonial Puerto Rican experience, in 1900–1901 the United States brought over ten thousand Puerto Rican men, women, and children to the Hawaiian Islands to work in the sugar cane plantations, often splitting up families and creating a class of cheap labor. Today, the descendants of those immigrants form an integral part of Hawaiian society influencing most areas of Hawaiian culture, particularly its cuisine and music. Morales, whose grandparents were part of a nearly forced migration to Hawaii in the early 1930s, represents the only prominent literary figure of Puerto Rican descent in Hawaii. And, more than any of the writers, he is representative of what could be the future of Puerto Rican literature in English.

Literature and the creative drive of the writer is primarily one of memory and conscience, of setting things right in the collective psyche of its people. Whether it is Ana Lydia Vega's chilling fictional account of a girl witnessing the Ponce Massacre in 1937 in "Liliane's Sunday" or Abraham Rodriguez, Jr.'s, poignant struggle of a grammar school boy with his father's ethics a half century later in the South Bronx in "The Boy Without a Flag," we are privy not only to tales of growing up Puerto Rican but perhaps to the coming of age of a literature, a culture, and a country with as much right to exist as any other, perhaps friendly to the United States, but with its visage fixed firmly on its own future.

—ED VEGA

ACKNOWLEDGMENTS

FIRST OF ALL, I WOULD LIKE TO THANK LIZABETH PARAVISINI-GEBERT for bringing this project to my attention and for her valuable support and guidance in all of my endeavors. I would also like to thank: Ed Vega and Susan Bergholz for giving me the opportunity to work with them. Suzanne Oboler and Leonard Tennenhouse for their insight and direction in the early stages of the project. The Department of American Civilization at Brown University for allowing me to incorporate the anthology into my graduate studies. Jason Hurd for convincing me I could squeeze the book into my schedule. Aimée Miller for her second opinions. Marlon Sanchez for accompanying me on all those trips to the library. Jocelyn De Jésus for her fresh perspective on the selections. And my patient editor, Doris Cooper, for her assistance and understanding from start to finish.

CONTENTS

FOREWORD by Ed Vega   v

ACKNOWLEDGMENTS   xiii

INTRODUCTION by Joy L. De Jesús   xvii

I. NEITHER HERE NOR THERE

"The Boy Without a Flag"
    by Abraham Rodriguez, Jr.   3

"Spanish Roulette"
    by Ed Vega   20

"Immigrants"
    by Aurora Levins Morales   33

"Ship of Dreams"
    by Rodney Morales   39

"The Ingredient"
    by Julio Marzán   50

II. FAMILY TIES

"Brothers Under the Skin"
    by Piri Thomas   63

"Silent Dancing"
    by Judith Ortiz Cofer   69

Contents

"Why Women Remain *Jamona*"
    by Esmeralda Santiago   79

"Every Sunday"
    by Magali García Ramis, *Trans. Carmen C. Esteves*   95

"Sofia"
    by Yvonne V. Sapia   112

III. SURVIVAL ON THE STREETS

"Kipling and I"
    by Jesús Colón   121

from *A Perfect Silence*
    by Alba Ambert   126

"The Champ"
    by Pedro Juan Soto   133

"Stoopball"
    by Edward Rivera   139

from *Carlito's Way*
    by Edwin Torres   157

"Johnny United"
    by Jack Agüeros   166

IV. ONCE ON THIS ISLAND

"There Is a Little Colored Boy in the Bottom of the Water"
    by José Luis González, *Trans. Lysander Kemp*   179

"Liliane's Sunday"
    by Ana Lydia Vega, *Trans. Lizabeth Paravisini-Gebert*   183

"Black Sun"
    by Emilio Díaz Valcárcel, *Trans. C. Virginia Matters*   194

"The Gift"
    by Rosario Ferré   202

PERMISSIONS   231

INTRODUCTION

"AmeRícan, defining myself my own way any way many
ways Am e Rícan, with the big R and the
accent on the í!"

—TATO LAVIERA

GROWING UP, I WAS AN AVID READER. I READ EVERYTHING FROM
the World Book Encyclopedia to *Anne of Green Gables* to *Gone With the
Wind*. But it wasn't until my first year of college that I encountered
literature written by a fellow Puerto Rican. Elated to finally find writing
that spoke in Spanglish, celebrated my African roots, moved to the
sounds of salsa, and showed no shame in being poor, I read and reread
Tato Laviera's collection of poetry, *AmeRícan*. The collection's title
poem, with its double entendre, has since defined for me what it means
to grow up Puerto Rican in the United States. I have always felt that I
am a product of both Puerto Rican culture and American society, but
neither wholly Puerto Rican nor just an American.

As I continued to explore Puerto Rican literature throughout the
remainder of my college education and into graduate school, it became
increasingly reassuring and a source of pride to know that aspects of my
life experience were being voiced by Puerto Rican writers. I was not
alone in my self-perceptions and culturally ambiguous environment.
"Brothers Under the Skin," in which Piri Thomas confronts racism
within his family and addresses his identity crisis as a black Puerto Rican
in the United States, reminds me of my own family's prejudices and how
dejected I used to feel when someone critiqued my kinky *pelo malo* (bad
hair). And the details of Judith Ortiz Cofer's autobiographical piece,
"Silent Dancing," resonate strongly with my own experience of growing

up in New Jersey, finding comfort in the familiar smell of rice and beans and the leisurely atmosphere of the corner *bodega.*

Researching and selecting the works for this anthology has allowed me to not only see myself mirrored in the narrative of others, but to better appreciate the variety of perspectives and experiences related to growing up Puerto Rican, both in the United States and on the Island. Excerpts like the one from Edwin Torres's *Carlito's Way,* which paints a dog-eat-dog New York City street life where the only way for a Puerto Rican kid to survive is by his fists, tricks, and general vice, have exposed me to a world that I have only witnessed in gangster movies. Although the scenario Torres describes may be exceptional or extreme, it certainly adds to the spectrum of experiences that fall under the rubric of growing up Puerto Rican. Then there are stories that have introduced me to little-known aspects of Puerto Rican history. For example, "Liliane's Sunday" by Ana Lydia Vega dramatically recounts one child's memories of the United States' 1937 ambush of a Puerto Rican nationalist demonstration in Ponce. And in "There Is a Little Colored Boy in the Bottom of the Water," José Luis González notes that black Puerto Ricans were once removed from certain parts of the island, forced to live literally on the margins of society.

In many ways, growing up Puerto Rican is not unlike growing up in any other ethnic culture. As young people we all need to decipher our increasingly complex relationships with family and friends, the legacy of our ancestors and the rollercoaster ride of love. What makes growing up Puerto Rican unique is trying to define yourself within the unsettling condition of being neither here nor there: "Am I black or white?" "Is my primary language Spanish or English?" "Am I Puerto Rican or American?" For the Puerto Rican child, the answers to these questions tend to be somewhere in between, and never simple.

Although this theme of being caught somewhere in the middle permeates several other stories in this anthology, I have grouped most of them in the first section, entitled "Neither Here nor There." Abraham Rodriguez's "The Boy Without a Flag" tells the story of one youth's intellectual struggle to reconcile his allegiance to Puerto Rico and his father's politics with his status as an American citizen. As a result of the Jones Act of 1917, which automatically made all Puerto Ricans United States citizens, the national identity of Puerto Ricans is a subject of on-going debate even for those residing on the Island. In "The Ingredient" by Julio Marzán, as in most stories written by Puerto Ricans who grew up in the United States, the protagonist's knowledge and use of Spanish often arises as a means of affirming his or her identity as a Puerto Rican. Marzán's protagonist is particularly interesting because of his half-Irish background, racist mother, and activist Latina love interest. "Ship of Dreams" by Rodney Morales explores the interaction among Puerto Rican, Japanese, and Native Hawaiian cultures, and "Immigrants" by Aurora Levins Morales is a sketch about the author's Russian-Jewish-American-Puerto Rican heritage. Both stories exemplify how Puerto Ricans have historically and successfully combined cultures, making for some children a truly multicultural upbringing.

The rest of the anthology is divided into three sections: "Family Ties," "Survival on the Streets," and "Once on This Island." The stories in "Family Ties" revolve around the notion that in the Puerto Rican com-munity, as in most cultures, family members are our first teachers. By way of example and admonishments, they instill in us the importance of family and faith and help us define our place in the world. In Magali García Ramis's story "Every Sunday," the adolescent protagonist is so mired in family traditions and the rituals of Catholicism that in order to escape from the routine, she resorts to her imagination and a secret love. Puerto Rican grandmothers, whether devout Catholics or just devoutly spiritual, tend to be bastions of faith within our families, taking quite seriously the responsibility of imparting Christian values to their grand-children. Lupe's grandmother in Yvonne Sapia's story, "Sofia," attends the Pentacostal Hallelujah Church, practices *santeria* avidly, and dabbles in a little magic, all the while impressing on young Lupe's mind that you need to have something that will comfort you when things go wrong and the unexpected leaves you alone. Esmeralda Santiago's autobio-graphical "Why Women Remain *Jamona*" identifies the kind of woman Negi does not want to be when she grows up, and critiques the role of parents in preserving the patriarchal double standard of Puerto Rican society.

The next section, "Survival on the Streets," depicts Puerto Ricans coming of age in New York City, amidst poverty, violence, and alienation, but getting by on the solid will to survive. Hard times can sometimes bring a family together and, at best, build character in a child; but more often, as these stories highlight, they abbreviate childhood. Overcoming the challenges of poverty lies at the core of "Kipling and I," in which Jesús Colón remembers cold and desperate times that called for mature and practical measures. The excerpt from Alba Ambert's novel *A Perfect Silence* shows how some children grow up exploited and violated, but survive on resiliency, imagination, and a little charity. The adversity and perseverance characterized by the writers in this section is in no way limited to the Puerto Rican community in New York City. It is also a central theme in Puerto Rican literature from the Island. In fact, because of the socioeconomic insecurity perpetuated by Puerto Rico's political status, the will to survive is commonly associated with the plight of Puerto Ricans in general.

The stories organized in the last section, "Once on This Island," are all set in Puerto Rico. More significantly, they bring to the fore the differences between growing up as a "have" and as a "have-not" on the Island. "Black Sun" by Emilio Diáz Valcárcel and José Luis González's "There Is a Little Colored Boy in the Bottom of the Water" substantiate the prominent role of poverty in the lives of some Puerto Rican children and its compounded effect when combined with racism on the part of fellow Puerto Ricans. Rosario Ferré's "The Gift" traces the evolving friendship between the privileged daughter of a family who built its fortune on the backs of dark sugar-mill workers and the Creole daughter of a *nouveau riche* dry goods merchant. Juxtaposed, these stories point to a society that limits childhood expectations based on a complicated caste system of wealth, race, and family name. Underlying this system, if not at its core, is Puerto Rico's long history of colonialism, instituted by the Spanish and since 1898 continued under the United States. This colonized status has affected not only youth on the Island, as exemplified Ana Lydia in Vega's "Liliane's Sunday," but also those Puerto Ricans in the United States who have grown to view the Island as neither country nor state.

The narratives brought together in *Growing Up Puerto Rican* give voice to a community that has been growing up in the United States and under its influence since the turn of the century. I have striven to make this a balanced collection, representing as many points of view as possible. That said, there will always be some perspectives missing. One of the most noticeable gaps is that of Puerto Ricans living in the United States *outside* of New York City. Puerto Rican migration to the United States between 1930 and 1950 was heavily dictated by the requirements of the labor market and available transportation routes. It is therefore not surprising that most Puerto Ricans settled primarily in New York City and formed communities that frequently reflected the *barrios* left behind. Today, Puerto Ricans reside in cities all over the United States, from Hartford to San Francisco, as well as in rural areas. However, stories that reflect growing up in these places are still hard to find compared to works written by "Nuyoricans" over the years. Finding stories about growing up gay and Puerto Rican also proved to be a challenge, probably more because of the general closeting of homosexuality than because of any mores specific to Puerto Rican culture.

Lastly, the collection has an overwhelmingly serious and pessimistic tone. I have no doubt this is due more to the gravity of some of the subjects explored, such as political and economic oppression, than to the lack of love, joy, and adventure experienced by Puerto Rican youth. My hope is that as more Puerto Ricans participate in literary production, more stories that celebrate Puerto Rican childhood will surface.

—JOY L. DE JESÚS

PART I

NEITHER HERE NOR THERE

THE BOY WITHOUT A FLAG

Abraham Rodriguez, Jr.

Abraham Rodriguez, Jr., was born in 1961 and grew up in the South Bronx, New York. Rodriguez began writing when he was ten years old after his father, a poet, bought him his first typewriter. Unchallenged at school and frustrated with the prevalence of drug use there, he dropped out at sixteen. He continued writing, and began writing songs and playing guitar. Rodriguez earned his high school equivalency and attended City College of New York for four years. He has published The Boy Without a Flag: Tales of the South Bronx *(1992) and a novel,* Spidertown *(1993). Several of his stories have also appeared in magazines.*

"The Boy Without a Flag" is the story of one youth's intellectual struggle to reconcile his allegiance to Puerto Rico with his status as an American citizen.

SWIRLS OF DUST DANCED IN THE BEAMS OF SUNLIGHT THAT CAME through the tall windows, the buzz of voices resounding in the stuffy auditorium. Mr. Rios stood by our Miss Colón, hovering as if waiting to catch her if she fell. His pale mouse features looked solemnly dutiful. He was a versatile man, doubling as English teacher and gym coach. He was only there because of Miss Colón's legs. She was wearing her neon pink nylons. Our favorite.

We tossed suspicious looks at the two of them. Miss Colón would smirk at Edwin and me, saying, "Hey, face front," but Mr. Rios would glare. I think he knew that we knew what he was after. We knew, because on Fridays, during our free period when we'd get to play records and eat stale pretzel sticks, we would see her way in the back by the tall windows, sitting up on a radiator like a schoolgirl. There would be a strange pinkness on her high cheekbones, and there was Mr. Rios, sitting beside her, playing with her hand. Her face, so thin and girlish, would blush. From then on, her eyes, very close together like a cartoon rendition of a beaver's, would avoid us.

Miss Colón was hardly discreet about her affairs. Edwin had first tipped me off about her love life after one of his lunchtime jaunts through the empty hallways. He would chase girls and toss wet bathroom napkins into classrooms where kids in the lower grades sat, trapped. He claimed to have seen Miss Colón slip into a steward's closet with Mr. Rios and to have heard all manner of sounds through the thick wooden door, which was locked (he tried it). He had told half the class before the day was out, the boys sniggering behind grimy hands, the girls shocked because Miss Colón was married, so married that she even brought the poor unfortunate in one morning as a kind of show-and-tell guest. He was an untidy dark-skinned Puerto Rican type in a colorful dashiki. He carried a paper bag that smelled like glue. His eyes seemed sleepy, his Afro an uncombed Brillo pad. He talked about protest marches, the sixties, the importance of an education. Then he embarrassed Miss Colón greatly by disappearing into the coat closet and falling asleep there. The girls, remembering him, softened their attitude toward her indiscretions, defending her violently. "Face it," one of them blurted out when Edwin began a new series of Miss Colón tales, "she married a bum and needs to find true love."

"She's a slut, and I'm gonna draw a comic book about her," Edwin said, hushing when she walked in through the door. That afternoon, he showed me the first sketches of what would later become a very popular comic book entitled "Slut at the Head of the Class." Edwin could draw really well, but his stories were terrible, so I volunteered to do the writing. In no time at all, we had three issues circulating under desks and hidden in notebooks all over the school. Edwin secretly ran off close to a hundred copies on a copy machine in the main office after school. It always amazed me how copies of our comic kept popping up in the unlikeliest places. I saw them on radiators in the auditorium, on benches in the gym, tacked up on bulletin boards. There were even some in the teachers' lounge, which I spotted one day while running an errand for Miss Colón. Seeing it, however, in the hands of Miss Martí, the pig-faced assistant principal, nearly made me puke up my lunch. Good thing our names weren't on it.

It was a miracle no one snitched on us during the ensuing investigation, since only a blind fool couldn't see our involvement in the thing. No bloody purge followed, but there was enough fear in both of us to kill the desire to continue our publishing venture. Miss Martí, a woman with a battlefield face and constant odor of Chiclets, made a forceful threat about finding the culprits while holding up the second issue, the one with the hand-colored cover. No one moved. The auditorium grew silent. We meditated on the sound of a small plane flying by, its engines rattling the windows. I think we wished we were on it.

It was in the auditorium that the trouble first began. We had all settled into our seats, fidgeting like tiny burrowing animals, when there was a general call for quiet. Miss Martí, up on stage, had a stare that could make any squirming fool sweat. She was a gruff, nasty woman who never smiled without seeming sadistic.

Mr. Rios was at his spot beside Miss Colón, his hands clasped behind his back as if he needed to restrain them. He seemed to whisper to her. Soft, mushy things. Edwin would watch them from his seat beside me, giving me the details, his shiny face looking worried. He always seemed sweaty, his fingers kind of damp.

"I toldju, I saw um holdin hands," he said. "An now lookit him, he's whispering sweet shits inta huh ear."

He quieted down when he noticed Miss Martí's evil eye sweeping over us like a prison-camp searchlight. There was silence. In her best military bark, Miss Martí ordered everyone to stand. Two lone, pathetic kids, dragooned by some unseen force, slowly came down the center aisle, each bearing a huge flag on a thick wooden pole. All I could make out was that great star-spangled unfurling, twitching thing that looked like it would fall as it approached over all those bored young heads. The Puerto Rican flag walked beside it, looking smaller and less confident. It clung to its pole.

"The Pledge," Miss Martí roared, putting her hand over the spot where her heart was rumored to be.

That's when I heard my father talking.

He was sitting on his bed, yelling about Chile, about what the CIA had done there. I was standing opposite him in my dingy Pro Keds. I knew about politics. I was eleven when I read William Shirer's book on Hitler. I was ready.

"All this country does is abuse Hispanic nations," my father said, turning a page of his *Post,* "tie them down, make them dependent. It says democracy with one hand while it protects and feeds fascist dictatorships with the other." His eyes blazed with a strange fire. I sat on the bed, on part of his *Post,* transfixed by his oratorical mastery. He had mentioned political things before, but not like this, not with such fiery conviction. I thought maybe it had to do with my reading Shirer. Maybe he had seen me reading that fat book and figured I was ready for real politics.

Using the knowledge I gained from the book, I defended the Americans. What fascism was he talking about, anyway? I knew we had stopped Hitler. That was a big deal, something to be proud of.

"Come out of fairy-tale land," he said scornfully. "Do you know what imperialism is?"

I didn't really, no.

"Well, why don't you read about that? Why don't you read about Juan Bosch and Allende, men who died fighting imperialism? They stood up against American big business. You should read about that instead of this crap about Hitler."

"But I like reading about Hitler," I said, feeling a little spurned. I didn't even mention that my fascination with Adolf led to my writing a biography of him, a book report one hundred and fifty pages long. It got an A-plus. Miss Colón stapled it to the bulletin board right outside the classroom, where it was promptly stolen.

"So, what makes you want to be a writer?" Miss Colón asked me quietly one day when Edwin and I, always the helpful ones, volunteered to assist her in getting the classroom spiffed up for a Halloween party.

"I don't know. I guess my father," I replied, fiddling with plastic pumpkins self-consciously while images of my father began parading through my mind.

When I think back to my earliest image of my father, it is one of him sitting behind a huge rented typewriter, his fingers clacking away. He was a frustrated poet, radio announcer, and even stage actor. He had sent for diplomas from fly-by-night companies. He took acting lessons, went into broadcasting, even ended up on the ground floor of what is now Spanish radio, but his family talked him out of all of it. "You should find yourself real work, something substantial," they said, so he did. He dropped all those dreams that were never encouraged by anyone else and got a job at a Nedick's on Third Avenue. My pop the counterman.

Despite that, he kept writing. He recited his poetry into a huge reel-to-reel tape deck that he had, then he'd play it back and sit like a critic, brow furrowed, fingers stroking his lips. He would record strange sounds and play them back to me at outrageous speeds, until I believed that there were tiny people living inside the machine. I used to stand by him and watch him type, his black pompadour spilling over his forehead. There was energy pulsating all around him, and I wanted a part of it.

I was five years old when I first sat in his chair at the kitchen table and began pushing down keys, watching the letters magically appear on the page. I was entranced. My fascination with the typewriter began at that point. By the time I was ten, I was writing war stories, tales of pain and pathos culled from the piles of comic books I devoured. I wrote unreadable novels. With illustrations. My father wasn't impressed. I guess he was hard to impress. My terrific grades did not faze him, nor the fact that I was reading books as fat as milk crates. My unreadable novels piled up. I brought them to him at night to see if he would read them, but after a week of waiting I found them thrown in the bedroom closet, unread. I felt hurt and rejected, despite my mother's kind words. "He's just too busy to read them," she said to me one night when I mentioned it to her. He never brought them up, even when I quietly took them out of the closet one day or when he'd see me furiously hammering on one of his rented machines. I would tell him I wanted to be a writer, and he would smile sadly and pat my head, without a word.

"You have to find something serious to do with your life," he told me one night, after I had shown him my first play, eighty pages long. What was it I had read that got me into writing a play? Was it Arthur

Miller? Oscar Wilde? I don't remember, but I recall my determination to write a truly marvelous play about combat because there didn't seem to be any around.

"This is fun as a hobby," my father said, "but you can't get serious about this." His demeanor spoke volumes, but I couldn't stop writing. Novels, I called them, starting a new one every three days. The world was a blank page waiting for my words to re-create it, while the real world remained cold and lonely. My schoolmates didn't understand any of it, and because of the fat books I carried around, I was held in some fear. After all, what kid in his right mind would read a book if it wasn't assigned? I was sick of kids coming up to me and saying, "Gaw, lookit tha fat book. Ya teacha make ya read tha?" (No, I'm just reading it.) The kids would look at me as if I had just crawled out of a sewer. "Ya crazy, man." My father seemed to share that opinion. Only my teachers understood and encouraged my reading, but my father seemed to want something else from me.

Now he treated me like an idiot for not knowing what imperialism was. He berated my books and one night handed me a copy of a book about Albizu Campos, the Puerto Rican revolutionary. I read it through in two sittings.

"Some of it seems true," I said.

"Some of it?" my father asked incredulously. "After what they did to him, you can sit there and act like a Yankee flag-waver?"

I watched that Yankee flag making its way up to the stage over indifferent heads, my father's scowling face haunting me, his words resounding in my head.

"Let me tell you something," my father sneered. "In school, all they do is talk about George Washington, right? The first president? The father of democracy? Well, he had slaves. We had our own Washington, and ours had real teeth."

As Old Glory reached the stage, a general clatter ensued.

"We had our own revolution," my father said, "and the United States crushed it with the flick of a pinkie."

Miss Martí barked her royal command. Everyone rose up to salute the flag.

Except me. I didn't get up. I sat in my creaking seat, hands on my knees. A girl behind me tapped me on the back. "Come on, stupid, get up." There was a trace of concern in her voice. I didn't move.

Miss Colón appeared. She leaned over, shaking me gently. "Are you sick? Are you okay?" Her soft hair fell over my neck like a blanket.

"No," I replied.

"What's wrong?" she asked, her face growing stern. I was beginning to feel claustrophobic, what with everyone standing all around me, bodies like walls. My friend Edwin, hand on his heart, watched from the corner of his eye. He almost looked envious, as if he wished he had thought of it. Murmuring voices around me began reciting the Pledge while Mr. Rios appeared, commandingly grabbing me by the shoulder and pulling me out of my seat into the aisle. Miss Colón was beside him, looking a little apprehensive.

"What is wrong with you?" he asked angrily. "You know you're supposed to stand up for the Pledge! Are you religious?"

"No," I said.

"Then what?"

"I'm not saluting that flag," I said.

"What?"

"I said, I'm not saluting that flag."

"Why the . . . ?" He calmed himself; a look of concern flashed over Miss Colón's face. "Why not?"

"Because I'm Puerto Rican. I ain't no American. And I'm not no Yankee flag-waver."

"You're supposed to salute the flag," he said angrily, shoving one of his fat fingers in my face. "You're not supposed to make up your own mind about it. You're supposed to do as you are told."

"I thought I was free," I said, looking at him and at Miss Colón.

"You are," Miss Colón said feebly. "That's why you should salute the flag."

"But shouldn't I do what I feel is right?"

"You should do what you are told!" Mr. Rios yelled into my face.

"I'm not playing no games with you, mister. You hear that music? That's the anthem. Now you go stand over there and put your hand over your heart." He made as if to grab my hand, but I pulled away.

"No!" I said sharply. "I'm not saluting that crummy flag! And you can't make me, either. There's nothing you can do about it."

"Oh yeah?" Mr. Rios roared. "We'll see about that!"

"Have you gone crazy?" Miss Colón asked as he led me away by the arm, down the hallway, where I could still hear the strains of the anthem. He walked me briskly into the principal's office and stuck me in a corner.

"You stand there for the rest of the day and see how you feel about it," he said viciously. "Don't you even think of moving from that spot!"

I stood there for close to two hours or so. The principal came and went, not even saying hi or hey or anything, as if finding kids in the corners of his office was a common occurrence. I could hear him talking on the phone, scribbling on pads, talking to his secretary. At one point I heard Mr. Rios outside in the main office.

"Some smart-ass. I stuck him in the corner. Thinks he can pull that shit. The kid's got no respect, man. I should get the chance to teach him some."

"Children today have no respect," I heard Miss Martí's reptile voice say as she approached, heels clacking like gunshots. "It has to be forced upon them."

She was in the room. She didn't say a word to the principal, who was on the phone. She walked right over to me. I could hear my heart beating in my ears as her shadow fell over me. Godzilla over Tokyo.

"Well, have you learned your lesson yet?" she asked, turning me from the wall with a finger on my shoulder. I stared at her without replying. My face burned, red hot. I hated it.

"You think you're pretty important, don't you? Well, let me tell you, you're nothing. You're not worth a damn. You're just a snotty-nosed little kid with a lot of stupid ideas." Her eyes bored holes through me, searing my flesh. I felt as if I were going to cry. I fought the urge. Tears rolled down my face anyway. They made her smile, her chapped lips twisting upwards like the mouth of a lizard.

"See? You're a little baby. You don't know anything, but you'd better learn your place." She pointed a finger in my face. "You do as you're told if you don't want big trouble. Now go back to class."

Her eyes continued to stab at me. I looked past her and saw Edwin waiting by the office door for me. I walked past her, wiping at my face. I could feel her eyes on me still, even as we walked up the stairs to the classroom. It was close to three already, and the skies outside the grated windows were cloudy.

"Man," Edwin said to me as we reached our floor, "I think you're crazy."

The classroom was abuzz with activity when I got there. Kids were chattering, getting their windbreakers from the closet, slamming their chairs up on their desks, filled with the euphoria of soon-home. I walked quietly over to my desk and took out my books. The other kids looked at me as if I were a ghost.

I went through the motions like a robot. When we got downstairs to the door, Miss Colón, dismissing the class, pulled me aside, her face compassionate and warm. She squeezed my hand.

"Are you okay?"

I nodded.

"That was a really crazy stunt there. Where did you get such an idea?"

I stared at her black flats. She was wearing tan panty hose and a black miniskirt. I saw Mr. Rios approaching with his class.

"I have to go," I said, and split, running into the frigid breezes and the silver sunshine.

At home, I lay on the floor of our living room, tapping my open notebook with the tip of my pen while the Beatles blared from my father's stereo. I felt humiliated and alone. Miss Martí's reptile face kept appearing in my notebook, her voice intoning, "Let me tell you, you're nothing." Yeah, right. Just what horrible hole did she crawl out of? Were those people really Puerto Ricans? Why should a Puerto Rican salute an American flag?

I put the question to my father, strolling into his bedroom, a tiny M-1 rifle that belonged to my G.I. Joe strapped to my thumb.

"Why?" he asked, loosening the reading glasses that were perched on his nose, his newspaper sprawled open on the bed before him, his cigarette streaming blue smoke. "Because we are owned, like cattle. And because nobody has any pride in their culture to stand up for it."

I pondered those words, feeling as if I were being encouraged, but I didn't dare tell him. I wanted to believe what I had done was a brave and noble thing, but somehow I feared his reaction. I never could impress him with my grades, or my writing. This flag thing would probably upset him. Maybe he, too, would think I was crazy, disrespectful, a "smart-ass" who didn't know his place. I feared that, feared my father saying to me, in a reptile voice, "Let me tell you, you're nothing."

I suited up my G.I. Joe for combat, slipping on his helmet, strapping on his field pack. I fixed the bayonet to his rifle, sticking it in his clutching hands so he seemed ready to fire. "A man's gotta do what a man's gotta do." Was that John Wayne? I don't know who it was, but I did what I had to do, still not telling my father. The following week, in the auditorium, I did it again. This time, everyone noticed. The whole place fell into a weird hush as Mr. Rios screamed at me.

I ended up in my corner again, this time getting a prolonged, pensive stare from the principal before I was made to stare at the wall for two more hours. My mind zoomed past my surroundings. In one strange vision, I saw my crony Edwin climbing up Miss Colón's curvy legs, giving me every detail of what he saw.

"Why?" Miss Colón asked frantically. "This time you don't leave until you tell me why." She was holding me by the arm, masses of kids flying by, happy blurs that faded into the sunlight outside the door.

"Because I'm Puerto Rican, not American," I blurted out in a weary torrent. "That makes sense, don't it?"

"So am I," she said, "but we're in America!" She smiled. "Don't you think you could make some kind of compromise?" She tilted her head to one side and said, "Aw, c'mon," in a little-girl whisper.

"What about standing up for what you believe in? Doesn't that matter? You used to talk to us about Kent State and protesting. You said those kids died because they believed in freedom, right? Well, I feel like them now. I wanna make a stand."

She sighed with evident aggravation. She caressed my hair. For a moment, I thought she was going to kiss me. She was going to say something, but just as her pretty lips parted, I caught Mr. Rios approaching.

"I don't wanna see him," I said, pulling away.

"No, wait," she said gently.

"He's gonna deck me," I said to her.

"No, he's not," Miss Colón said, as if challenging him, her eyes taking him in as he stood beside her.

"No, I'm not," he said. "Listen here. Miss Colón was talking to me about you, and I agree with her." He looked like a nervous little boy in front of the class, making his report. "You have a lot of guts. Still, there are rules here. I'm willing to make a deal with you. You go home and think about this. Tomorrow I'll come see you." I looked at him skeptically, and he added, "to talk."

"I'm not changing my mind," I said. Miss Colón exhaled painfully.

"If you don't, it's out of my hands." He frowned and looked at her. She shook her head, as if she were upset with him.

I reread the book about Albizu. I didn't sleep a wink that night. I didn't tell my father a word, even though I almost burst from the effort. At night, alone in my bed, images attacked me. I saw Miss Martí and Mr. Rios debating Albizu Campos. I saw him in a wheelchair with a flag draped over his body like a holy robe. They would not do that to me. They were bound to break me the way Albizu was broken, not by young, smiling American troops bearing chocolate bars, but by conniving, double-dealing, self-serving Puerto Rican landowners and their ilk, who dared say they were the future. They spoke of dignity and democracy while teaching Puerto Ricans how to cling to the great coat of that powerful northern neighbor. Puerto Rico, the shining star, the great lap dog of the Caribbean. I saw my father, the Nationalist hero, screaming from his podium, his great oration stirring everyone around him to acts of bravery. There was a shining arrogance in his eyes as he stared out over the sea of faces mouthing his name, a sparkling audacity that invited and incited. There didn't seem to be fear anywhere in him, only the urge to rush to the attack, with his arm band and revolutionary tunic. I stared up at him, transfixed. I stood by the podium, his personal adjutant, while his voice rang through the stadium. "We are not, nor will we ever be, Yankee flag-wavers!" The roar that followed drowned out the whole world.

The following day, I sat in my seat, ignoring Miss Colón as she neatly

13

drew triangles on the board with the help of plastic stencils. She was using colored chalk, her favorite. Edwin, sitting beside me, was beaning girls with spitballs that he fired through his hollowed-out Bic pen. They didn't cry out. They simply enlisted the help of a girl named Gloria, who sat a few desks behind him. She very skillfully nailed him with a thick wad of gum. It stayed in his hair until Edwin finally went running to Miss Colón. She used her huge teacher's scissors. I couldn't stand it. They all seemed trapped in a world of trivial things, while I swam in a mire of oppression. I walked through lunch as if in a trance, a prisoner on death row waiting for the heavy steps of his executioners. I watched Edwin lick at his regulation cafeteria ice cream, sandwiched between two sheets of paper. I was once like him, laughing and joking, lining up for a stickball game in the yard without a care. Now it all seemed lost to me, as if my youth had been burned out of me by a book.

Shortly after lunch, Mr. Rios appeared. He talked to Miss Colón for a while by the door as the room filled with a bubbling murmur. Then he motioned for me. I walked through the sudden silence as if in slow motion.

"Well," he said to me as I stood in the cool hallway, "have you thought about this?"

"Yeah," I said, once again seeing my father on the podium, his voice thundering.

"And?"

"I'm not saluting that flag."

Miss Colón fell against the doorjamb as if exhausted. Exasperation passed over Mr. Rios's rodent features.

"I thought you said you'd think about it," he thundered.

"I did. I decided I was right."

"*You* were right?" Mr. Rios was losing his patience. I stood calmly by the wall.

"I told you," Miss Colón whispered to him.

"Listen," he said, ignoring her, "have you heard of the story of the man who had no country?"

I stared at him.

"Well? Have you?"

"No," I answered sharply; his mouse eyes almost crossed with anger at my insolence. "Some stupid fairy tale ain't gonna change my mind anyway. You're treating me like I'm stupid, and I'm not."

"Stop acting like you're some mature adult! You're not. You're just a puny kid."

"Well, this puny kid still ain't gonna salute that flag."

"You were born here," Miss Colón interjected patiently, trying to calm us both down. "Don't you think you at least owe this country some respect? At least?"

"I had no choice about where I was born. And I was born poor."

"So what?" Mr. Rios screamed. "There are plenty of poor people who respect the flag. Look around you, dammit! You see any rich people here? I'm not rich either!" He tugged on my arm. "This country takes care of Puerto Rico, don't you see that? Don't you know anything about politics?"

"Do you know what imperialism is?"

The two of them stared at each other.

"I don't believe you," Mr. Rios murmured.

"Puerto Rico is a colony," I said, a direct quote of Albizu's. "Why I gotta respect that?"

Miss Colón stared at me with her black saucer eyes, a slight trace of a grin on her features. It encouraged me. In that one moment, I felt strong, suddenly aware of my territory and my knowledge of it. I no longer felt like a boy but some kind of soldier, my bayonet stained with the blood of my enemy. There was no doubt about it. Mr. Rios was the enemy, and I was beating him. The more he tried to treat me like a child, the more defiant I became, his arguments falling like twisted armor. He shut his eyes and pressed the bridge of his nose.

"You're out of my hands," he said.

Miss Colón gave me a sympathetic look before she vanished into the classroom again. Mr. Rios led me downstairs without another word. His face was completely red. I expected to be put in my corner again, but this time Mr. Rios sat me down in the leather chair facing the principal's desk. He stepped outside, and I could hear the familiar *clack-clack* that could only belong to Miss Martí's reptile legs. They were talking in whispers. I expected her to come in at any moment, but the principal walked in instead. He came in quietly, holding a folder in his hand. His soft brown eyes and beard made him look compassionate, rounded cheeks making him seem friendly. His desk plate solemnly stated: Mr. Sepulveda, PRINCIPAL. He fell into his seat rather unceremoniously, opened the folder, and crossed his hands over it.

"Well, well, well," he said softly, with a tight-lipped grin. "You've created quite a stir, young man." It sounded to me like movie dialogue.

"First of all, let me say I know about you. I have your record right here, and everything in it is very impressive. Good grades, good attitude, your teachers all have adored you. But I wonder if maybe this hasn't gone to your head? Because everything is going for you here, and you're throwing it all away."

He leaned back in his chair. "We have rules, all of us. There are rules even I must live by. People who don't obey them get disciplined. This will all go on your record, and a pretty good one you've had so far. Why ruin it? This'll follow you for life. You don't want to end up losing a good job opportunity in government or in the armed forces because as a child you indulged your imagination and refused to salute the flag? I know you can't see how childish it all is now, but you must see it, and because you're smarter than most, I'll put it to you in terms you can understand.

"To me, this is a simple case of rules and regulations. Someday, when you're older," he paused here, obviously amused by the sound of his own voice, "you can go to rallies and protest marches and express your rebellious tendencies. But right now, you are a minor, under this school's jurisdiction. That means you follow the rules, no matter what you think of them. You can join the Young Lords later."

I stared at him, overwhelmed by his huge desk, his pompous mannerisms and status. I would agree with everything, I felt, and then, the following week, I would refuse once again. I would fight him then, even though he hadn't tried to humiliate me or insult my intelligence. I would continue to fight, until I . . .

"I spoke with your father," he said.

I started. "My father?" Vague images and hopes flared through my mind briefly.

"Yes. I talked to him at length. He agrees with me that you've gotten a little out of hand."

My blood reversed direction in my veins. I felt as if I were going to collapse. I gripped the armrests of my chair. There was no way this could be true, no way at all! My father was supposed to ride in like the cavalry, not abandon me to the enemy! I pressed my wet eyes with my fingers. It must be a lie.

"He blames himself for your behavior," the principal said. "He's already here," Mr. Rios said from the door, motioning my father inside. Seeing him wearing his black weather-beaten trench coat almost asphyxiated me. His eyes, red with concern, pulled at me painfully. He came over to me first while the principal rose slightly, as if greeting a head of state. There was a look of dread on my father's face as he looked at me. He seemed utterly lost.

"Mr. Sepulveda," he said, "I never thought a thing like this could happen. My wife and I try to bring him up right. We encourage him to read and write and everything. But you know, this is a shock."

"It's not that terrible, Mr. Rodriguez. You've done very well with him, he's an intelligent boy. He just needs to learn how important obedience is."

"Yes," my father said, turning to me, "yes, you have to obey the rules. You can't do this. It's wrong." He looked at me grimly, as if working on a math problem. One of his hands caressed my head.

There were more words, in Spanish now, but I didn't hear them. I felt like I was falling down a hole. My father, my creator, renouncing his creation, repentant. Not an ounce of him seemed prepared to stand up for me, to shield me from attack. My tears made all the faces around me melt.

"So you see," the principal said to me as I rose, my father clutching me to him, "if you ever do this again, you will be hurting your father as well as yourself."

I hated myself. I wiped at my face desperately, trying not to make a spectacle of myself. I was just a kid, a tiny kid. Who in the hell did I think I was? I'd have to wait until I was older, like my father, in order to have "convictions."

"I don't want to see you in here again, okay?" the principal said sternly. I nodded dumbly, my father's arm around me as he escorted me through the front office to the door that led to the hallway, where a multitude of children's voices echoed up and down its length like tolling bells.

"Are you crazy?" my father half-whispered to me in Spanish as we stood there. "Do you know how embarrassing this all is? I didn't think you were this stupid. Don't you know anything about dignity, about respect? How could you make a spectacle of yourself? Now you make us all look stupid."

He quieted down as Mr. Rios came over to take me back to class. My father gave me a squeeze and told me he'd see me at home. Then I walked with a somber Mr. Rios, who, oddly, wrapped an arm around me all the way back to the classroom.

"Here you go," he said softly as I entered the classroom, and everything fell quiet. I stepped in and walked to my seat without looking at anyone. My cheeks were still damp, my eyes red. I looked like I had been tortured. Edwin stared at me, then he pressed my hand under the table.

"I thought you were dead," he whispered.

Miss Colón threw me worried glances all through the remainder of the class. I wasn't paying attention. I took out my notebook, but my strength ebbed away. I just put my head on the desk and shut my eyes, reliving my father's betrayal. If what I did was so bad, why did I feel more ashamed of him than I did of myself? His words, once so rich and vibrant, now fell to the floor, leaves from a dead tree.

At the end of the class, Miss Colón ordered me to stay after school. She got Mr. Rios to take the class down along with his, and she stayed with me in the darkened room. She shut the door on all the exuberant hallway noise and sat down on Edwin's desk, beside me, her black pumps on his seat.

"Are you okay?" she asked softly, grasping my arm. I told her everything, especially about my father's betrayal. I thought he would be the cavalry, but he was just a coward.

"Tss. Don't be so hard on your father," she said. "He's only trying to do what's best for you."

"And how's this the best for me?" I asked, my voice growing hoarse with hurt.

"I know it's hard for you to understand, but he really was trying to take care of you."

I stared at the blackboard.

"He doesn't understand me," I said, wiping my eyes.

"You'll forget," she whispered.

"No, I won't. I'll remember every time I see that flag. I'll see it and think, 'My father doesn't understand me.' "

Miss Colón sighed deeply. Her fingers were warm on my head, stroking my hair. She gave me a kiss on the cheek. She walked me downstairs, pausing by the doorway. Scores of screaming, laughing kids brushed past us.

"If it's any consolation, I'm on your side," she said, squeezing my arm. I smiled at her, warmth spreading through me. "Go home and listen to the Beatles," she added with a grin.

I stepped out into the sunshine, came down the white stone steps, and stood on the sidewalk. I stared at the towering school building, white and perfect in the sun, indomitable. Across the street, the dingy row of tattered, uneven tenements where I lived. I thought of my father. Her words made me feel sorry for him, but I felt sorrier for myself. I couldn't understand back then about a father's love and what a father might give to ensure his son safe transit. He had already navigated treacherous waters and now couldn't have me rock the boat. I still had to learn that he had made peace with The Enemy, that The Enemy was already in us. Like the flag I must salute, we were inseparable, yet his compromise made me feel ashamed and defeated. Then I knew I had to find my own peace, away from the bondage of obedience. I had to accept that flag, and my father, someone I would love forever, even if at times to my young, feeble mind he seemed a little imperfect.

Spanish Roulette

Ed Vega

Ed Vega is the pen name of Edgardo Vega Yunqué. He was born in Puerto Rico in 1936, where he lived in the town of Cidra until his family moved to the Bronx, New York, in 1949. Vega is the author of two novels, The Comeback *(1985) and* Mendoza's Dreams *(1987), and a collection of short stories,* Casualty Report *(1991). He has received fellowships from the National Endowment for the Arts and the New York Foundation for the Arts. Vega lives in New York City, where he has taught at several colleges and universities, and is currently cofounder and president of the Clemente Soto Vélez Cultural Center.*

"Spanish Roulette" depicts a young poet's psychological turmoil over avenging the rape of his sister to protect his family's honor, or standing firm against violence as a means of retaliation. At the core of this protagonist's dilemma are the mixed messages he has received over the years from his family and from "mainstream" America.

SIXTO ANDRADE SNAPPED THE GUN OPEN AND SHUT SEVERAL TIMES and then spun the cylinder, intrigued by the kaleidoscopic pattern made by the empty chambers. He was fascinated by the blue-black color of the metal, but more so by the almost toylike quality of the small weapon. As the last rays of sunlight began their retreat from the four-room tenement flat, Sixto once again snapped the cylinder open and began loading the gun. It pleased him that each brass and lead projectile fit easily into each one of the chambers and yet would not fall out. When he had finished inserting the last of the bullets, he again closed the cylinder and, enjoying the increased weight of the gun, pointed it at the ceiling and pulled back the hammer.

"What's the piece for, man?"

Sixto had become so absorbed in the gun that he did not hear Willie Collazo, with whom he shared the apartment, come in. His friend's question came at him suddenly, the words intruding into the world he had created since the previous weekend.

"Nothing," he said, lowering the weapon.

"What do you mean, 'nothing'?" said Willie. "You looked like you were ready to play Russian roulette when I came in, bro."

"No way, man," said Sixto, and as he had been shown by Tommy Ramos, he let the hammer fall back gently into place. "It's called Spanish roulette," he added, philosophically.

Willie's dark face broke into a wide grin, and his eyes, just as if he were playing his congas, laughed before he did. "No kidding, man," he said. "You taking up a new line of work? I know things are rough, but sticking up people and writing poetry don't go together."

Sixto put the gun on the table, tried to smile but couldn't, and recalled the last time he had read at the cafe on Sixth Street. Willie had played behind him, his hands making the drums sing a background to his words. "I gotta take care of some business, Willie," he said solemnly, and, turning back to his friend, walked across the worn linoleum to the open window of the front room.

"Not like that, *panita,*" Willie said as he followed him.

"Family stuff, bro."

"Who?"

"My sister," Sixto said without turning.

"Mandy?"

Sixto nodded, his small body taut with the anger he had felt when Mandy had finished telling him of the attack. He looked out over the street four flights below and fought an urge to jump. It was one solution but not *the* solution. Despairingly, he shook his head at the misery below: burned-out buildings, torched by landlords because it was cheaper than fixing them; empty lots, overgrown with weeds and showing the ravages of life in the neighborhood. On the sidewalk, the discarded refrigerator still remained as a faceless sentinel standing guard over the lot, its door removed too late to save the little boy from Avenue B. He had been locked in it half the day while his mother, going crazy with worry, searched the streets, so that by the time she saw the blue-faced child, she was too far gone to understand what it all meant.

He tried to cheer himself up by focusing his attention on the children playing in front of the open fire hydrant, but could not. The twilight rainbow within the stream of water, which they intermittently shot up in the air to make it cascade in a bright arc of white against the asphalt, was an illusion, *un engaño,* a poetic image of his childhood created solely to contrast his despair. He thought again of the crushed innocence on his sister's face, and his blood felt like sand as it ran in his veins.

"You want to talk about it?" asked Willie.

"No, man," Sixto replied. "I don't."

Up the street, in front of the *bodega,* the old men were already playing dominoes and drinking beer. Sixto imagined them joking about each other's weaknesses, always, he thought ironically, with respect. They had no worries. Having lived a life of service to that which now beckoned him, they could afford to be light-hearted. It was as if he had been programmed early on for the task now facing him. He turned slowly, wiped an imaginary tear from his eyes, and recalled his father's admonition about crying: "*Usted es un machito y los machos no lloran,* machos don't cry." How old had he been? Five or six, no more. He had fallen in the playground and cut his lip. His father's friends had laughed at the remark, but he couldn't stop crying and his father had shaken him. "*Le dije que usted no es una chancleta. ¡Apréndalo bien!*" "You are not a girl, understand that once and for all!"

Concerned with Sixto's mood, once again Willie tried drawing him out. "*Coño,* bro, she's only fifteen," he said. "*¿Qué pasó?*"

The gentleness and calm that Sixto so much admired had faded from Willie's face and now mirrored his own anguish. It was wrong to involve his friend, but perhaps that was part of it. Willie was there to test his resolve. He had been placed there by fate to make sure the crime did not go unpunished. In the end, when it came time to act, he'd have only his wits and manhood.

"It's nothing, bro," Sixto replied, walking back into the kitchen. "I told you, family business. Don't worry about it."

"Man, don't be like that."

There was no injury in Willie's voice, and as if someone had suddenly punched him in the stomach to obtain a confession, the words burst out of Sixto.

"*Un tipo la mangó en el rufo,* man. Some dude grabbed her. You happy now?"

"Where?" Willie asked, knowing that uttering the words was meaningless. "In the projects?"

"Yeah, last week. She got let out of school early and he grabbed her in the elevator and brought her up to the roof."

"And you kept it all in since you came back from your mom's Sunday night?"

"What was I supposed to do, man? Go around broadcasting that my sister got took off?"

"I'm sorry, Sixto. You know I don't mean it like that."

"I know, man. I know."

"Did she know the guy? *Un cocolo,* right? A black dude. They're the ones that go for that stuff."

"No, man. It wasn't no *cocolo.*"

"But she knew him."

"Yeah, you know. From seeing him around the block. *Un bonitillo,* man. Pretty dude that deals coke and has a couple of women hustling for him. A dude named Lino."

"*¿Bien blanco?* Pale dude with Indian hair like yours?"

"Yeah, that's the guy."

"Drives around in a gold Camaro, right?"

"Yeah, I think so." Willie nodded several times and then shook his head.

"He's Shorty Pardo's cousin, right?" Sixto knew about the family connection but hadn't wanted to admit it until now.

"So?" he said defiantly.

"Those people are crazy, bro," said Willie.

"I know."

"They've been dealing *tecata* up there in El Barrio since forever, man. Even the Italians stay clear of them, they're so crazy."

"That doesn't mean nothing to me," said Sixto, feeling his street manhood, the bravado that everyone develops growing up in the street, surfacing. Bad talk was the antidote to fear, and he wasn't immune to it. "I know how crazy they are, but I'm gonna tell you something. I don't care who the dude is. I'm gonna burn him. Gonna set his heart on fire with that piece."

"Hey, go easy, *panita,*" said Willie. "Be cool, bro. I know how you feel but that ain't gonna solve nothing. You're an artist, man. You know that? A poet. And a playwright. You're gonna light up Broadway one of these days." Willie was suddenly silent as he reflected on his words. He sat down on one of the kitchen chairs and lowered his head. After a few moments he looked up and said, "Forget what I said, man. I don't know what I'm talking about. I wouldn't know what to do if that happened to one of the women in my family. I probably would've done the dude in by now. I'm sorry I said anything. I just don't wanna see you messed up. And I'm not gonna tell you to go to the cops, either."

Sixto did not answer Willie. They both knew going to the police would serve no purpose. As soon as the old man found out, he'd beat her for not protecting herself. It would become a personal matter, as if it had been he who had submitted. He'd rant and rave about short skirts and lipstick and music and then compare everything to the way things were on the island and his precious hometown, his beloved Cacimar, like it was the center of the universe and the place where all the laws governing the human race had been created. But Sixto had nothing to worry about. He was different from his father. He was getting an education, had been enlightened to truth and beauty and knew about equality and justice. Hell, he was a new man, forged out of steel and concrete, not old banana leaves and coconuts. And yet he wanted to strike back and was sick to his stomach because he wanted Lino Quintana in front of him, on his knees, begging for mercy. He'd smoke a couple of joints and float back uptown to the Pardos' turf and then blast away at all of them like he was the Lone Ranger.

He laughed sarcastically at himself and thought that in the end he'd probably back down, allow the matter to work itself out, and let Mandy live with the scar for the rest of her life. And he'd tell himself that rape was a common thing, even in families, and that people went on living and working and making babies like a bunch of zombies, like somebody's puppets without ever realizing who was pulling the strings. It was all crazy. You were born and tagged with a name: Rodríguez, Mercado, Torres, Cartagena, Pantoja, Maldonado, Sandoval, Ballester, Nieves, Carmona. All of them, funny-ass Spanish names. And then you were told to speak English and be cool because it was important to try and get over by imitating the Anglo-Saxon crap, since that's where all the money and success were to be found. Nobody actually came out and said it, but it was written clearly in everything you saw, printed boldly between the lines of books, television, movies, advertising. And at the place where you got your love, your mother's milk, your rice and beans, you were told to speak Spanish and be respectful and defend your honor and that of the women around you.

"I'm gonna burn him, Willie," Sixto repeated. "Gonna burn him right in his *quevos*. Burn him right there in his balls so he can feel the pain before I blow him away and let God deal with him. He'll understand, man, because I don't." Sixto felt the dizzying anger blind him for a moment. "*Coño,* man, she was just fifteen," he pleaded, as if Willie could absolve him of his sin before it had been committed. "I have to do it, man. She was just a kid. *Una nena,* man. A little innocent girl who dug Latin music and danced only with her girlfriends at home and believed all the nonsense about purity and virginity, man. And now this son of a bitch went and did it to her. *Le hizo el daño.*"

That's what women called it. The damage. And it was true. Damaged goods. He didn't want to believe it, but that's how he felt. In all his educated, enlightened splendor, that's how he felt. Like she had been rendered untouchable, her femaleness soiled and smeared forever. Like no man would want to love her knowing what had happened. The whole thing was so devastating that he couldn't imagine what it was like to be a woman. If they felt even a little of what he was experiencing, it was too much. And he, her own brother, already talking as if she were dead. That's how bad it was. Like she was a memory.

"I'm gonna kill him, Willie," said Sixto once more, pounding on the wall. "*¡Lo mato, coño! Lo mato, lo mato,*" he repeated the death threat over and over in a frenzy. Willie stood up and reached for his arm, but Sixto pulled roughly away. "It's cool, man," he said, and put his opened hands in front of him. "I'm all right. Everything's cool."

"Slow down," Willie pleaded. "Slow down."

"You're right, man. I gotta slow down." Sixto sat down but before long was up again. "Man, I couldn't sleep the last couple of nights. I kept seeing myself wearing the shame the rest of my life. I gave myself every excuse in the book. I even prayed, Willie. Me, a spic from the streets of the Big Apple, hip and slick, writing my *jíbaro* poetry; *saliéndome las palabras de las entrañas; inventando foquin mundos* like a god; like *foquin* Juracán pitching lightning bolts at the people to wake them from their stupor, man. Wake them up from their lethargy and their four-hundred-year-old sleep of self-induced tyranny, you know?"

"I understand, man."

"Willie, man, I wanted my words to thunder, to shake the earth *pa' que la gente le pida a Yuquiyú que los salve.*"

"And it's gonna be that way, bro. You're the poet, man. The voice."

"And me praying. Praying, man. And not to Yuquiyú, but to some distorted European idea. I'm messed up, bro. Really messed up. Writing all this jive poetry that's supposed to incite the people to take up arms against the oppressor and all the while my heart is dripping with feelings of love and brotherhood and peace like some programmed puppet, Willie."

"I hear you."

"I mean, I bought all that stuff, man. All that liberal American jive. I bought it. I marched against the war in Vietnam, against colonialism and capitalism, and for the Chicano brothers cracking their backs in the fields, marched till my feet were raw, and every time I saw lettuce or grapes, I saw poison. And man, it felt right, Willie."

"It was a righteous cause, man."

"And I marched for the independence of the island, of Puerto Rico, Willie: *de Portorro, de Borinquen, la buena, la sagrada, el terruño, madre de todos nosotros; bendita seas entre todas las mujeres y bendito sea el fruto de tu vientre pelú.* I marched for the land of our people and it felt right."

"It is right, man."

"You know, once and for all I had overcome all the anger of being a

26

colonized person without a country and my culture being swallowed up, digested, and thrown back up so you can't even recognize what it's all about. I had overcome all the craziness and could stand above it; I could look down on the brothers and sisters who took up arms in '50 and '54 when I wasn't even a fantasy in my pop's mind, man. I could stand above all of them, even the ones with their bombs now. I could pay tribute to them with words but still judge them crazy. And it was okay. It felt right to wear two faces, to go back and forth from poetic fury to social condescension, or whatever you wanna call it. I thought I had it beat with the education and the poetry and opening up my heart like some long-haired, brown-skinned hippy. And now this. I'm a hypocrite, man.''

Like the water from the open fire hydrant, the words had rushed out of him. And yet he couldn't say exactly what it was that troubled him about the attack on his sister, couldn't pinpoint what it was that made his face hot and his blood race angrily in his veins. Willie, silenced by his own impotence, sat looking at him. He knew he could neither urge him on nor discourage him and inevitably he would have to stand aside and let whatever was to happen run its course. His voice almost a whisper, he said, "It's okay, Sixto. I know how it feels. Just let the pain come out, man. Just let it out. Cry if you have to.''

But the pain would never leave him. Spics weren't Greeks, and the word *katharsis* had no meaning in private tragedy. Sixto's mind raced back into time, searching for an answer, knowing, even as it fled like a wounded animal seeking refuge from its tormentors, that it was an aimless search. It was like running a maze. Like the rats in the psychology films and the puzzles in the children's section of weekend newspapers. One followed a path with a pencil until he came to a dead end, then retraced his steps. Thousands of years passed before him in a matter of minutes.

The Tainos: a peaceful people, some history books said. No way, he thought. They fought the Spaniards, drowned them to test their immortality. And their *caciques* were as fierce and as brave as Crazy Horse or Geronimo. Proud chiefs they were. Jumacao, Daguao, Yaureibo, Caguax, Agueybaná, Mabodamaca, Aymamón, Urayoán, Orocobix, Guarionex all fought the Spaniards with all they had . . . *guasábara* . . . *guasábara* . . . *guasábara* . . . their battle cry echoing through the hills like an eerie phantom; they fought their horses and dogs; they fought their swords and guns, and when there was no other recourse, rather than submitting, they climbed sheer cliffs and, holding their children to their breasts, leaped into the sea.

And the blacks: *los negros,* whose blood and heritage he carried. They didn't submit to slavery but escaped and returned to conduct raids against the oppressors, so that the whole *negrito lindo* business, so readily accepted as a term of endearment, was a joke, an appeasement on the part of the Spaniards. The *bombas* and *bembas* and *ginganbó* and their all-night dances and *oraciones* to Changó: warrior men of the Jelofe, Mandingo, Mende, Yoruba, Dahomey, Ashanti, Ibo, Fante, Baule, and Congo tribes, choosing battle over slavery.

And the Spaniards: certainly not a peaceful people. For centuries they fought each other and then branched out to cross the sea and slaughter hundreds of thousands of Indians, leaving an indelible mark on entire civilizations, raping and pillaging and gutting the earth of its riches, so that when it was all done and they laid in a drunken stupor four hundred years later, their pockets empty, they rose again to fight themselves in civil war.

And way back, way back before El Cid Campeador began to wage war: The Moors. *Los moros . . . alhambra, alcázar, alcohol, almohada, alcalde, alboroto . . .* NOISE . . . CRIES OF WAR . . . A thousand years the maze traveled and it led to a dead end with dark men atop fleet Arabian stallions, dark men, both in visage and intent, raising their scimitars against those dishonoring their house . . . they had invented algebra and Arabic numbers and it all added up to war . . . there was no other way. . . .

"I gotta kill him, bro," Sixto heard himself say. "I gotta. Otherwise I'm as good as dead."

One had to live with himself and that was the worst part of it; he had to live with the knowledge and that particular brand of cowardice that eroded the mind and destroyed one's soul. And it wasn't so much that his sister had been wronged. He'd seen that. The injury came from not retaliating. He was back at the beginning. Banana leaves and coconuts and machete duels at sundown. Just like his father and his *jíbaro* values. For even if the aggressor never talked, even if he never mentioned his act to another soul for whatever reason, there was still another person,

28

another member of the tribe, who could single him out in a crowd and say to himself, "That one belongs to me and so does his sister."

Sixto tried to recall other times when his manhood had been challenged, but it seemed as if everything had happened long ago and hadn't been important. Kid fights over mention of his mother, rights of ownership of an object, a place in the hierarchy of the block, a word said of his person, a lie, a bump by a stranger on a crowded subway train— nothing ever going beyond words or at worst, a sudden shoving match quickly broken up by friends.

But this was different. His brain was not functioning properly, he thought. He tried watching himself, tried to become an observer, the impartial judge of his actions. Through a small opening in his consciousness, he watched the raging battle. His heart called for the blood of the enemy and his brain urged him to use caution. There was no thought of danger, for in that region of struggle, survival meant not so much escaping with his life, but conquering fear and regaining his honor.

Sixto picked up the gun and studied it once more. He pushed the safety to make sure it was locked and placed the gun between the waistband of his pants and the flesh of his stomach. The cold metal sent slivers of ice running down his legs. It was a pleasant sensation, much as if a woman he had desired for some time had suddenly let him know, in an unguarded moment, that intimacy was possible between them. Avoiding Willie's eyes, he walked around the kitchen, pulled out his shirt and let it hang out over his pants. It was important that he learn to walk naturally and reduce his self-consciousness about the weapon. But it was his mind working tricks again. Nobody would notice. The idea was to act calmly. That's what everyone said: the thieves, the cheap stickup men who mugged old people and taxi drivers; the burglars who, like vultures, watched the movement of a family until certain that they were gone, swooped down and cleaned out the apartment, even in the middle of the day; the check specialists, who studied mailboxes as if they were bank vaults so they could break them open and steal welfare checks or fat letters from the island on the chance they might contain money orders or cash. They all said it. Even the young gang kids said it. Don't act suspiciously. Act as if you were going about your business.

Going to shoot someone was like going to work. That was it. He'd carry his books and nobody would suspect that he was carrying death. He laughed inwardly at the immense joke. He'd once seen a film in which Robert Mitchum, posing as a preacher, had pulled a derringer out of a Bible in the final scene. Why not. He'd hollow out his Western Civilization text and place the gun in it. It was his duty. The act was a way of surviving, of earning what was truly his. Whether a paycheck or an education, it meant nothing without self-respect.

But the pieces of the puzzle did not fit and Sixto sat down dejectedly. He let his head fall into his hands and for a moment thought he would cry. Willie said still nothing and Sixto waited, listening, the void of silence becoming larger and larger, expanding so that the sounds of the street, a passing car, the excitement of a child, the rushing water from the open hydrant, a mother's window warning retreated, became fainter and seemed to trim the outer edges of the nothingness within the silence. He could hear his own breathing and the beating of his heart and still he waited.

And then slowly, as if waking from a refreshing sleep, Sixto felt himself grow calmer and a pleasant coldness entered his body as heart and mind finally merged and became tuned to his mission. He smiled at the feeling and knew he had gone through the barrier of doubt and fear that had been erected to protect him from himself, to make sure he did not panic at the last moment. War had to be similar. He had heard the older young men, the ones who had survived Vietnam, talk about it. Sonny Maldonado with his plastic foot, limping everywhere he went, quiet and unassuming, talked about going through a doorway and into a quiet room where one died a little and then came out again, one's mind alive but the rest of the body already dead to the upcoming pain.

It had finally happened, he thought. There was no anger or regret, no rationalizations concerning future actions. No more justifications or talk about honor and dignity. Instead, Sixto perceived the single objective coldly. There was neither danger nor urgency in carrying out the sentence and avenging the wrong. It seemed almost too simple. If it took years, he knew the task would be accomplished. He would study the habits of his quarry, chart his every movement, and one day he'd strike. He would wait in a deserted hallway some late night, calmly walk out of the shadows, only his right index finger and his brain connected, and say, "How you doing, Lino?" and his voice alone would convey the terrible message. Sixto smiled to himself and saw, as in a slow-motion cinematic shot, his mind's ghost delicately squeeze the trigger repeatedly, the small animal muzzle of the gun following Lino Quintana's body as it fell slowly and hit the floor, the muscles of his victim's face twitching and life ebbing away forever. It happened all the time and no one was ever discovered.

Sixto laughed, almost too loudly. He took the gun out from under his shirt and placed it resolutely on the table. "I gotta think some more, man," he said. "That's crazy, rushing into the thing. You wanna beer, Willie?"

Willie was not convinced of his friend's newly found calm. Reluctantly, he accepted the beer. He watched Sixto and tried to measure the depth of his eyes. They had become strangely flat, the glint of trust in them absent. It was as if a thin, opaque veil had been sewn over the eyes to mask Sixto's emotions. He felt helpless but said nothing. He opened the beer and began mourning the loss. Sixto was right, he thought. It was Spanish roulette. Spics were born and the cylinder spun. When it stopped, one was handed the gun and, without looking, had to bring it to one's head, squeeze the trigger, and take one's chances.

The belief was pumped into the bloodstream, carved into the flesh through generations of strife, so that being was the enactment of a ritual rather than the beginning of a new life. One never knew one's own reactions until faced with Sixto's dilemma. And yet the loss would be too great, the upcoming grief too profound, and the ensuing suffering eternal. The violence would be passed on to another generation to be displayed as an invisible coat of arms, much as Sixto's answer had come to him as a relic. His friend would never again look at the world with wonder, and poetry would cease to spring from his heart. If he did write, the words would be guarded, careful, full of excuses and apologies for living. Willie started to raise the beer in a toast but thought better of it and set the can on the table.

"Whatever you do, bro," he said, "be careful."

"Don't worry, man," Sixto replied. "I got the thing under control." He laughed once again and suddenly his eyes were ablaze with hatred. He picked up the gun, stuck it back into his pants, and stood up. "No good, man," he said, seemingly to himself, and rushed out, slamming the door of the apartment behind him.

Beyond the sound of the door, Willie could hear the whirring cylinder as it began to slow down, each minute click measuring the time before his friend had to raise the weapon to his head and kill part of himself.

IMMIGRANTS

Aurora Levins Morales

Aurora Levins Morales has a Ph.D. in Women's Studies from the Union Institute in Cincinnati. Author of fiction, essay, poetry, and documentary scripts and plays, she has published in Ms., The American Voice, *and* La Nuez, *and with her mother, she coauthored* Getting Home Alive *(1986). She and her family live in Berkeley, California.*

In her autobiographical sketch "Immigrants," Levins Morales expounds on her Russian-Jewish-American-Puerto Rican heritage, exemplifying how Puerto Ricans have historically and successfully mixed cultures.

FOR YEARS AFTER WE LEFT PUERTO RICO FOR THE LAST TIME, I would wake from a dream of something unbearably precious melting away from my memory as I struggled desperately to hold on, or at least to remember that I had forgotten. I am an immigrant, and I forget to feel what it means to have left. What it means to have arrived.

There was hail the day we got to Chicago and we joked that the city was hailing our arrival. The brown brick buildings simmered in the smelly summer, clenched tight all winter against the cold and the sooty sky. It was a place without silence or darkness, huddled against a lake full of dying fish whose corpses floated against the slime-covered rocks of the south shore.

Chicago is the place where the slack ended. Suddenly there was no give. In Indiera there was the farm: the flamboyan tree, the pine woods,

33

the rainforest hillsides covered with *alegría*, the wild joyweed that in English is called impatiens. On the farm there were hideouts, groves of bamboo with the tiny brown hairs that stuck in your skin if you weren't careful. Beds of sweet-smelling fern, drowsy-making under the sun's heat, where the new leaves uncurled from fiddleheads and tendrils climbed and tangled in a spongy mass six feet deep. There were still hillsides, out of range of the house, where I could watch lizards hunt and reinitas court, and stalk the wild cuckoos, trying to get up close. There were mysteries and consolations. There was space.

Chicago was a wasteland. Nowhere to walk that was safe. Killers and rapists everywhere. Police sirens. Ugly, angry looks. Bristling hostility. Worst of all, nowhere to walk. Nowhere to go if it was early morning and I had to get out. Nowhere to go in the late afternoon or in the gathering dusk that meant fireflies and moths at home. Nowhere to watch animal life waking into a new day. The animal life was rats and dogs, and they were always awake because it never got dark here; always that sickly purple and orange glow they call sky in this place. No forest to run wild in. Only the lot across Fifty-fifth Street with huge piles of barren earth, outlines of old cellars, and a few besieged trees in a scraggly row. I named one of them Ceres, after the goddess of earth and plenty who appeared in my high school production of *The Tempest:* bounteous Ceres, queen of the wasteland. There were no hills to race down, tumbling into heaps of fern, to slide down, on a slippery banana leaf; no place to get muddy. Chicago had grime, but no mud. Slush, but no slippery places of the heart, no genuine moistness. Only damp alleyways, dank brick, and two little humps in the middle of Fifty-fifth Street over which grass had been made to grow. But no real sliding. No slack.

There are generations of this desolation behind me, desolation, excitement, grief, and longing all mixed in with the dirty air, the noise, seasickness, and the strangeness of wearing a winter coat.

My grandmother Lola was nineteen the day she married my grandfather and sailed away to Nueva York in 1929. She had loved someone else, but his family disapproved and he obeyed their orders to leave for the States. So her family married her to a son of a neighboring family because the family store was doing poorly and they could no longer support so many children. Two months after her first love left, she found herself married and on the boat. She says, "I was a good Catholic girl. I thought it was my duty to marry him, that it was for the good of my family." I have pictures of her, her vibrant beauty wrapped up but not smothered in the winter coats and scarves, in my grandfather's violent possessiveness and jealousy. She is standing in Central Park with her daughters, or with her arms around a friend or cousin. Loving the excitement. Loving the neighbors and the hubbub. In spite of racist landlords. In spite of the girdle factory. In spite of Manolin's temper and the poverty and hunger. Now, retired to Manolin's dream of a little house in Puerto Rico with a yard and many plants to tend, she longs for New York or some other U.S. city where a woman can go out and about on her own, live among many voices speaking different languages, out of the stifling air of that house, that community, that family.

My mother, the child in that Central Park photo, grew up an immigrant child among immigrants. She went to school speaking not a word of English, a small Puerto Rican girl scared out of her wits, and learned fast: learned accentless English in record time, the sweet cadence of her mother's open-voweled words ironed out of her vocabulary, the edges flattened down, made crisp, the curls and flourishes removed. First generation.

The strangeness. The way time worked differently. The way being on time mattered. Four second bells. Four minutes of passing time between classes. A note from home if you were ten minutes late, which you took to the office and traded for a late pass. In Indiera the classroom emptied during coffee season, and they didn't bother to send the inspector up unless we were out for longer than four or five weeks. No one had a clock with a second hand. We had half days of school because there were only four rooms for six grades. Our room was next to the bakery, and the smell of the warm *pan de agua* filled our lungs and stomachs and mouths. Things happened when they were ready, or *"cuando Dios quiere."* The público to town, don Paco's bread, the coffee ripening, the rain coming, growing up.

The stiffness. The way clothing mattered with an entirely different kind of intensity. In Indiera, I wore the same wine-colored jumper to school each day with the same white blouse, and only details of the buttons or the quality of the cloth or the presence or absence of earrings, only the shoes gave information about the homes we left at dawn each day, and I was grateful to be able to hide my relative wealth. In Chicago, there were rituals I had never heard of. Knee socks and plaid skirts and sweaters matching each other according to a secret code I didn't understand. Going steady and wearing name tags. First date, second date, third date, score. The right songs to be listening to. The right dances. The coolness.

In the middle of coolness, of stiffness, of strangeness, my joyful rushing up to say, "I come from Puerto Rico, a nest of beauty on the top of a mountain range." Singing, "Beauty, beauty, beauty." Trying to get them to see in their minds' eyes the perfect edge of a banana leaf against a tropical blue sky, just wanting to speak of what I longed for. Seeing embarrassed faces turning away, getting the jeering voices, singing, "Puerto Riiiico, my heart's devotion . . . let it sink into the ocean!" Learning fast not to talk about it, learning excruciatingly slowly how to dress, how to act, what to say, where to hide. The exuberance, the country-born freshness going quietly stale. Made flat. Made palatable. Made unthreatening. Not different, really. Merely "exotic."

I can remember the feelings, but I forget to give them names. In high school we read novels about immigrant families. In college we discussed the problems of other first generations, talked about displacement, talked about families confused and divided, pride and shame. I never once remembered that I was an immigrant, or that both my parents are the first U.S.-born generations of their families.

My father is the First American Boy. His mother, Ruth, was born in Russia. Took the boat with her mother, aunt, and uncle when she was two. My grandfather Reuben was the second son of Lev Levinsky, the first one born in the new country, but born into the ghetto. Lev and the first son, Samuel, were orthodox, old-country Jews, but Reuben and his younger brother, Ben, went for the new. They worked three or four jobs at once. They ran a deli in shifts and went to law school in their free hours. So Rube grew up and out of the immigrant poverty, still weak and bent from childhood hungers, still small and vulnerable. The sicker he got, the harder he worked to safeguard his wife and sons, adding on yet another job, yet another project until he worked himself to death at the age of forty-six.

My father was the First American Boy: the young genius, the honors student, the Ph.D. scientist. Each milestone recorded in home movies.

His letters and report cards hoarded through the decades, still exhibited to strangers. The one who knew what was what. The expert. The one who carried the family spark, the one to boast about. The one with the weight of the family's hope on his shoulders. First generation.

And what am I?

The immigrant child of returned immigrants who repeated the journey in the second generation. Born on the island with firsthand love and the stories of my parents' Old Country—New York; and behind those, the secondhand stories of my mother's father, of the hill town of his long-ago childhood, told through my mother's barrio childhood. Layer upon layer of travel and leaving behind, an overlay of landscapes, so that I dream of all the beloved and hated places, and endlessly of trains and paths and roads and ships docking and leaving port and a multitude of borders and officials waiting for my little piece of paper.

I have the passport with which my great-grandmother Leah, traveling as Elisavieta, and her sister, Betty (Rivieka), and her brother, Samuel, and her mother, Henke, and my grandmother, Riva, a round two-year-old to be known all her life as Ruth, and a neighbor who traveled with them as a relative, all came together into New York. I touch the seal of Russia, the brown ink in which their gentile names were recorded, the furriness of the old paper, the place where the date is stamped: June 1906. My great-grandfather Abe had come alone, fleeing the draft, by way of England and Canada, two years earlier.

I don't know what it looked like, the Old Country they left, the little farm in the Ukraine. I will never know. The town of Yaza was utterly destroyed in two gory days in 1942, eight thousand shot and buried in long trenches. My aunt Betty was unable to speak by the time I wanted to ask her: What was it like, a girl of fifteen, to come from that countryside to New York, to suddenly be working ten hours a day in a factory? I have the tiniest fragments, only the dust clinging to their shoes. The dreamy look on my great-grandmother's face one morning when I was ten, watching me play jacks. "There was a game we used to play on the farm, just like that, but with round little stones from the river, tossed from the fronts to the backs of our hands: how many times before they fall?" Pop's, my great-grandfather's painting of the farm he grew up on, and a dozen pages he left in phonetic yiddishy English about the place he grew up in, the horses, the pumpkins, the potatoes, the family decision for him to marry, to flee to New York, where you had to use *tsikolodzi* (psychology) to stay on top.

My grandmother Ruth unexpectedly answering my questions about her earliest memories with a real story, one whole, shining piece of her life: *"Dancing. We were on the boat from Russia. The sun was shining. The place we slept was smelly, stuffy, dark, so all the people were out on the deck as much as possible, sharing food, talking, laughing, playing music. Some of the other passengers were playing accordions and fiddles and I began to dance in the middle of the deck. I danced and danced and all the people around me were laughing and clapping and watching me as I spun round and round in my short skirts. It was the happiest moment of my life!"*

My children will be born in California. It's not strange anymore, in this part of the world, in this time, to be born a thousand miles from the birthplace of your mother. My children will hear stories about the *coquís* and coffee flowers, about hurricanes and roosters crowing in the night, and will dig among old photographs to understand the homesick sadness that sometimes swallows me. Living among these dry golden hills, they will hear about rain falling for months, every afternoon at two o'clock, and someday I'll take them there, to the farm on the top of Indiera, redolent of my childhood, where they can play, irreverent, in the ruins of my house. Perhaps they will lie in bed among the sounds of the rain forest, and it will be the smell of eucalyptus that calls to them in their dreams.

SHIP OF DREAMS

Rodney Morales

Rodney Morales is the author of a collection of short stories, The Speed of Darkness *(1988), and the editor of* Ho 'iHo 'i Hou: A Tribute to George Helm and Kimo Mitchell *(1984). Morales is a two-time Grand Prize winner of the* Honolulu *Magazine Fiction Contest, and is also anthologized in* Rereading America: Cultural Contexts for Reading and Writing. *A descendant of Puerto Ricans who were part of a large contingent who journeyed to Hawaii in 1900 to labor on sugar and pineapple plantations, Morales lives in Honolulu.*

In "Ship of Dreams" Morales explores the interface between Puerto Rican, Japanese, and Native Hawaiian cultures through the experiences of Takeshi, a young man captivated by the sounds of Puerto Rican music and the beauty of a girl named Linda.

TAKESHI *KNEW* THAT IT MUST HAVE BEEN MANUEL AND TONY WHO stole the largest squash from his family's vegetable garden. He had seen them hanging around a couple of times, peeking through the wooden fence before picking up groceries at his family's store. It must have been them. But why? What for? Masaharu, Takeshi's father, suspected the same. "It was dose damn Puerto Rican boys," he said. "Had to be dose damn borinkees."

But they had left it at that. In the midst of the booming town of Palama in west Honolulu during a time that immigrants of different backgrounds were finding common ground in their shared plight, it was not good to make waves. No more fights among the workers. Cooperation, instead, was to prevail. Sharing of food, drink, and dreams.

The year was 1922. At nineteen, Takeshi was growing up with the century that had three years on him. It had been a century of mixed blessings, mixed promises thus far. *The* war had ended. The League of Nations would prevent any more. Yet during Takeshi's last year at McKinley High School, his teacher, Mr. Armstrong, often stated that the worst was yet to come. What was happening in Russia, he would say cryptically, would have unprecedented impact on the rest of the world. His classmates—children of the plantations—paid little attention. The world, the century, was theirs to conquer. America, which claimed them as its own, offered unlimited opportunities. Never mind that the glories of the Hawaiian monarchy were dimming, for the legacies of Prince Kuhio and Queen Liliuokalani were torches lit, *malamalama*. More important, the legacy of democracy existed now for the benefit of all. This legacy was being tested by, among other things, the many strikes on plantations by Japanese, Filipinos, and Puerto Ricans. . . .

But Takeshi's father had had enough of that. After saving bits of his meager earnings for twenty-odd years, and thanks to *tanomoshi* and a small bank loan, he finally obtained enough capital to quit the plantation and start his own small store.

The family lived in back of the store, though Takeshi had managed to gather enough scrap lumber to build himself a little loft above. He needed *some* privacy, what with four younger brothers and sisters doing what young children do.

Takeshi spent his mornings *hapai*-ing rice in hundred-pound burlap bags, stacking potatoes, oranges, yams, stocking shelves with cans of soup and meat, as well as other everyday needs like flour, milk, lard, beans, and shoyu.

He missed going to school. His dream of being a lawyer had left with the ship that brought him and his father their first load of goods at Honolulu Harbor. Whether that ship of dreams would return remained to be seen.

★　★　★

The Puerto Ricans—at least what Takeshi knew of them—were a complicated lot. Boisterous in their manners, relationships, and very much like the Hawaiians in their openness, their sense of family. Yet they were awfully repressed in their Catholicity in a way that Hawaiians—who had converted to all shades of Christianity—were not. While Hawaiian girls were still quite casual about their dress—in the rural areas one would occasionally see women bare-topped and unaffected—Puerto Rican girls appeared intriguingly puritanical in dresses that covered their bodies from their necks on down to the ground they walked on. Takeshi recalled a story told one night when Masaharu and a Japanese friend remembered in their drunken revelry (thanks to some homemade brew) how shocked the Puerto Rican women—some Portuguese women, too—were when the Japanese men paraded down the dirt road in only towels on their way to the *furo*. "Da girls, dey wen' scream," the friend said, "and we nevah know what dey was screaming about!" They roared, falling on the ground in laughing fits. Then, after they finally recovered for brief silent moments of sober reflection, one of them came up with another "old times" story that had been told and heard a hundred times before.

Those same Puerto Rican women really loosened up on Saturday nights, however. What Masaharu and others called "kachi-kachi" music thumped from the social hall on School Street where the Puerto Ricans congregated, along with some Portuguese, Hawaiians, a smattering of whites and Filipinos. (The Chinese, Japanese, and Koreans still preferred far-eastern means of expressing themselves, like sake and *kachashi*.)

Some of the younger Asian kids, like Takeshi, spent much of their Saturday evenings on one of the mango trees outside the social hall, peering inside, entranced by the goings-on. Takeshi would gaze in wild-eyed wonder at these weekend bursts of exuberance—the *changa-changa* strumming of different-sized guitars, the maracas doing things with time that no hourglass would, the joyful if other-worldly singing, and that *da kine, ah, wha-cha-ma-call-it* thing that made the scratchy sound that held it all together, the wild fits of . . . *dancing*? And the drunken fistfights and arguments by men concerning their women that culminated each dream-like Saturday night.

Takeshi was surprised that brisk April evening when he saw his half-drunk father struggling to climb up the tree to join him and some other young boys. He knew he had nothing to fear, though, as the sake seemed to break down the differences between the *issei* and *nisei* males and inspired boylike camaraderie.

"Dese damn borinkees. Dey no quit, eh?" Masaharu said when he finally reached the limb his son sat on.

"Hey, be careful, Papa. You can fall, you know."

"Me fall?" Masaharu laughed. "Me monkey, you know. Jes' like you." As he said this, he slipped and would have fallen if his son had not grabbed him by the shirt with lightning speed.

"I tole you be careful."

Masaharu snickered as Takeshi helped him get safely settled where two branches forked and formed a somewhat comfortable chair. For minutes they silently watched the romp and revelry. Finally Masaharu spoke.

"Dass . . . dass my squash!" he said, pointing into the hall accusingly.

"What?" Takeshi answered. "What'chu talking about?"

Already his father was climbing down the tree, pressing tightly against the tree trunk, seemingly sobered. Takeshi was bewildered. He saw no squash. He swung down the tree and followed his father, who stormed into the hall and through the crowded dance floor till he stood in front of the band, specifically the *jíbaro,* who relentlessly dictated rhythm with the scratcher.

The music stopped. Takeshi felt the heat of a thousand eyes on him and his crazy father.

"Dass my squash!" he declared, pointing at the scratcher, a finely carved, etched, and painted gourd that any Japanese would normally be appreciative of. The musicians laughed. An old Puerto Rican man, also quite drunk, made his way up front.

"Whasamatta, Masaharu-san?" he said, partly inquisitive, partly annoyed. "Why you come bodda us?"

"You," Masaharu said, recognizing Pablo, a former plantation coworker. "Yo' sons . . . ," he said, getting bug-eyed, "dey wen steal . . . my squash!"

"Manny! Get yo' okole ovah heah right now!" the old man shouted.

Takeshi shook his head. He pressed his nose-bridge with his index finger and thumb, shut his eyes for several seconds, thinking, *This isn't happening. This isn't happening.* He then opened his eyes to see a well-dressed young man emerging from the crowd. "How you get dis *guiro*?" Pablo said, referring to the scratcher.

"No was me, dad. Was Tony dem."

"No lie," a female voice from the crowd said. "Was *you* and Tony, Manny." The accuser emerged from the crowd. Takeshi recognized Manny's sister, Linda. He and Linda had been school chums a few years back. But he hadn't seen her in school during the last two years.

"*Sinverguenza!*" Pablo slapped his much larger son in the head.

"Was Tony's idea," Manny said, cowering. "He—" The father grabbed him by the frilly sleeve of his shirt.

"No, Pablo," Masaharu said, pleading. "Nevah mind. Let him go."

Pablo didn't hear. He was cursing his son in Spanish, pushing him out toward the door as everyone followed. Takeshi could not help but steal quick glances at Linda. She was beautiful now, he thought. The full breasts, the color on her cheeks. Half the crowd, Takeshi and his father included, followed Pablo and Manny out of the hall. By then Pablo had removed his belt and was yelling, "Wheah's Tony? Wheah da hell is dat damn kid?" Pablo was still deaf to Masaharu's pleas of "Nevah mind, nevah mind," as he led his son up the dirt road and into the darkness.

The crowd went in.

The music went on.

Takeshi was back on the tree when Masaharu finally returned from wherever he had disappeared to and again was struggling to climb up. Takeshi hadn't noticed his father climbing up the tree. His ears were attuned to the music, but his eyes were too focused to be enjoying the generalities of the partying and scuffling. He seemed captivated. What Masaharu saw in his son's eyes was not the stare of mere enchantment. One look and he knew his son was more lost than anyone he ever knew had ever been in this crazy sugar and pineapple paradise.

Takeshi was stricken by *love*.

Masaharu peered into the hall from his roost, squinting his Japanese eyes till he, too, noticed the radiance. *Must be the one that glows.* Masaharu slapped his son's head. "Go home! Now! *Hayaku!*"

Takeshi, jarred out of his dream world, sadly swung on an outhanging branch, his feet just barely reaching yet landing on another branch in a way only one brought up around trees could. Simultaneously, his knees collapsed as his hands grasped that same branch and the movement was repeated. He then made a short drop, feetfirst, to the ground. Again his father struggled down, sliding down the trunk, arms and legs wrapped tightly, and still he fell on his ass.

Masaharu got up and again slapped his son on the head, muttering, "*Bakatare* . . . stoopid boy . . . stoo-pid boy. Mo' bettah send back Japan . . ."

That night in bed Takeshi closed his eyes to clearly see Linda's face, the way she dimpled when she smiled. He imagined touching her large breasts, unraveling her braided hair. He pretended, as best he could, that he was having sex with her. For as long as he could handle it. Finally, with the vague image of her thighs no longer pounding through his head, and after having felt simultaneously the ecstasy and pain of his wild imagination and fruitless dreams, Takeshi fell asleep on the wet spot, snoring snores as long in time as the stroke of a rough-hewn stick across a shining gourd.

The cock crowed. It was four A.M. Takeshi groaned. Then he remembered it was Sunday. He would get two whole hours more of sleep. He thanked God for resting that day so he could too, and hummed himself back to sleep.

Takeshi was pulling weeds in the family garden that afternoon when she came.

"Ah, excuse me," she said.

That voice. "Wha'?" Takeshi muttered as he looked up and saw Linda standing over him carrying a package. He had no shirt on, no footwear, only an old pair of khakis rolled up to knee length. He was suddenly very aware of his appearance.

She blushed, the color of cinnamon. She wore a *kinuli* shirt and faded denim overalls, her hair in two pigtail braids. She took something out of the package. "Dis fo' your faddah." It was the gourd in its new state, an explicit and implicit piece of art. "And dis fo' your family. Ah, um. Spanish rice with gandule beans. . . . My faddah said he real sorry about what da boys did."

"Nah . . . 'ass okay. No problem." Takeshi managed to say as he tried to grab the gourd and package without making contact with the girl of his most recent dream. Still, the back of his left hand brushed against her left breast in the exchange. She smiled. He blushed. "Ah . . . tanks. But you guys should've kept dis . . . ah . . ."

"Oh, you dunno my fadda. . . ."

"Well . . . tanks." He felt more nervous each second. "Ah . . . you wen change school?"

"No," she said frankly. "I had to quit . . . I heard you wen' graduate." Takeshi nodded. "Too good. . . . Well, I bettah go." Linda started to leave.

"How come you wen' quit?" She turned toward him and shrugged her shoulders.

"You should come to da dance Saturday night," she said suddenly, then turned and began walking away. There was an inch-wide hole in her pants that revealed some flesh.

Wait. I love you, he wanted to cry out. But he kept his mouth shut. *She must have a dozen suitors,* he thought. *And I'm Japanese.* It would be easier to climb Mount Fuji *hadashi* than to get permission from mama and papa. Especially papa. And what about *her* parents? They might have already arranged a marriage for her.

Takeshi did not know the customs of Puerto Ricans, how they went about such things. But he understood one thing, one thing that cut through all beliefs and customs: What he felt had to be dealt with. He could not keep his feelings hidden for long. He felt as if love had carved its way into his chest, and his entire being trembled from the feeling. He got chicken skin. With his free hand he rubbed his opposite arm hard to soothe the myriad bumps. He gazed at the gourd. The care that had gone into shaping the wood—the perfectly aligned grooves—and then painting in the achote red lines like Indian warpaint was almost—almost Japanese. If he could look that good in her eyes. . . .

That night Takeshi dreamed about the guiro. He had taken it with him out to the southern side of Sand Island and placed it, hole side up, with stick inside, into the ocean. He gently pushed it away. It returned. He pushed it away again. Again it returned, this time altered. Each time he pushed it away, it returned in a slightly different form: a double-hulled canoe, a schooner, a steamer . . . Then he noticed that an old Hawaiian woman, dressed in a *kikepa,* stood behind him and off to the side. She wore a faint smile, and shook her head slowly. He shuddered. The last time a wave brought it in, Takeshi noticed a piece of paper inside. He quickly took it out of the Chinese junk that it now resembled.

The paper was blank.

The message was clear.

The image of Linda walking away in her puka overalls stayed with him for days. During those same days Takeshi—stomach warmed by miso—sailed through the morning routine that began with daybreak at the docks with its oranges and blues, unloading crates that were to stock empty shelves, mulching, weeding, and *hanawai*-ing the garden, gathering the ready vegetables, nurturing the sizable squashes his father proudly grew, always noticing the broken vine where the stolen one had been, secretly proud of his new plaything, practicing on it every chance he could.

He took the gourd on his afternoon journeys up the Kapalama Stream. His escape. *Scrrape, chuk-chuk. Scrrape, chuk-chuk.* He became obsessed with trying to capture the rhythm. Playing out his dream, he placed the gourd in the water. It did not return. Instead it was quickly swept downstream. Takeshi chased it alongside the bank, dashing like a mongoose through the thicket, and finally dived, fully clothed, to capture it.

He laughed like a child.

Masaharu had not believed his son when Takeshi had told him about what he had done that Saturday night. Takeshi showed him the guiro as evidence. Masaharu reacted by staying sober all week, trying to remember. Takeshi knew his father had finally pieced together the events when Masaharu began telling his son, over and over, *"Japanese girl good fo' you. Odda kine girl, no good."*

Takeshi was restless in bed all that week. Sometimes he carried hundred-pound bags in his sleep, stacking them head high. He would wake up and remind himself that work was *pau. Pau hana,* he told himself. Rest time. He tried to think of other things. Like Linda. A future.

The mango wars didn't help. That was what Takeshi called the season's first falling of mango on the Quonset roofs. *BOOM! WHABAM!* It sounded like another World War.

The night moans of his parents from the next room did not help either. Was that his destiny? To moan at night from the aches of too many years of long hours of backbreaking work?

Saturday came. Mr. Armstrong walked into the store. Takeshi had been sitting behind the jars of pickled plum and dried fruit practicing his stroke on the guiro.

"So this is the family store," Mr. Armstrong said.

"Yeah. Dis is it," Takeshi said. They shook hands.

"Say, this is a strange-looking calabash." Mr. Armstrong had noticed the carved gourd. Takeshi handed it over to him.

"Nice, yeah?"

"Very nice." Mr. Armstrong held the gourd up. "This is the baby form of Lono, the god of fertility, agriculture, music . . . everything nice."

"Wha'chu talking about?"

"Lono. The Hawaiian god who oversees the Makahiki festivities." He looked at his former student, stating matter-of-factly, "You don't know that?" Takeshi shrugged his shoulders. "This is the very stuff the schools ought to be teaching, the meaningful stuff."

"Hey, ah . . . ," Takeshi said. "But dass Puerto Rican. Not Hawaiian."

"Hmmmm . . . I *knew* there was something different about this. Different yet same. Nice." He handed the gourd back to Takeshi. "Well, I'd better get what I came for." Mr. Armstrong began gathering groceries. Afterward he and Takeshi talked a bit more, about Takeshi's fellow McKinley graduates who spent their days diving for coins dropped from passenger ships like the *Lurline* at Pier 10, about those who were *furyoshonin,* pool hall bums, about the general lack of opportunities for nonwhites, especially Orientals, who were seen by the white oligarchy as a threat. Before he left, Mr. Armstrong, as if he were again lecturing Takeshi in a class, as if he could read his former student's mind, stated, "You know, I've missed so many boats in my lifetime, I thought I'd never get anywhere. But look now, I'm here. All the way from New York. And, believe me, this is paradise. No matter what anybody says. . . . I guess what I'm trying to say is that another boat will always come. See you later." He left.

Takeshi was carrying the guiro—which was tied on a string to his left hand—that night when he climbed the mango tree outside the social hall. It was nine o'clock and the place was starting to explode. Those who drank were drunk by now. Two fistfights had started out of the blue and had ended in a manner even more vague. The guitarists—playing guitars of all sizes—strummed harder and harder, shouting out their Spanish words to be heard above the din. And the poor guiro player—playing a gourd half the size of the one Takeshi carried—struggled to keep up with the demands for increased volume. Takeshi, numbed observer of all the madness, could not resist the temptation to start scraping his own guiro from his unique position. At first he played softly, not even attracting the attention of those around him. But then he, too, got lost in the rhythm, and before Manny made him realize it, had begun to dictate it from afar.

"Ay! Get yo' ass down here, Japanee." The voice was Manny's. Takeshi was hesitant but saw the futility of not complying. He silently cursed his father for not passing on to him his knowledge of *jujitsu* and, holding the gourd in one hand and the stick in his mouth, made the easy jump down. Takeshi had seen enough Saturday-night scrapes to be pretty sure he would be involved in the next one.

"Ay," said Manny, leaning quite a bit and grinning wide. "If you like play da music, you go *in*side. Not out here. Come on." Manny grabbed Takeshi by the arm.

"No," Takeshi said, pulling back. "Ass okay. I no like."

"Come on. No be shame! We all da same, ovah here. No be shame," Manny repeated. "Everybody too drunk fo' notice anyway." Takeshi found himself being pulled into the hall and to the front in midsong. Manny urged him on, pantomiming the art of guiro playing and shouting, *"Toca! Toca, Japonesa!"*

Takeshi finally succumbed to the strong will of Manny, playing softly, with hesitation. Smiles from the band, some familiar faces, comforted him. Shame gave way to relief.

"Da feel!" one band member shouted. "Yeah. You get da feeling, my friend."

"Welcome aboard!" another shouted as Takeshi slipped onto the stage.

Takeshi knew he had broken through some godawful barrier—within himself. He couldn't help but smile at the thought that was forming, the thought of being the helmsman of the ship that would sail on through the night, through the sea of dancers, across the ocean of lost opportunities. . . . He just wanted to steer her right.

Then there was Linda. Takeshi spotted her (it wasn't hard), her eyes shining like beacons in the darkness, her unbraided hair flowing in waves about her shoulders, dancing to the rhythms, and her smile. . . . When Linda spotted him, she winked him on, snapping her fingers like castanets.

THE INGREDIENT

Julio Marzán

Julio Marzán is a graduate of Columbia University's Graduate Writing Pro-gram. He has published a collection of poems, Translations Without Originals *(1986),* The Spanish American Roots of William Carlos Williams *(1994), and* The Numinous Site: The Poetry of Luis Palés Matos *(1995). His short stories have been published in several anthologies and literary journals. He is a professor of English and resides in New York.*

Half Irish and half Puerto Rican, the protagonist of "The Ingredient" finds himself simultaneously embarrassed by and attracted to his Puerto Rican back-ground. He is challenged to establish a sense of identity between these two poles, represented by his alienated dark-skinned Puerto Rican grandmother and a blond and blue-eyed Puerto Rican love interest.

WHEN VINCENT FINALLY LOOKED DOWN FROM THE ROOF ACROSS from his grandmother's building, he realized how crazily he was behav-ing. Why had he come up here? Just to catch a glimpse of Robert and confirm with his own eyes that his friend was fucking Magda? The idea of coming up, now executed, seemed stupid—even dangerous, but there was a kind of beauty to the view. The setting October sun behind him reflected golden in rows of windows. In every building an assortment of old people, teenagers, housewives leaned out, one or two talking to people below. On the sidewalks children jumped rope or chased a rubber ball or simply each other. From the far end of the street rose the shouting voices of a stickball game in progress. At the nearest corner, a steady trickle of men and women, returning from work, turned and paraded to their respective buildings. From up here a kind of peace indeed washed over everything. Unlike the baked street, the gray and black rooftops had a breeze blowing over them. The moment made him think of lines he had underlined in Wordsworth's "The Prelude" the day before as his professor lectured:

> *Whate'er mission, the soft breeze can come*
> *To none more grateful than to me; excaped*
> *From the vast city, where I long had pined*
> *A discontented sojourner . . .*

But he was in the city and he noticed just then that a faint crosscurrent of salsa and merengue danced in the dusk air. Louder still was the rap music from below, from a suitcase-sized boom box beside a guy sitting on the top step of his grandmother's stoop. He was gesturing to Vincent's side of the street, to a one-legged guy seated on a car fender. That had to be Rafy the Vietnam Vet, who hadn't been there when Vincent entered the building. Contemplating those two characters prompted Vincent to ask himself how it could have occurred to him to show up in this shit neighborhood to stupidly surprise Magda with a visit, especially since he should have seen the signs that she had no interest in him. *Slam!* A metal door had shut loudly behind him. On the roof of the building to his right walked a man and little boy whose entire body was shielded by a white plastic kite. The man took the kite from the boy and walked toward the roof wall. Raising the kite with one hand, he waved off the kid, who took backward steps as he unspooled the cord. The kite wafted briefly before teetering-tottering back down. The man picked it up and ordered the kid to run holding up the cord. It was aloft. Blown away . . . like him, as if Magda had just puckered her lips and exhaled a gust that set him sailing up on this roof, with no hope of having her and without a best friend.

Robert had been like his second brother at Fieldston. This year they entered Columbia together. They both signed up for Intermediate Spanish, although Vincent needed it more than Robert, who only took the course to boost his average. Robert spoke Spanish fluently. His diplomat father had been stationed throughout the Americas, where Robert grew up. If he hadn't taken the initiative to join the Spanish Club, Vincent wouldn't have joined because, to begin with, he didn't speak Spanish fluently and it was going to be a chore. At Fieldston he took French. Now he would have given anything to be fluent in Spanish, just to be able to defend himself against the Spanish Club snobs who expected that, because his father was Puerto Rican, he should speak it. Robert didn't have those problems. The Spanish club welcomed him. He even possessed the confidence to try to join the more militant Latin Students Association, although he was let known straight out he wasn't wanted. The L.S.A. students were the type who used their campus roles to fantasize having the power they were denied in the real world, which Vincent had always assumed was more his domain. He hadn't planned to join the L.S.A. until he learned that Magda, the president of the Spanish Club, was also a leader of the L.S.A.

Vincent picked up his backpack by the straps. Inside were books, syringes, and insulin, his mother's only apparent legacy, and hard candy because chocolate melted in summer. He heard the boy complaining as the man spooled the cord. Before turning to depart, Vincent noticed that in the low sun lost behind buildings, the lighted apartments were sharply visible through their windows. His grandmother was in the kitchen, stirring something in a pot. He had eaten her food only a few times, never forgetting the roasted pork loin on Christmas. As they grew up, his father stopped taking his sons to visit her, and they never felt compelled to visit on their own. He couldn't recall ever looking directly at her, studying her, as he was doing now. What irony. Magda had told Robert about Rafy the Vietnam Vet, the one-legged drug dealer who hung out on the stoop two doors from her building. Robert passed it on to Vincent that this street was where they could score some pot. Vincent kept to himself that that street was his grandmother's.

Slam! The man and kid were gone. Vincent looked around the tar-coated roof. Anything could happen up here in the dark. He had to get back to his real world, after an hour's subway ride to the West Side. He took a last look at his grandmother's window. Behind the sofa, she had dinner with a younger, heavier woman. What must they be talking about? What was the world of that gray-haired dark-skinned woman whose blood ran in him and whom he hardly knew? Of her two grandsons only he was burdened with her brown complexion. Vincent's father was fair-skinned, like his father, who had died before Vincent was born. He had only seen his grandfather in an old wedding photograph. In its yellowing sepia, his grandmother looked as blond as his grandfather. It was difficult for him to imagine that the young woman in the photograph and the old woman in the window contained a past connected to his present. He could cite no folklore or bedtime stories passed on by her. Neither he nor his brother ever called her. Nor she them. Because she and his Irish mother disliked each other, his father never forced her on the family.

Vincent last saw her when he was in the ninth grade. She was supposed to be very sick, and his father insisted the boys come with him. She didn't appear that sick and wasn't very loving or grateful. Their coming down from nice Riverdale to this part of the Bronx was a psychological chore and a half, but she never displayed an ounce of sympathy for the difficulty of their coming down to her. Instead she looked at them with a kind of shame, exhibiting no sense of being the source of so much embarrassment to them in their world, in which her blood line elicited from others a look that enveloped them in an isolating cellophane. Afterwards he complained about her attitude to his mother, who considered herself "an American, just that," and whose only past, to speak of, was embodied in a brother in Philadelphia, whom she rarely saw. She thought Vincent's identity concerns were a waste of time. She got impatient with him. "You don't have to identify with her, because you and she have nothing in common," she advised him. Then what was he supposed to say his father's last name was? "Tell them you're French, that's all, Beauchamp is French."

Magda had looked shocked to find him standing at her door. As usual her eyes refused to meet his. He had always thought the gap between them was cultural. She was the president of the Spanish Club, member of the Latin Students Association governing board, organizer of protest marches in favor of every cause: Latin Women's Rights, Puerto Rican Independence, and the Ad Hoc Committee on Fairness in Admission Practices. In every respect she embodied the single motivation for his and Robert's moving in on the Latin scene: to meet Latin women. Robert thought they were the sexiest-looking and Vincent couldn't agree more. Everything else about the Latin students he and Robert mocked in private. They felt above the few José's, Manuel's, and Tito's—studying on minority scholarships, which his mother turned down—with their sleazy mustached-look, their ghetto English that always just sounded black. Robert theorized that their hot ladies were also hot for social mobility and a better class of man.

Caught up in his friend's sexual agenda, Vincent shared Robert's fair-haired confidence, forgetting his being different. Additionally, Magda's magnetism further inspired him to overcome his insecurity among Latins. She always wore a dress or skirt that revealed her full, proportioned legs. Her long ash-blond hair, halfway down her back, bounced with her constant exuberance. Her every gesture excited him. In pursuit of her he made every effort to bridge the cultural distance between them. He plowed into Spanish, practicing for hours in the language lab. He signed up for every elective on Latin American culture and literature that fit his schedule. He wouldn't have minded at all coming to these streets to take her home. He had gone as far as to think about a way of breaking the news to his mother.

At that very second Robert had to be sitting in Magda's living room, holding her hand. Maybe her mother was about to serve fried green plantains and pan-fried steaks with sautéed onions and white rice with red beans, a dish his grandmother once prepared so deliciously. After dinner they might discuss his future career plans, with Robert giving an Oscar performance. Vincent's jealousy inflamed his mind. He had to wipe his soul clean of the whole episode, begin a new chapter. He contemplated the twin peaks of the Triboro Bridge outlined in blue lights, the blackness of the surrounding night, and heaved a deep breath. Another girl, what the fuck, just another girl. He turned, frightened of the intense dark, finally come to his senses that he had to get back.

When he opened the steel door, a hard-bassed rap music resonated in the stairwell, a flight or two below. He shut the door and listened to the music become louder. He ran to the darkest spot, behind the chimney base, and squatted there, wedged between the chimney and the roof wall. The metal door opened. The guy who had been standing in front of his grandmother's building with the boom box stepped out on the roof and leaned his back against the open door. In the triangular light from the stairwell, out came Rafy, who had climbed, incredibly, five flights on crutches. His skin was smooth brown and his hair wavy black, combed straight back. He wore baggy jeans with one leg rolled up and an Army fatigue shirt with the sleeves torn at the wriggling biceps. He hopped out in front of the stairwell door as Boombox turned off the boom box and placed it in the center of the light. Rafy leaned against the door while Boombox tied it open from behind, then disappeared behind the stairwell to bring out a milk crate that he placed at the edge of the light. Rafy sat on it, laying his crutches beside the crate, and immediately pulled on the Velcro strip that held together his rolled-up pants leg.

Boombox kneeled beside the leg and unrolled it flat. Out of pockets sewn along the inside of the leg, he removed an inventory of small manila and plasticine envelopes and an assortment of vials. He straightened his torso and took out of his side pocket a wad of bills and a small notepad. He counted the bills, wrote in the pad, then returned both into his pocket. Out of his back pocket he took out a folded knife and whipped out its blade. Tilting back the boom box, he wedged open the right lower speaker. The grid, covering no speaker, popped off. From that cavity, he removed merchandise that he stuffed into the appropriate flap-covered compartment in Rafy's pants leg.

Vincent's sugar level dropped. He needed to suck on a candy but was afraid to move. It occurred to him that these two guys represented all he knew about that half of his past that the world had thrust upon him. Robert knew a better kind, that's why he had no problem with getting close to them. He tried to keep poised, resisting the dizziness and lethargy from his need for sugar. He thought of his father, who near the end looked at the entire family as if from a distance, the way Vincent was observing Rafy and Boombox. His successful father, a chemist and later a pharmaceutical's representative, had risen far away from this street. Even though he felt oddly left out of the mainstream in which his father had left him, he always thought that that was where he belonged. What gene caused him to gravitate to this neighborhood and these broken people? His hands pressed against the roof wall and the chimney, holding him up as his head seemed to spin in a low-blood-sugar vertigo.

Boombox commented to Rafy about the white guy who had been scoring some pot. Boombox had made the sale, then gave a sign to Rafy, who, across the street, went into the hallway to get the stuff from his pants leg. He came out and as usual leaned against a car to drop the envelope on the curb beside a tire. This time a patrol car was coming up the street. Boombox whistled. Rafy hobbled into his hallway and Boombox vanished into his. The white guy panicked and yelled into Boombox's hallway that he'd come back for it later. Boombox was laughing because that guy, Bob, thought the street was some Kmart with a layaway plan. "He left his shit on the street, man, he fucking gave it away," as far as Boombox was concerned.

Their restocking done, now they were sharing a joint. Boombox sucked fervently on the roach as he looked down from the roof wall. He was fat and wore a white T-shirt over a pair of baggy, pink knee-length shorts. His high-necked sneakers were loosely tied. He looked up and down the length of the street. Then, bursting out in laughter, he pointed down and looked back to Rafy because that white guy was back, coming up the block. "One unique dumb motherfucker coming back to KMart." They both laughed wildly at that. Boombox described Bob's motions in front of the building across the street. Bob went into the hallway. He came out and looked around. He crossed the street and looked along the curb. "Guess what? He didn't find nothing." They cackled. Now Bob was going back down the block. Boombox returned to Rafy. "We better go downstairs and do some business." Boombox held the crutches upright for Rafy, who mounted his armpits over the pads. Boombox put away the milk crate, picked up his boom box, and untied the door. The metal door sounded like a shot, leaving the roof totally black. Rap music resounded in the hall.

Drenched with sweat, Vincent came out of the fetal position he had assumed to hide in the shadow. He sat against the roof wall and felt in the dark through his backpack for the cellophane-covered candies. He sucked and bit into one desperately. He waited for the sugar to kick in. As he relaxed, relieved of his discomfort, the only thing he could think about was the name Bob.

★   ★   ★

... Over her loud stereo playing Rubén Blades, one of the few Latin singers whose music he knew, Vincent had had to identify himself three times. Magda's repeating "Who?" to herself cut mortally into his confidence. When she finally opened, instead of inviting him in she had demanded to know why he was there. He asked to be let in. She warned him that she was waiting for Bob. Bob who? "Your friend." Vincent had always known Robert as Robert. He hadn't expected to be turned down, not in a million years. Robert knew how he felt about Magda. Nevertheless, Vincent kept to his script. He needed to talk to her, could she lower the volume. No, she wouldn't. He sat on her sofa, sensing the need to talk fast. He explained that he was brought up very differently from her, but that because of her he had taken Spanish and joined the Latin American Students Association. Magda cut him off. "What are you getting at?"

"Because of your commitment and sense of identity. You're like the star of everything Latin, Magda, you know that."

"Well, so what?"

"I just thought you saw me as some assimilated guy from Riverdale and I wanted to get close to you. I was ashamed I couldn't speak Spanish fluently, for instance."

"And what if you could?"

"Then you would pay some attention to me. I like you a lot, Magda."

Magda rolled her eyes upward and went to get her pocketbook. She took out a pack of cigarettes. Shaking her head, she opened the pack and lit up. She started to speak but paused. When she found the right words, she spoke looking at her lap, as if speaking to herself, the red-tipped cigarette punctuating every word, "I just told you I'm waiting for Bob. Wasn't that enough of a hint?"

"I didn't know that when I worked up the courage to come here. And, right now, I don't care."

"I'm going to tell you something, Vinny. I'm going to be frank with you." She took a deep drag, dispelling the smoke hard, her eyes toward the window. Her long hair wore the afternoon light coming in from the window. Her blue eyes were Bermudan coves in travel posters. She began the next sentence with "I . . . ," then looked into his eyes for the first time. "I don't go out with Rican guys. Okay?"

His words flowed out thickly: "Bob only likes Latin girls because he thinks they all look like sluts. Those are his words, Magda."

"Well, I'm no slut and he knows it. So I think it's just better if you get out."

Downstairs Rafy and Boombox were back at work. The asphalt looked smoother and cleaner in the yellow streetlights. Some kids still played in the dark. A mother leaning out a lighted window hollered out a name. A kid answered her from the sidewalk. Vincent's grandmother sat in a sofa facing the window. The younger, heavy-set woman sat in a chair. They watched TV as he watched them, a portrait framed by the window. Suddenly his mind came up with an answer to a question he hadn't consciously asked: He hadn't joined the Latin Students Association or his Spanish classes because of Magda. He had joined because of the inevitable "What are you?" Later he was told he looked "Spanish" and he responded he wasn't, that he was born in the Bronx and he was half Irish. Nobody believed the Irish part and the other half stuck in his throat. In high school this identity crap seemed like a stupid game, but in college it had become all important. Until that afternoon, Magda was the one person who could help him. She was the solution to his solitude. Magda, he realized that very second, reminded him of his grandmother in his father's old photograph.

The streets below looked fathoms deep. The city's lights formed a labyrinth he was seeing for the first time. Robert's path in it started at any point in this country and led to Riverdale, the West Side, the South Bronx, and to wherever on the planet he wanted. Rafy and Boombox had only one, this street to their island and back. On the same path belonged his grandmother and also Magda, who coveted Robert's, on which she would find Vincent's mother and blond brother. But what was his father's path? Did he have one of his own or was that why he married his mother? The thought was cruel, but he felt angry. Nobody ever told him he would grow up deprived of a path. Now, losing Robert, he had lost the path on which he had been a guest. *What dwelling shall receive me? in what vale Shall be my harbour? underneath what grove Shall I take up my home?* And that afternoon Magda had shoved him out into nowhere, alone with his father's treacherous gene and his mother's diabetes. Maybe that's why he had come up to this roof: because he was walking in a maze he had intuited and not yet acknowledged. Or maybe to observe in his grandmother the ingredient that caused Magda to reject him, that thread bonding him to even Rafy and Boombox. This defect for his entire life was, after all, inherited from his grandmother, who would vibrate in his bones like Boombox's music behind the metal roof door, which he had just opened. The chipped-beige halls around him were identical to those he remembered in his grandmother's building. In the naked-bulb light, he descended to what borrowed path would get him to Columbia.

PART II

FAMILY TIES

Brothers Under the Skin

Piri Thomas

Piri Thomas was born in 1928 in El Barrio (Spanish Harlem), New York. Thomas, now a prominent Puerto Rican lecturer, short-story writer, playwright, and poet, was originally limelighted by the success of his autobiography Down These Mean Streets *(1967). This was the first coming-of-age memoir, written in English by a second-generation Puerto Rican, to become a best-seller in the United States. Similar to his other major works,* Savior, Savior Hold My Hand *(1972),* Seven Long Times *(1974), and* Stories from El Barrio *(1978), it chronicles his experience with life on the streets and in prison from the 1930s to the 1960s.*

"Brothers Under the Skin" is one of the few chapters in Down These Mean Streets *that focuses on Thomas's home life. Here he poignantly recounts coming to terms with his identity as a black Puerto Rican in the United States, while confronting his own family's racism and denial.*

MY DAYDREAMING WAS SPLINTERED BY MY BROTHER JOSÉ KICKING at the door in sheer panic. "Hey, who's in there?" he yelled.

"Me, man, me," I yelled back. "Whatta ya want?"

"Let me in. I gotta take a piss so bad I can taste it."

"Taste good?" I asked softly.

"Dammit, open up!"

I laughed, and reached out a dripping hand and flipped the latch. José rushed in like his behind was on fire. His face had a pained look on it. "Chri-sus sake," he said, "you made me piss all over my pants."

"It'll dry, man, it'll dry."

"Aggh," he said as he relieved himself. "That feels good."

I looked at my brother. *Even his peter's white,* I thought, *just like James's. Only ones got black peters is Poppa and me, and Poppa acts like his is white, too.*

"Poppa's home."

"Yeah. Hand me the towel, simple."

"Damn, Piri, you made me piss all over my pants," José said again. He pulled back the towel he was offering me and began to wipe his pants with it.

"Man, turkey, what you doin'?" I said. "You drying that piss and I gotta wipe my face with that towel."

"It'll dry, man, it'll dry."

I yanked the towel outta his hand and carefully wiped with what seemed to be the part he hadn't used. "You know somethin', José?" I said.

"What? Jesus, I hope this piss don't stink when it dries."

"I'm goin' down South."

"Where?"

"Down South."

"What for?"

"Don't know all the way," I said, "except I'm tryin' to find somethin' out."

"Down South!" He said it like I was nuts.

"*Sí.* I want to see what a *moyeto*'s worth and the paddy's weight on him," I said.

"Whatta ya talking about? You sound like a *moto* who's high on that *yerba* shit. And anyway, what's the spade gotta do with you?"

"I'm a Negro."

"You ain't no nigger," José said.

"I ain't?"

"No. You're a Puerto Rican."

"I am, huh?" I looked at José and said, "'Course, you gotta say that. 'Cause if I'm a Negro, then you and James is one too. And that ain't leavin' out Sis and Poppa. Only Momma's an exception. She don't care what she is."

José didn't look at me. He decided that looking at the toilet bowl was better. "So whatta you got to find out, eh?" he said. "You're crazy, stone loco. We're Puerto Ricans, and that's different from being *moyetos*." His voice came back very softly and his hand absentmindedly kept brushing the drying wet patch on his pants.

"That's what I've been wanting to believe all along, José," I said. "I've been hanging on to that idea even when I knew it wasn't so. But only pure white Puerto Ricans are white, and you wouldn't even believe that if you ever dug what the paddy said."

"I don't give a good shit what you say, Piri. We're Puerto Ricans, and that makes us different from black people."

I kept drying myself even though there was nothin' to dry. I was trying not to get mad. I said, "José, that's what the white man's been telling the Negro all along, that 'cause he's white he's different from the Negro; that he's better'n the Negro or anyone that's not white. That's what I've been telling myself and what I tried to tell Brew."

"Brew's that colored guy, ain't he?" José said.

"Yeah—an' like I'm saying, sure there's stone-white Puerto Ricans, like from pure Spanish way back—but it ain't us. Poppa's a Negro and, even if Momma's *blanca*, Poppa's blood carries more weight with Mr. Charlie," I said.

"Mr. Charlie, Mr. Charlie. Who the fuck is he?"

"That's the name Brew calls the paddies. Ask any true *corazón* white motherfucker what the score is," I said.

"I'm not black, no matter what you say, Piri."

I got out of the shower and sat on the edge of the tub. "Maybe not outside, José," I said. "But you're sure that way inside."

"I ain't black, damn you! Look at my hair. It's almost blond. My eyes are blue, my nose is straight. My mother-fuckin' lips are not like a baboon's ass. My skin is white. White, goddammit! White! Maybe Poppa's a little dark, but that's the Indian blood in him. He's got white blood in him and—"

"So what the fuck am I? Something Poppa an' Momma picked out the garbage dump?" I was jumping stink inside and I answered him like I felt it. "Look, man, better believe it, I'm one of 'you-all.' Am I your brother or ain't I?"

"Yeah, you're my brother, and James an' Sis, and we all come out of Momma an' Poppa—but we ain't Negroes. We're Puerto Ricans, an' we're white."

"Boy, you, Poppa, and James sure are sold on that white kick. Poppa thinks that marrying a white woman made him white. He's wrong. It's just another nigger marrying a white woman and making her as black as him. That's the way the paddy looks at it. The Negro just stays black. Period. Dig it?"

José's face got whiter and his voice angrier at my attempt to take away his white status. He screamed out strong, "I ain't no nigger! You can be if you want to be. You can go down South and grow cotton, or pick it, or whatever the fuck they do. You can eat that cornbread or whatever shit they eat. You can bow and kiss ass and clean shit bowls. But—I—am—*white*! And you can go to hell!"

"And James is *blanco*, too?" I asked quietly.

"You're damn right."

"And Poppa?"

José flushed the toilet chain so hard it sounded as if somebody's neck had broken. "Poppa's the same as you," he said, avoiding my eyes, "Indian."

"What kinda Indian?" I said bitterly. "Caribe? Or maybe Borinquén? Say, José, didn't you know the Negro made the scene in Puerto Rico way back? And when the Spanish spics ran outta Indian coolies, they brought them big blacks from you know where. Poppa's got *moyeto* blood. I got it. Sis got it. James got it. And, mah deah brudder, you-all got it! Dig it! It's with us till game time. Like I said, man, that shit-ass poison I've been living with is on its way out. It's a played-out lie about me—us—being white. There ain't nobody in this fucking house can lay any claim to bein' paddy exceptin' Momma, and she's never made it a mountain of fever like we have. You and James are like houses—painted white outside, and blacker'n a mother inside. An' I'm close to being like Poppa—trying to be white on both sides."

José eased by me and put his hand on the doorknob.

"Where you going?" I said. "I ain't finished talking yet."

José looked at me like there was no way out. "Like I said, man, you can be a nigger if you want to," he said, as though he were talking with a ten-ton rock on his chest. "I don't know how you come to be my brother, but I love you like one. I've busted my ass, both me and James, trying to explain to people how come you so dark and how come your hair is so curly an'—"

I couldn't help thinking, *Oh, Crutch, you were so right. We shouldn't have moved to Long Island.* I said, "You and James hadda make excuses for *me?* Like for me being *un Negrito?*" I looked at the paddy in front of me. "Who to?" I said. "Paddies?"

Lights began to jump into my head and tears blurred out that this was my brother before me. The burning came up out of me and I felt the shock run up my arm as my fists went up the side of his head. I felt one fist hit his mouth. I wondered if I had broken any of his nice white teeth.

José fell away and bounced back with his white hands curled into fists. I felt the hate in them as his fists became a red light of exploding pain on my tender, flat-nose. *Oh, God!* I tried to make the lights go away. I made myself creep up a long sinking shit-hole agony and threw myself at José. The bathroom door flew open and me, naked and wet with angry sweat, and José, his mouth bleedin', crashed out of the bathroom and rolled into the living room. I heard all kinds of screaming and chairs turning over and falling lamps. I found myself on top of José. In the blurred confusion I saw his white, blood-smeared face and I heard myself screaming, "You bastard! Dig it, you bastard. You're bleeding, and the blood is like anybody else's—red!" I saw an unknown face spitting blood at me. I hated it. I wanted to stay on top of this unknown what-was-it and beat him and beat him and beat him and beat him and *beat beat beat beat beat*—and feel skin smash under me and—and—and—

I felt an arm grab me. It wasn't fair; it wasn't a *chevere* thing to do. In a fair rumble, nobody is supposed to jump in. "Goddammit, are you crazy?" a voice screamed. "Goddamn you for beating your brother like that. My God!—"

I twisted my head and saw Poppa. And somewhere, far off, I heard a voice that sounded like Momma crying, "What's it all about? What's it all about? Why do brothers do this to each other?"

I wanted to scream it out, but that man's arm was cutting my air from sound. I twisted and forced out, "Lemme go, Poppa. *Coño,* let me go!" And the arm was gone. I stayed on bended knees. My fists were tired and my knuckles hurt at this Cain and Abel scene. As the hurting began to leave me, I slowly became a part of my naked body. I felt weak with inside pain. I wondered why.

"José, José," Momma screamed, and I wondered why she didn't scream for me, too. Didn't she know I had gotten hurt the worst?

"Why in God's name?" Poppa was saying.

Fuck God! I thought.

"Why in God's name?"

I looked at Poppa. "'Cause, Poppa," I said, "him, you and James think you're white, and I'm the only one that's found out I'm not. I tried hard not to find out. But I did, and I'm almost out from under that kick you all are still copping out to." I got up from my knees. "Poppa," I added, "what's wrong with not being white? What's so wrong with being *tre-geño*? Momma must think it's great, she got married to you, eh? We gotta have pride and dignity, Poppa; we gotta walk big and bad. I'm me and I dig myself in the mirror and it's me. I shower and dig my peter and it's me. I'm black, and it don't make no difference whether I say good-bye or *adiós*—it means the same."

Nobody said anything; everyone just stood there. I said, "I'm proud to be a Puerto Rican, but being Puerto Rican don't make the color." Still there was silence. "I'm going," I said.

"Where?" Poppa asked.

"I don't know . . ."

"He's going down South," said José, sitting on the floor with his head in his hands and the almost-blond hair, the good, straight hair that could fall down over his forehead.

"Where?" Poppa asked.

I looked at José and felt sorry for me. I looked at the wall and said, "Down South. I joined the merchant marine and me and Brew's going, and—"

"Who? Brew? That's that colored boy, ain't it?" Poppa said.

"—and I wanna find out what's happening, and . . ." I wondered why everything I was saying didn't sound like it was so important to anybody, including me. I wondered why James wasn't there. I wondered why Sis wasn't there. . . .

I walked away. Momma put her hand on me and she asked, "Why does it hurt you so to be *un Negrito*?"

I shook my head and kept walking. I wished she could see inside me. I wished she could see it didn't hurt—so much.

Silent Dancing

Judith Ortiz Cofer

Judith Ortiz Cofer was born in Hormigueros, Puerto Rico, in 1952. She is the author of a novel, The Line of the Sun *(1989); two poetry collections,* Terms of Survival *(1987) and* Reaching for the Mainland *(1987); a compilation of poems and personal essays,* Silent Dancing: A Partial Remembrance of a Puerto Rican Childhood *(1990); and* The Latin Deli: Prose and Poetry *(1993). Cofer's work has appeared in numerous literary journals and anthologies and she has received fellowships from the National Endowment for the Arts and the Whitter Binner Foundation. She resides in Georgia, where she is a professor of English and creative writing at the University of Georgia.*

Most of Cofer's work reflects her struggle to create a history for herself out of a culturally ambiguous childhood spent traveling back and forth between the United States and Puerto Rico. In "Silent Dancing" she colorfully pieces together the images, sounds, smells, and faces of Puerto Rico in New Jersey.

WE HAVE A HOME MOVIE OF THIS PARTY. SEVERAL TIMES MY MOTHER and I have watched it together, and I have asked questions about the silent revelers coming in and out of focus. It is grainy and of short duration but a great visual aid to my first memory of life in Paterson at that time. And it is in color—the only complete scene in color I can recall from those years.

We lived in Puerto Rico until my brother was born in 1954. Soon after, because of economic pressures on our growing family, my father joined the United States Navy. He was assigned to duty on a ship in

Brooklyn Yard, New York City—a place of cement and steel that was to be his home base in the States until his retirement more than twenty years later.

He left the Island first, tracking down his uncle, who lived with his family across the Hudson River, in Paterson, New Jersey. There he found a tiny apartment in a huge apartment building that had once housed Jewish families and was just being transformed into a tenement by Puerto Ricans overflowing from New York City. In 1955 he sent for us. My mother was only twenty years old, I was not quite three, and my brother was a toddler when we arrived at *El Building,* as the place had been christened by its new residents.

My memories of life in Paterson during those first few years are in shades of gray. Maybe I was too young to absorb vivid colors and details, or to discriminate between the slate blue of the winter sky and the darker hues of the snow-bearing clouds, but the single color washes over the whole period. The building we lived in was gray, the streets were gray with slush the first few months of my life there, the coat my father had bought for me was dark in color and too big. It sat heavily on my thin frame.

I do remember the way the heater pipes banged and rattled, startling all of us out of sleep until we got so used to the sound that we automatically either shut it out or raised our voices above the racket. The hiss from the valve punctuated my sleep, which has always been fitful, like a nonhuman presence in the room—the dragon sleeping at the entrance of my childhood. But the pipes were a connection to all the other lives being lived around us. Having come from a house made for a single family back in Puerto Rico—my mother's extended-family home—it was curious to know that strangers lived under our floor and above our heads, and that the heater pipe went through everyone's apartments. (My first spanking in Paterson came as a result of playing tunes on the pipes in my room to see if there would be an answer). My mother was as new to this concept of beehive life as I was, but had been given strict orders by my father to keep the doors locked, the noise down, ourselves to ourselves.

It seems that Father had learned some painful lessons about prejudice while searching for an apartment in Paterson. Not until years later did I hear how much resistance he had encountered with landlords who were panicking at the influx of Latinos into a neighborhood that had been Jewish for a couple of generations. But it was the American phenomenon of ethnic turnover that was changing the urban core of Paterson, and the human flood could not be held back with an accusing finger.

"You Cuban?" the man had asked my father, pointing a finger at his name tag on the navy uniform—even though my father had the fair skin and light brown hair of his northern Spanish family background and our name is as common in Puerto Rico as Johnson is in the U.S.

"No," my father had answered, looking past the finger into his adversary's angry eyes, "I'm Puerto Rican."

"Same shit." And the door closed. My father could have passed as European, but we couldn't. My brother and I both have our mother's black hair and olive skin, and so we lived in El Building and visited our great-uncle and his fair children on the next block. It was their private joke that they were the German branch of the family. Not many years later that area, too, would be mainly Puerto Rican. It was as if the heart of the city map were being gradually colored in brown—*café-con-leche* brown. Our color.

The movie opens with a sweep of the living room. It is "typical" immigrant Puerto Rican decor for the time: the sofa and chairs are square and hard-looking, upholstered in bright colors (blue and yellow in this instance, and covered in the transparent plastic) that furniture salesmen then were adept at making women buy. The linoleum on the floor is light blue, and if it was subjected to the spike heels as it was in most places, there were dime-sized indentations all over it that cannot be seen in this movie. The room is full of people dressed in mainly two colors: dark suits for the men, red dresses for the women. I have asked my mother why most of the women are in red that night, and she shrugs, "I don't remember. Just a coincidence." She doesn't have my obsession for assigning symbolism to everything.

The three women in red sitting on the couch are my mother, my eighteen-year-old cousin, and her brother's girlfriend. The "novia" is just up from the Island, which is apparent in her body language. She sits up formally, and her dress is carefully pulled over her knees. She is a pretty girl, but her posture makes her look insecure, lost in her full-skirted red dress which she has carefully tucked around her to make room for my gorgeous cousin, her future sister-in-law. My cousin has grown up in Paterson and is in her last year of high school. She doesn't have a trace of what Puerto Ricans call la mancha *(literally, the stain: the mark of the new immigrant—something about the posture, the voice, or the humble demeanor, making it obvious to everyone that that person has just arrived on the mainland; has not yet acquired the polished look of the city dweller). My cousin is wearing a tight red-sequined cocktail dress. Her brown hair has been lightened with per-oxide around the bangs, and she is holding a cigarette very expertly between her fingers, bringing it up to her mouth in a sensuous arc of her arm to her as she talks animatedly with my mother, who has come to sit between the two women, both only a few years younger than herself. My mother is somewhere halfway between the poles they represent in our culture.*

It became my father's obsession to get out of the barrio, and thus we were never permitted to form bonds with the place or with the people who lived there. Yet the building was a comfort to my mother, who never got over yearning for *la isla*. She felt surrounded by her language: the walls were thin, and voices speaking and arguing in Spanish could be heard all day. Salsas blasted out of radios turned on early in the morn-ing and left on for company. Women seemed to cook rice and beans perpetually—the strong aroma of red kidney beans boiling permeated the hallways.

Though Father preferred that we do our grocery shopping at the su-permarket when he came home on weekend leaves, my mother insisted that she could cook only with products whose labels she could read, and so, during the week, I accompanied her and my little brother to La Bodega—a hole-in-the-wall grocery store across the street from El Building. There we squeezed down three narrow aisles jammed with various products. Goya and Libby's—those were the trademarks trusted by her mamá, and so my mother bought cans of Goya beans, soups, and condiments. She bought little cans of Libby's fruit juices for us. And she bought Colgate toothpaste and Palmolive soap. (The final *e* is pro-nounced in both those products in Spanish, and for many years I believed that they were manufactured on the Island. I remember my surprise at first hearing a commercial on television for the toothpaste in which *Col-gate* rhymed with *ate*.)

We would linger at La Bodega, for it was there that mother breathed best, taking in the familiar aromas of the foods she knew from Mamá's kitchen, and it was also there that she got to speak to the other women of El Building without violating outright Father's dictates against fraternizing with our neighbors.

But he did his best to make our "assimilation" painless. I can still see him carrying a Christmas tree up several flights of stairs to our apartment, leaving a trail of aromatic pine. He carried it formally, as if it were a flag in a parade. We were the only ones in El Building that I knew of who got presents on both Christmas Day and on *Día de Reyes,* the day when the Three Kings brought gifts to Christ and to Hispanic children.

Our greatest luxury in El Building was having our own television set. It must have been a result of Father's guilt feelings over the isolation he had imposed on us, but we were one of the first families in the barrio to have one. My brother quickly became an avid watcher of Captain Kangaroo and Jungle Jim. I loved all the family series, and by the time I started first grade in school, I could have drawn a map of Middle America as exemplified by the lives of characters in *Father Knows Best, The Donna Reed Show, Leave It to Beaver, My Three Sons,* and (my favorite) *Bachelor Father,* where John Forsythe treated his adopted teenage daughter like a princess because he was rich and had a Chinese houseboy to do everything for him. Compared to our neighbors in El Building, we were rich. My father's navy check provided us with financial security and a standard of life that the factory workers envied. The only thing his money could not buy us was a place to live away from the barrio—his greatest wish and Mother's greatest fear.

In the home movie the men are shown next, sitting around a card table set up in one corner of the living room, playing dominoes. The clack of the ivory pieces is a familiar sound. I heard it in many houses on the Island and in many apartments in Paterson. In Leave It to Beaver, *the Cleavers played bridge in every other episode; in my childhood, the men started every social occasion with a hotly debated round of dominoes: the women would sit around and watch, but they never participated in the games.*

Here and there you can see a small child. Children were always brought to parties and, whenever they got sleepy, put to bed in the host's bedrooms. Baby-sitting was a concept unrecognized by the Puerto Rican women I knew: a re-

sponsible mother did not leave her children with any stranger. And in a culture where children are not considered intrusive, there is no need to leave the children at home. We went where our mother went.

Of my preschool years I have only impressions: the sharp bite of the wind in December as we walked with our parents toward the brightly lit stores downtown, how I felt like a stuffed doll in my heavy coat, boots, and mittens; how good it was to walk into the five-and-dime and sit at the counter drinking hot chocolate.

On Saturdays our whole family would walk downtown to shop at the big department stores on Broadway. Mother bought all our clothes at Penney and Sears, and she liked to buy her dresses at the women's specialty shops like Lerner's and Diana's. At some point we would go into Woolworth's and sit at the soda fountain to eat.

We never ran into other Latinos at these stores or eating out, and it became clear to me only years later that the women from El Building shopped mainly at other places—stores owned either by other Puerto Ricans or by Jewish merchants who had philosophically accepted our presence in the city and decided to make us their good customers, if not neighbors and friends. These establishments were located not downtown but in the blocks around our street, and they were referred to generically as *La Tienda, El Bazar, La Bodega, La Botánica*. Everyone knew what was meant. These were the stores where your face did not turn a clerk to stone, where your money was as green as anyone else's.

On New Year's Eve we were dressed up like child models in the Sears catalogue—my brother in a miniature man's suit and bow tie, and I in black patent leather shoes and a frilly dress with several layers of crinolines underneath. My mother wore a bright red dress that night, I remember, and spike heels; her long black hair hung to her waist. Father, who usually wore his navy uniform during his short visits home, had put on a dark civilian suit for the occasion: we had been invited to his uncle's house for a big celebration. Everyone was excited because my mother's brother, Hernán—a bachelor who could indulge himself in such luxuries—had bought a movie camera, which he would be trying out that night.

Even the home movie cannot fill in the sensory details such a gathering left imprinted in a child's brain. The thick sweetness of women's perfume mixing with the ever-present smells of food cooking in the kitchen: meat and plantain *pasteles,* the ubiquitous rice dish made special with pigeon peas—*gandules*—and seasoned with the precious *sofrito* sent up from the Island by somebody's mother or smuggled in by a recent traveler. *Sofrito* was one of the items that women hoarded, since it was hardly ever in stock at La Bodega. It was the flavor of Puerto Rico.

The men drank Palo Viejo rum and some of the younger ones got weepy. The first time I saw a grown man cry was at a New Year's Eve party. He had been reminded of his mother by the smells in the kitchen. But what I remember most were the boiled *pasteles*—boiled plantain or yucca rectangles stuffed with corned beef or other meats, olives, and many other savory ingredients, all wrapped in banana leaves. Everyone had to fish one out with a fork. There was always a "trick" pastel—one without stuffing—and whoever got that one was the "New Year's Fool."

There was also the music. Long-playing albums were treated like precious china in these homes. Mexican recordings were popular, but the songs that brought tears to my mother's eyes were sung by the melancholic Daniel Santos, whose life as a drug addict was the stuff of legend. Felipe Rodríguez was a particular favorite of couples. He sang about faithless women and broken-hearted men. There is a snatch of a lyric that has stuck in my mind like a needle on a worn groove: *"De piedra ha de ser mi cama, de piedra la cabecera . . . la mujer que a mi me quiera . . . ha de quererme de veras. Ay, Ay, corazón, ¿por qué no amas . . . ?"* I must have heard it a thousand times since the idea of a bed made of stone, and its connection to love first troubled me with its disturbing images.

The five-minute home movie ends with people dancing in a circle. The creative filmmaker must have asked them to do that so that they could file past him. It is both comical and sad to watch silent dancing. Since there is no justification for the absurd movements that music provides for some of us, people appear frantic, their faces embarrassingly intense. It's as if you were watching sex. Yet for years, I've had dreams in the form of this home movie. In a recurring scene, familiar faces push themselves forward into my mind's eye, plastering their features into distorted close-ups. And I'm asking them, "Who is she? Who is the woman I don't recognize? Is she an aunt? Somebody's wife? Tell me who she is. Tell me who these people are."

"No, see the beauty mark on her cheek as big as a hill on the lunar landscape of her face—well, that runs in the family. The women on your father's side of the family wrinkle early; it's the price they pay for that fair skin. The young girl with the green stain on her wedding dress is *La Novia*—just up from the island. See, she lowers her eyes as she approaches the camera, like she's supposed to. Decent girls never look you directly in the face. *Humilde,* humble, a girl should express humility in all her actions. She will make a good wife for your cousin. He should consider himself lucky to have met her only weeks after she arrived here. If he marries her quickly, she will make him a good Puerto Rican–style wife; but if he waits too long, she will be corrupted by the city, just like your cousin there."

"She means me. I do what I want. This is not some primitive island I live on. Do they expect me to wear a black *mantilla* on my head and go to Mass every day? Not me. I'm an American woman and I will do as I please. I can type faster than anyone in my senior class at Central High, and I'm going to be a secretary to a lawyer when I graduate. I can pass for an American girl anywhere—I've tried it—at least for Italian, anyway. I never speak Spanish in public. I hate these parties, but I wanted the dress. I look better than any of these *humildes* here. My life is going to be different. I have an American boyfriend. He is older and has a car. My parents don't know it, but I sneak out of the house late at night sometimes to be with him. If I marry him, even my name will be American. I hate rice and beans. It's what makes these women fat."

"Your *prima* is pregnant by that man she's been sneaking around with. Would I lie to you? I'm your great-uncle's common-law wife—the one he abandoned on the Island to marry your cousin's mother. I was not invited to this party, but I came anyway. I came to tell you that story about your cousin that you've always wanted to hear. Remember that comment your mother made to a neighbor that has always haunted you? The only thing you heard was your cousin's name and then you saw your mother pick up your doll from the couch and say, 'It was as big as this doll when they flushed it down the toilet.' This image has bothered you for years, hasn't it? You had nightmares about babies being flushed down the toilet, and you wondered why anyone would do such a horrible thing. You didn't dare ask your mother about it. She would only tell you that you had not heard her right and yell at you for listening to adult conversations. But later, when you were old enough to know about abortions, you suspected. I am here to tell you that you were right. Your cousin was growing an *Americanito* in her belly when this movie was made. Soon after, she put something long and pointy into her pretty self, thinking maybe she could get rid of the problem before breakfast and still make it to her first class at the high school. Well, *Niña,* her screams could be heard downtown. Your aunt, her mamá, who had been a mid-wife on the Island, managed to pull the little thing out. Yes, they prob-ably flushed it down the toilet, what else could they do with it—give it a Christian burial in a little white casket with blue bows and ribbons? Nobody wanted that baby—least of all the father, a teacher at her school with a house in West Paterson that he was filling with real children, and a wife who was a natural blonde.

"Girl, the scandal sent your uncle back to the bottle. And guess where your cousin ended up? Irony of ironies. She was sent to a village in Puerto Rico to live with a relative on her mother's side: a place so far away from civilization that you have to ride a mule to reach it. A real change in scenery. She found a man there. Women like that cannot live without male company. But believe me, the men in Puerto Rico know how to put a saddle on a woman like her. *La Gringa,* they call her. Ha, ha. ha. *La Gringa* is what she always wanted to be. . . ."

The old woman's mouth becomes a cavernous black hole I fall into. And as I fall, I can feel the reverberations of her laughter. I hear the echoes of her last mocking words: *La Gringa, La Gringa!* And the conga line keeps moving silently past me. There is no music in my dream for the dancers.

When Odysseus visits Hades asking to see the spirit of his mother, he makes an offering of sacrificial blood, but since all of the souls crave an audience with the living, he has to listen to many of them before he can ask questions. I, too, have to hear the dead and the forgotten speak in my dream. Those who are still part of my life remain silent, going around and around in their dance. The others keep pressing their faces forward to say things about the past.

My father's uncle is last in line. He is dying of alcoholism, shrunken and shriveled like a monkey, his face is a mass of wrinkles and broken veins. As he comes closer, I realize that in his features I can see my whole family. If you were to stretch that rubbery flesh, you could find my father's face, and deep within *that* face—mine. I don't want to look into those eyes ringed in purple. In a few years he will retreat into silence, and take a long, long time to die. *Move back, Tío,* I tell him. *I don't want to hear what you have to say. Give the dancers room to move, soon it will be midnight. Who is the New Year's Fool this time?*

WHY WOMEN REMAIN *JAMONA*

Esmeralda Santiago

Esmeralda Santiago is a graduate of Harvard University and has an M.F.A. from Sarah Lawrence College. She has published an autobiography, When I Was Puerto Rican *(1993), and a novel,* America's Dream *(1996), both of which she has translated into Spanish. Santiago's work has appeared in* The New York Times, *the* Boston Globe, *the* Christian Science Monitor, *and* Si *magazine. A sequel to her autobiography is forthcoming. With her husband she owns CANTOMEDIA, a film production company. They have two children and live in Westchester County, New York.*

When I Was Puerto Rican vividly recounts Santiago's early years, from growing up in rural Puerto Rico among seven siblings and warring parents, through high school in New York City. In "Why Women Remain Jamona*," Santiago observes the peculiar lifestyle of her grandparents, and her parents' failing marriage, critiquing the expectation that wives should be infinitely tolerant of their husbands' behavior and consider themselves fortunate to have one.*

La verdad, aunque severa, es amiga verdadera.

Truth, although severe, is a true friend.

ONE SUNDAY MAMI STARCHED AND IRONED MY WHITE PIQUÉ DRESS, packed a few changes of clothes in a small bag, and told me I was to spend a few days with Papi's mother.

"Your *abuela* is old, so you be a good helper," Mami told me as she braided my hair.

"How long will I be there?"

"About a week. Papi will take you, and he'll pick you up next Sunday. Don't look so worried. You'll have fun!"

Papi dressed in his best clothes, and while the day was still cool, we set out for Santurce. The *público* made many stops on the way, to pick up and drop off passengers, most of them, like us, dressed for a journey. When we reached Bayamón, the closest city to Macún, we had to change *públicos*. We were early, so we walked to the *plaza del mercado*. It was a square cement building with stalls along the walls and in the middle, forming a labyrinth of aisles dead-ending into kiosks with live chickens in wire cages, shelves of canned food, counters stacked high with *ñames* and *yautías,* coffee beans and breadfruit. Colored lights swung from the rafters where pigeons and warblers perched, forcing vendors to put up awnings against bird droppings.

"Are you hungry?" Papi asked, and I nodded, searching for the food stalls I smelled but could not see. We turned at the corner where a tall stack of rabbit hutches butted against a stack of dove cages.

"I smell *alcapurrias,*" I said as Papi led me past a long table on which a tall gray woman arranged plaster heads of Jesus crowned with thorns, blood dripping into his upturned eyes, in an expression similar to the one Norma took on when she was annoyed. The woman set a Jesus down, her fingers caressing the thorns, and watched us, her long, mournful face horselike, her large eyes almond-shaped, the corners pointing down as if weighed by many tears. The space around her felt cold, and I changed sides with Papi as we passed her on our way to the far end of the market, which was light and noisy with birds chirping overhead and a few well-placed speakers through which blared my favorite *chachachá,* "Black Eyes, Cinnamon Skin."

"What can I get you?" the counterman asked as he wiped in front of us with a rag that spread a thin film of grease on the Formica surface.

"Let me have a couple of those *alcapurrias* and two Coca-Colas," Papi said. "You do want a Coca-Cola, don't you?" he asked, and I nodded my head as I whirled on the stool, which rattled as it spun me faster and faster. Colors blended into one another in streaks of red, yellow, brown, and orange. Music came in and out of my ears, a syncopated half song that was familiar and foreign at the same time.

"You'd better stop that, or you'll hurt yourself."

I tried to brake the stool by sticking my leg out and hooking my foot on the one next to it. That threw me off balance and I fell, spinning to the ground. Papi was next to me in a flash.

"Are you okay?" he asked, but I felt heavy and light at the same time. My legs were wobbly, and when I looked around, there were two of everything. Two Papis and two of the gray woman next to him like shadows.

"She's all right," he said to her, and drew me back to the stool. I was floating in a fog of colors and smells and warbling birds and voices singing, "I like you, and you, and you, and no one else but you, and you, and you."

"Jesus doesn't love children who don't behave," the gray woman said. Her voice crackled like a worn record. "And he will punish them."

"Just ignore her," the counterman said. "She's crazy." He set a hot *alcapurria* and a frosty Coca-Cola in front of me. "Leave my customers alone," he shouted at her and waved the greasy rag the way Don Berto used to wave his sharp *machete*. "That's what happens to women when they stay *jamonas*," he said with a snort, and Papi laughed with him. The gray woman retreated to her bleeding heads.

"Papi, what's a *jamona?*" I asked as we left the market, our bellies full.

"It's a woman who has never married."

"I thought that was a *señorita*."

"It's the same thing. But when someone says a woman is *jamona*, it means she's too old to get married. It's an insult."

"How come?"

"Because it means no one wants her. Maybe she's too ugly to get married. . . . Or she has waited too long. . . . She ends up alone for the rest of her life. Like that woman in the *mercado*."

"She was ugly, that's for sure."

"That's probably why she stayed *jamona*."

"I hope that never happens to me."

"No, that won't happen to you. . . . There's our *público*. Let's run for it."

We dodged across the street holding hands, avoiding cars, people, and stray dogs sunning themselves on the sidewalk.

"What do they call a man who never marries?" I asked as we settled ourselves in the front of the *público*.

"Lucky," the driver said, and the rest of the passengers laughed, which made me mad, because it felt as if he were insulting me in the worst possible way.

"*¡Ay Santo Dios, bendícemela!*" Abuela hugged me and crossed herself. "She's so big!"

Her hands were large-knuckled, wrinkled; her palms the color and texture of an avocado pit. She rubbed my hair back and held my chin in her strong fingers.

"She looks just like you, Pablito," she told Papi, which made both of us feel good. "Look at the line of her hair. The same shape as yours. . . . A large forehead," she said as she led us into her house, "is a sign of intelligence."

"She's the best student in her class," Papi said, which wasn't entirely true. Juanita Marín was much smarter. "And you should hear her recite poetry!"

"Just like you, Pablito. You were always memorizing poems."

Abuela's house was two stories high and made of cement, with a front garden in which grew medicinal herbs and flowers. She and my grandfather, Don Higinio, lived on the ground floor, and her son, Bartolo, and his family lived upstairs. Abuela's Miami windows were draped with white crocheted curtains, as was the glass-topped table, the sofa, the doors to all the rooms, and all the beds and dressers. The tablecloth was bordered with yellow and brown pineapples. Red crocheted roses on bright green petals hemmed the doilies on the side tables.

Abuela fed us *sancocho,* a vegetable stew thickened with mashed tubers, with cornmeal dumplings floating on top. Papi and I sat at the table while she drifted in and out of the kitchen bringing us food, water, a chunk of bread, and finally, a steaming cup of sweetened *café con leche.* As soon as we'd finished eating, Papi stood up from the table and stretched.

"I'd better get going, Mamá. It's a long way to Macún."

"But we just came, Papi. It doesn't take so long to get home. . . ."

"I have to see some people on the way," he snapped, his back to me. He unhooked his hat from the nail by the door, knelt in front of me, and pushed the hair off my forehead. His eyes had a peculiar expression, as if he were begging. He kissed and hugged me, and in his arms there was a plea. I was confused by the rage that thudded into my stomach like a fist. I was certain that he was not going home to Mami and my sisters and brothers and that somehow I had been used.

I didn't return his embrace. I stood stiff and solid, swallowing the bitter lump that had formed in my throat, and swore to myself I wouldn't cry, wouldn't beg him not to go, wouldn't even miss him when he left. I pulled out of his arms.

"Now, you be a good girl and do as Abuela tells you," he said, trying to sound stern. "I'll come get you next week."

I sat on the sofa, stuck my legs out in front of me, and studied the scabs on my shins, the brown scars of countless wounds and scrapes. "*Sí.*"

I felt his eyes on me and knew he knew I knew. He kissed Abuela's forehead. "Bless me, Mamá," he said in a near murmur. She touched his shoulder and mumbled softly, "May the Good Lord keep you on your journey, Son, and may He watch over you." She crossed the air in front of him and, without looking back, he left. She watched him go, her head shaking from side to side as if she felt sorry for him.

"Come, let me show you where you'll sleep," she said as she led me to the back of the house.

I followed Abuela into the room next to hers, where she had laid out fresh sheets and a pillow. The bed was large, covered with a crocheted spread on which two peacocks stood beak to beak. The drape covering the blinds also had peacocks on it, only they faced forward, their plumage spread into a thousand blue-green eyes that seemed to watch us.

"Change into something comfortable," she told me, and showed me where to put my belongings. "I have some things to do in the kitchen."

When she was done, she sat on her rocking chair facing the door, took up a basket of crochet, and began working. She worked quietly. The needle flashed as her fingers flew in, around, and out. I could find nothing to do, so I sat on the sofa and watched, not daring to speak for fear I'd break her concentration. After a long time, she put the work in her basket, covered it with a cloth, and stood up from her chair, knees creaking.

"I'm going to say my prayers," she said. "If you get hungry, have some crackers from the tin." She disappeared into her room.

I sat on the stoop and watched the street beyond the garden fence. People came and went, dressed in their Sunday clothes, some looking as if they were going somewhere, others wrinkled and worn, as if they'd already been away and couldn't wait to get home. Every so often a car or truck rumbled up the hill, chased by scrawny dogs whose barks sounded hoarse and exhausted. Next door was a shack not much better than ours in Macún. My aunt Generosa lived there with my cousins, most of whom were older than I was. I had met Titi Generosa when we lived in Santurce and liked the sound of her loud, coarse voice and the way she moved her hands when she spoke, as if she were kneading words.

As evening fell, the street slowed, and all life and sound came from inside, as if it were time for secrets. But nothing could remain private in the echoing treble of cement walls and ceilings. People talked, or fought, or sang *boleros* while they showered, and every sound was amplified in the cul-de-sac where Abuela's house sat. Spoons clanked against pots, and the street filled with the steamy smells of garlic, hot oil, and spices. Radios blared frenzied *merengues* from one house, while from another, an evangelist exhorted his listeners to abandon their sinful lives and seek salvation in the arms of Jehovah, *Aleluya,* Amen!

I wondered where Papi had gone, who he had to see on a Sunday afternoon in San Juan. I remembered Margie and her mother and imagined them in New York, wearing beautiful clothes and eating bright yellow eggs. I mulled over Mami's words that men were always up to one *pocavergüenza* or another. That, Mami claimed in one of her bean-shucking discussions with Doña Lola, was men's nature. And Doña Lola had nodded and then shook her head so that I wasn't sure if she was agreeing with Mami or not.

I wondered if it were true, as Mami claimed when she and Papi fought, that he saw other women behind her back. And if he did, was it because he didn't love us? My eyes watered, my mouth filled with a salty taste, but if I cried, Abuela would hear me and think I didn't want to be with her. From the stoop, I could hear the rhythmic clicks of her rosary beads and the soft hum of her voice reciting prayers whose music was familiar to me, but whose words I'd never learned. And I wished that I knew how to pray, because then I could speak to God and maybe He or one of His saints could explain things to me. But I didn't know any prayers, because Mami didn't believe in churches or holy people, and Papi, even though he read the Bible and could lead novenas for the dead, never talked to us about God.

I determined not to cry, because if she asked me, I didn't want to tell Abuela why. But the pressure was too much, and as the tears came, I looked around for something with which to hurt myself so that when Abuela asked, I could show her a reason for the tears. I put my hand in the doorjamb and slammed the door shut.

The pain burned across my knuckles, through my fingers, and a scream, louder than I had intended, brought Abuela to my side. She hugged me, walked me to the sink, where she poured cool water over my hand, dried it with the soft hem of her dress, rubbed Vicks VapoRub on the pain, and held me against her bosom. She half carried me to her chair, pulled me onto her lap, and rocked me back and forth, back and forth, humming a lullaby I'd never heard.

Later Abuela wrapped my hand in a white rag and tucked me into bed. She shuttered the house and, after making sure I was settled, went into her bedroom, where I heard her moving about, the springs of her bed creaking as she sat on it and got up again, sat, got up, until it seemed as if she were rocking herself to sleep.

My hand throbbed. I shushed the pain by rubbing the inside of my arm and told myself that next time I shouldn't slam the door so hard. The chinks on the window slats changed color, from russet to an intensely dark blue that deepened into impenetrable darkness, until it didn't matter if my eyes were open or closed. I dropped into a solid sleep unbroken by the distant sounds of cars and barking dogs, or the careful unlatching of the door when my grandfather came back in the middle of the night, fed himself from whatever was left in the kitchen, went into his own room, slept, and woke up and left before the sun rose. It was days before I realized he lived in the small room near the front door, the only room in the house unadorned by Abuela's crochet.

Abuelo slept in a narrow metal cot with a thin mattress wrapped in white sheets. There was a small table and a chair in his room, and on the wall a picture of Jesus wearing the same exasperated expression as the statues in the *mercado,* his wounded hands palm up as if he were saying, "Not again!" A coconut-palm frond knotted into a cross was nailed above the picture.

By comparison, Abuela's room was opulent, with its double bed, thick mattress, four bedposts from which to tie the mosquito netting, pillows, and a small crocheted rug. Her dresser held a brush and comb, an altar to the Virgin and Child, a rosary, a Bible, candles, a missal, a small bottle filled with holy water, a picture of Papa Pío, the pope, and cards on which were printed prayers to saints with names like San Francisco, Santa Ana, Santa Bárbara, and San José. Papi had told me that Abuela didn't know how to read, and I wondered what words looked like to her. Did she recognize any of them? Or were they just a pattern, like crochet stitches?

After the first night, she closed the doors and windows right after supper but didn't make me go to bed. I stayed up reading the day-old newspaper Abuelo left behind or traced the flower patterns on paper napkins with a ballpoint pen.

One rainy afternoon Abuela pulled out her needlework basket. "Would you like to learn?" she asked timidly, as if she'd been working up the courage to ask.

"*Sí,* I would!" I had looked closely at the elaborate motifs of her tablecloths and doilies and had tried to draw them on lined notebook paper or on flattened grocery bags. I had sat mesmerized in the almost holy silence in which she worked, as she wove the needle in and out of stitches, forming pictures with thread.

She found a needle with a large hook and had me sit on the stoop, between her legs, so that she could look over my head and adjust my fingers as she helped me guide the thread in and out of the loops. She taught me how to count stitches, how to make chains that became rows, how to join rounds, when to fill in, and when to build space around stitches. After a while, I learned why the silence in which she worked seemed so magical. To crochet well, I had to focus on the work, had to count and keep track of when and where I increased or decreased stitches, and keep a picture in my head of what the finished cloth should look like, all the while estimating how much cotton thread it would take, and making sure when I ran out of one spool that the other was joined in as seamlessly as possible. Sounds dwindled into dull, distant murmurs, backgrounds receded into a blur, and sensations waned as I slid under the hypnotic rhythm of a hook pulling up thread, the finished work growing into my palm until its very weight forced me to stretch it out on my lap and look, and admire, and be amazed at what my hands had made.

Abuelo was a quiet man who walked with his head down, as if he had lost something long ago and was still trying to find it. He had sparse white hair and eyes the color of turquoise. When he spoke, it was in a low rasp, in the *jíbaro* dialect, his lips in an apologetic half smile. His hands were rough, the nails yellowed and chipped, the fingertips scarred. He left the house before dawn, pushing before him a cart he had fashioned from pieces of plywood and bicycle parts. At the produce market he stacked a pyramid of oranges on the top and kept two more sackfuls in the cabinet underneath.

He spent his days at the corner of Calle San Cristóbal in Old San Juan, peeling oranges with his pocket knife and scooping out a triangular hole through which tourists could suck the sweet juice. Each orange brought him five cents. He slipped the nickels into his right-hand pocket, to jingle as he walked home at the end of the day, the pocket sagging against his thigh.

Evenings when I heard the rattle of his cart I ran out to open the garden gate for him, and each time, he searched the lower cabinet to see if he had any oranges left. There was always one in the farthest corner, and once he'd secured his cart against the side of the house, he sat on the stoop and peeled it for me in one long ribbon that curled and whirled and circled on itself orange, white, orange.

★ ★ ★

Sunday morning before breakfast Abuela handed me my piqué dress, washed and ironed.

"We're going to Mass," she said, pulling out a small white *mantilla,* which I was to wear during the service.

"Can we have breakfast first, Abuela? I'm hungry."

"No. We have to fast before church. Don't ask why. It's too complicated to explain."

I dressed and combed my hair, and she helped me pin the *mantilla* to the top of my head.

"All the way there and back," she said, "you should have nothing but good thoughts, because we're going to the house of God."

I'd never been to church and had never stopped to classify my thoughts into good ones and bad ones. But when she said that, I knew what she meant and also knew bad thoughts would be the only things on my mind all the way there and back.

I tried to look as holy as possible, but the white *mantilla* tickled my neck and the sides of my face. I wished I didn't have to wear it, and that was a bad thought, since all the women and girls walking in front of us wore theirs without any complaints.

I love my mother, my father, all my sisters and brothers, my *abuela* and *abuelo,* all my cousins, the governor of Puerto Rico, Doña Lola, my teacher. A boy went by too fast and bumped into me, so I bumped him back, and that was bad, because Jesus said we should turn the other cheek, which seemed stupid, and there went another bad thought.

I counted all the squares on the sidewalk up to the steps of the church, then I counted the steps, twenty-seven. No bad thoughts.

The church was cool, dark, and sweet-smelling. Abuela dipped her fingers into a bowl at the entrance and crossed herself. I dipped my fingers, and there was nothing but water. I tasted it, and she gave me a horrified look and crossed herself. She took my hand and walked me down the aisle lined with pews. When we came to the front, she half knelt, looking up to the altar, and crossed herself again before sliding in to take her seat. I did the same thing.

We were early. Music came from somewhere behind us. When I

turned around to see, Abuela leaned down and whispered, "Face forward. You should never look behind you in church." I was about to ask why, but Abuela put her fingers to her lips and shushed me as everyone stood up. I couldn't see anything except the back of the man in front of me. He wore a wrinkled brown suit that stretched into folds around his waist because he was so fat. That must have been a bad thought.

The church's windows were of colored glass, each window a scene with Jesus and his cross. The two I could see without turning my head were beautiful, even though Jesus looked like He was in a lot of pain. The priest said something, and everyone knelt. The altar had an enormous Jesus on his cross at the center, the disciples at his feet. Tall candles burned in steps from the rear of the altar to the front, where the priest, dressed in purple and yellow robes, moved his hands up and down and recited poetry that everyone in the church repeated after him. Two boys wearing white lace tunics helped him, and I was jealous, because their job seemed very important. Envy, I knew, was a bad thought.

I counted the times people stood up, knelt down, stood up. That didn't seem right. I shouldn't be in church counting things. I should feel holy, blessed. But I got an itch in the space between my little toe and the sole of my foot. I scraped my shoe against the kneeling bench on the floor. The itch got worse. We knelt again, so I leaned back and took the shoe off to scratch my foot. But I had to get up, because the person next to me wanted to get through. And other people in the same pew got up and squeezed past me, kicking my shoe toward the aisle in the process. Abuela leaned down. "I'm going to take communion. You wait right here."

As soon as she was gone, I slid over to the end of the pew and looked up the aisle. No shoe. I felt for it with my foot all along under the pew but couldn't find it. It was wrong to look back in church, so it seemed that it would be worse to look down. But I didn't want Abuela to come back and find me with one shoe missing.

The people who went up to the altar knelt in front of the priest so he could put something into their mouths. As soon as Abuela knelt, I dove under the pew and looked for my shoe. It was under the pew behind us, so I crawled under ours, over the kneeling bench, and stretched to get the shoe. I crawled up just as Abuela came down the aisle. I knelt piously, my hands in prayer, and stared in front of me, trying to look like I was having nothing but the very best thoughts. Abuela went into the pew in front of me, looked over, seemed confused, got out, then knelt next to me. "How foolish. I thought we were one pew up," she whispered.

When everyone had come back, I realized the man with the wrinkled brown suit was two pews up, and I looked up at Jesus on his cross and prayed, "Please, Jesus, don't let her find out I moved during the service." Which I knew was a bad thought.

I packed my clothes and put the doily I had made for Mami into a corner of my small bag. Abuela made fish-head soup with plantain dumplings, and we ate some for lunch.

"Don't take your dress off," she said. "When he comes to pick you up, Pablito might be in a hurry to get back."

But Papi didn't come. Sunday stretched long and hot, through siesta time. Abuela made coffee in the late afternoon, and we sat at the table with a stack of soda crackers.

"He'll probably come for dinner," she said. But the blue haze of evening shrouded the street, stifled sounds, and sent everyone indoors to their secrets, and Papi didn't come. Abuela went in to say her prayers. "He must have been held up. Why don't you change into something comfortable."

I took off my white piqué dress, which was no longer clean and starched. I thought, *The minute I change clothes he's going to show up.* But he didn't, and when Abuela came out from her prayers, we sat by the door, working our needles in, around, up, and out, silently making patterns with thread that might have told a story had either one of us known how to transform our feelings into shape.

Instead, she worked an altar cloth she'd promised Father David, and I added red flowers to the doily I'd made for Mami. And neither one of us said what we both knew. That Papi wasn't coming. That perhaps the person he had to see the Sunday before needed him again, and he went there, and maybe that person needed him so much that he had forgotten about us, just like he sometimes forgot about Mami chasing after babies in Macún. We worked our crochet until it was too dark to see, until after Abuelo had brought his cart into the yard and tied it up against the fence, until he'd peeled an orange in one long ribbon, until we'd closed up the house and gone into our separate rooms and had wrapped ourselves in the white cotton sheets edged with crocheted scallops.

And I thought about how many nights Mami had left food warming on the ashes of the *fogón,* how often she'd sat on her rocking chair, nursing a baby, telling us to be still, that Papi would be coming any minute, but in the morning he wasn't there and hadn't been. I thought about how she washed and pressed his clothes until they were new-looking and fresh, how he didn't have to ask where anything was because nothing he ever wore stayed dirty longer than it took Mami to scrub it against the metal ripples of the washboard, to let it dry in the sun so that it smelled like air. I wondered if Mami felt the way I was feeling at this moment on those nights when she slept on their bed alone, the springs creaking as she wrestled with some nightmare, or whether the soft moans I heard coming from their side of the room were stifled sobs, like the ones that now pressed against my throat, so that I had to bury my face in the pillow and cry until my head hurt.

Every night, right after dinner, Abuela slipped into her room, put on a faded green nightgown embroidered with small yellow flowers, and undid her hair. Two twisted ropes of hair fell past her knees, one over each shoulder. She combed first one side, then the other, loosening the ropes into strands of white, gray, and a few black hairs, her fingers weaving in and out of them until each side looked like a serene waterfall against a pale forest.

"Our Father, who art in heaven . . . ," I repeated after Abuela.

"Hallowed be thy name. . . ."

"What does that mean?"

She raked her fingers through her hair, fluffing it, untangling the knots. "It means His name is holy."

"Hallowed be thy name. . . ."

"Thy kingdom come . . ." Abuela fed me the prayer in short phrases that echoed the rhythm I'd heard when Papi led novenas and when she clicked her beads at night before bed. It was like learning a song. If I left something out, the rhythm didn't work.

"Give us this day our daily bread . . ." I imagined a long loaf of *pan de agua,* the kind the baker made with a coconut frond down the center of its crunchy crust.

"And forgive us our trespasses . . ."

"What does that mean?"

"We're asking God to forgive any sins we might commit by mistake."

"Forgive us our trespasses . . ."

"And lead us not into temptation . . ." She didn't wait for me to ask: "That means we're asking God to keep us from sinning."

When I'd repeated the prayer several times and could recite most of it without stumbling, she taught me how to cross myself.

"Cross your thumb over your pointing finger, like this. . . . No, not with that hand. . . . You must always use your right hand," she said, holding it out to make sure I knew the difference.

"Why?"

"Because the left hand is the hand of the Devil."

I wondered if that meant the Devil had two left hands, but didn't dare ask because just saying the word *Devil* made Abuela drop her voice into a near whisper, as if the Devil were in the next room.

"Then you go straight down to your heart. . . . Then across . . . No, this side first." I'd seen women cross themselves so many times, it had never occurred to me there was a right way and a wrong way to do it. "Then you kiss the cross on your fingers." I did as she showed me. "You must always cross yourself before and after saying the Lord's Prayer. Let me see if you can say the whole thing."

I tried to look grave, eyes down, face expressionless, the way people in *velorios* looked when Papi led them in prayer. I lowered my voice to a near mumble, quieted my lips until they barely moved, and let the rhythm guide the words out and up to the sky, where Abuela said Papa Dios, my other Father, lived.

"¡Hola, Negrita!" Mami wore a printed dress she called a muumuu, which stretched across her pregnant belly like a round plot of exotic

flowers. I couldn't get enough of her to hug, so I clung to her hand as she huffed up the three steps into Abuela's house. "How are you, Doña Margara?" she asked cheerily as if she knew the answer.

"Oh, I'm fine, *m'hija,* just fine," Abuela said, pulling out a chair for Mami to sit in. "How about some lemonade?"

"Wonderful!" Mami's cheeks were flushed, partly from the hot walk down the street, partly because she'd colored them. Her hair was twisted up and held with pins that she kept pushing in so they wouldn't fall out.

"I hope you don't mind that I came to bring Negi home. I've missed her." Now that she was sitting, I could hug her around the neck, kiss her soft, powdered face, smell the fruity perfume she put on for special occasions.

"I missed you too, Mami," I whispered, and she pulled me close and kissed the top of my head.

Abuela brought in a pitcher of lemonade and three glasses. "I thought Pablito was coming on Sunday. We waited all afternoon. . . ."

Mami's face flashed into the hard expression I'd come to expect when she talked about Papi. "You know how he is," she said to his mother.

Abuela nodded and poured us lemonade. "Who's watching the children?"

"My neighbor's daughter."

"Who?" I asked. Mami turned to me as if she'd just remembered who I was.

"Gloria." She sipped her drink. "Guess what? We have electricity!"

"Really?"

"Yes! We only use the *quinqués* if the lights go out." She turned to Abuela. "Which is every time the wind blows hard." They laughed.

I leaned against Mami and sipped my drink, listening to them talk about people whose names were familiar, but whom I hadn't met—Flor, Concha, Chía, Cándida, Lalo. They talked about whose daughter had run off with whose son, who'd had babies, who had died, the price of groceries, the hot weather, the rickety buses between San Juan and Santurce. They talked as if they were good friends, and I wondered how that could be since they seldom saw each other. They came back to the subject of Macún, how things seemed to be better now that we had electricity and running water was weeks away.

93

"Of course," Mami said, "with Pablo gone all the time it's hard to know. . . ." Her face darkened again. She looked down at the floor, rubbed circles on her belly. The silence around her was total, not rich and full like Abuela's when she crocheted, but empty and sad and lonesome.

"Negi," Abuela said, "go take a shower and get ready so that your mother doesn't have to wait for you." I didn't want to leave Mami, but Abuela's eyes were stern, and with her head, she signaled in the direction of the bathroom.

I set my glass down and went. Although I leaned against the bathroom door, trying to hear what they said, I only caught snatches: "always been that way . . . ," "upsets the kids . . . ," "think of yourself . . . ," "alone with children . . . ," "make it work . . . ," "don't know how. . . ." And, in a louder voice, "Negi, why don't we hear water running?"

I opened the faucets and let cool water wash over me, wishing it could melt away the fear that made the thumps of my heart louder than usual. When I came out, my hair dripping, the tips of my fingers wrinkled, Mami and Abuela still sat across from each other. Abuela's face was sad, and she looked older, as if years, rather than minutes, had passed since I last saw her. Mami's rouge was streaked, and her eyes were swollen. She pretended to smile, and I pretended not to see it as I went by wrapped in a towel, stepping lightly, as if the floor would break under my weight.

I dressed to their murmurs in the other room, their voices soft but strained, and I wondered if men ever talked like this, if their sorrows ever spilled into these secret cadences. I combed my hair, put on my socks, buckled my leather shoes. And still they talked, and I couldn't understand a word they said. But their pain bounced off the walls and crawled under my skin, where it settled like prickly bristles.

It seemed to me then that remaining *jamona* could not possibly hurt this much. That a woman alone, even if ugly, could not suffer as much as my beautiful mother did. I hated Papi. I sat on the bed in his mother's house and wished he'd die, but as soon as the thought flashed, I slapped my face for thinking such a thing. I packed my bag and stepped into the room where Mami and Abuela sat. When they looked up at me, it seemed as if we were all thinking the same thing. I would just as soon remain *jamona* than shed that many tears over a man.

EVERY SUNDAY

Magali García Ramis

Translated by Carmen C. Esteves

Born in Santurce, Puerto Rico, in 1946, Magali García Ramis started her professional life as a journalist. Her first collection of short stories, La familia de todos nosotros, *appeared in 1976. García Ramis's novel* Felices días, Tío Sergio *(1989), a testimonial told in the simple, everyday language of a young middle-class adolescent girl, established her as one of Puerto Rico's best contemporary writers. She received a Guggenheim Fellowship to work on her second novel,* Las horas del sur, *and her recent publications include a collection of essays and a collection of short stories.*

The young narrator of "Every Sunday" tries to escape the ennui of her family's weekly gatherings in the country through the auspices of her imagination, an abandoned house, and a secret love.

NONE OF US HAS EVER DIED, SO I HAVE TO ANSWER NO.

"No, ma'am, no, no one in my family has died, at least since I was born." Her deep black eyes dig into my sleepy eyes. The feeble early-morning light filters through the cracks of the hut. Doña Amparo closes her eyes again. She is in a trance, I think.

"I see it there, next to you. It's the spirit of a girl who died, you know. She was about eighteen, you know, but I don't know how she died. It's always next to you. You say that no sister of yours has died. . . ."

"I have no sisters."

"Or a girlfriend."

"I have no girlfriends."

"It's someone who is very close to you, you know, like from your house."

Yes, it could be from my house, I think. Doña Amparo's constant "you knows" distract me. She tries to look inside of me, to that part of me that not even I know, and I feel myself clamming up.

"I can't see anymore, there are interferences. Take three baths and put flowers in the water, you know, so the spirits won't control you."

So that I don't control myself, yes, yes, ma'am, I say to her. I am about to tell her that spirits bore me, but as with many other things, I say it in silence and I store it in my memory. I get up from the small wooden bench and I'm about to give her a dollar. I try to remember my cousin's instructions: "You put it in the small can she has on the desk." Doña Amparo looks at me without saying a word and I get nervous. I throw the dollar in the first can I see without noticing that it has water inside.

"No, not there,"

She says, alarmed. I look into the rusty blue can. For a second I see my reflection on the water. I see myself double. My spirit and I, I think, and I smile to myself. "I am sorry," I say, and I take out the wet bill and give it to her. Then I remember that spiritualists are supposed to be able to feel spirit vibrations in water. I'm about to lift the old curtain to leave the room, but she calls me one last time.

"Listen, be careful, be careful of your house and of things that push like the wind."

Of my house. So she has looked inside of me. No one pushes me, not even the wind, only I, but it isn't worth explaining to her.

"Yes, yes, okay. Good day and thank you."

★   ★   ★

Be careful, always be careful. Be careful of my house. Be careful of the wind. Be careful of the world. Live carefully, keep out of trouble, people repeat every day; that is why they don't understand.

In the waiting room a dozen people are waiting their turn. To know what the future will bring. To know if it's worth marrying him although he drinks a lot. And to know who has cast an evil eye on the kid. And who the husband's lover is. To know everything that witchcraft has known from time immemorial and mankind has searched for—to know.

The humidity, the tropical humidity, the humidity of December in summer, the morning humidity that announces a sticky Sunday, runs through the nearby fields and touches my neck and face as I leave the hut of Doña Amparo, the spiritualist. I breathe a bit of fresh air. In the distance I see the mountains undressing from the cloak of mist that covered them through the night. My cousins are waiting in the car. They are bursting, with faith and incredulity; hoping that it might be true and doubting if it will be, speaking excitedly about what Doña Amparo said to them.

"Did you like it?"

"Yes, tell me what she said to you!"

"She told me that everything will come out okay with Jorge! She told me that. . . ."

I get comfortable in the backseat. I let them talk. Today is Sunday. I would also let them talk if it were Saturday or Monday. I'm not interested. I only want to get home. Today is Sunday, and every Sunday my family, where no one ever dies, must gather in their country house, while I, if I don't go to my house, I die of boredom. I hate Sundays, but if it were not for Sundays I would never go to my house. As we drive I'm in a daze as I look at the mountains. Mountains, a mountain, any mountain is the strongest force that exists. The wind comes through the window and kisses my eyes. I look at the mountains again; in a few hours I will be within them.

★   ★   ★

The sign, the sign of the cross. Everyone makes the sign of the cross. The dark-mustached husband to the tiny wife. The godmother to the godchild. The older brother to the younger, all at once sprinkling holy water all over his face. The grandmother to the impatient grandson. The mother to the babe in arms. The entire town, generation after generation, wet their fingers in the same font of yellowish water and all make the sign of the cross when they leave the old church for the hot Sunday that awaits outside. And I, as usual, out of habit, as I enter the church that smells of melted wax and small-town dust, I make the sign of the cross.

And next to me, at the threshold, the idiot makes the sign of the cross, without rhyme or reason. During the entire Mass I look at him instead of at the altar. He stares out of the corners of his green, watery eyes at all the churchgoers who shy away from him. He stinks like a chicken, like a chicken house during a drought, from the grime that eats away his clothes. While, from the altar, the American priest, blond and extremely tall like the angels on religious cards, sweats with an American accent his Our Father: *padreí nuestro que estais en lous cielous* . . . the town idiot, deformed from his waist down, staggers toward a corner and scatters holy water and signs of the cross that remain floating in the air.

"Hail Mary . . ."

is the first thing I hear when I return to the Mass. It is almost over; either the priest is breaking a speed record, or I was distracted with the idiot for a long time. It is better to come for Mass to a small-town church than to the parish church in Santurce, to hear the sermons of the Spanish priest, but today it has gone by so fast!

"For God's sake, child, why didn't you take today holy communion with the rest of the family?"

★   ★   ★

This is the first thing I hear when I leave the church. Here comes Aunt Pía with one of her nagging sessions. Her real name is Elena, but I call her Pía for her piety. . . .

"Today all of us took Holy Communion together because it is your father's name day. Even your younger brother went with him to the altar, and you as always . . ."

And as always, I invent an excuse.

"I forgot that we were all going to take communion and I ate a banana a little while ago. . . ."

It's a cheap excuse, but she would not understand if I were to tell her that I was looking at the idiot making signs of the cross in the air, because she would say, "You are the idiot." I move away from her and I greet grandparents, uncles, aunts, everyone. We get into the cars and we go by the cock ring to pick up Papi and Uncle Gustavo. They do not have to go to Mass. They are the family heretics, according to Aunt Pía. I would like to be a heretic but I don't dare.

We arrive at the country house. It's Sunday. I know everything by heart. My cousins' and brothers' laughter in the yard. The view from the house's balcony with a tiny San Juan in the distance. The smell of rice and chicken, a chicken just killed by Aunt Pía's chubby hands. The rum stink of Uncle Alberto's breath. Grandpa and Grandma's obsessions with miniskirts. My cousins' chats about dances and boyfriends. The only thing that changes is color. Sundays in the countryside are blue and green or gray and green. Today is a blue and green Sunday.

It's lunchtime. The grown-ups eat at a table on the balcony, the little ones in the yard at a table made for them from wooden planks placed over the enormous rocks that surround the house. Since there is no intermediate table I sit with my cousins and brothers on the rocks. With them one eats comfortably since they don't ask silly questions. Gustavo José, the more mischievous of my twin brothers, has a small lizard tied with a ribbon and he puts it on the table. We make it the guest of honor and feed it. Then we baptize it with cologne, and since it is Sunday we name it Pious Sunday.

After lunch they all give in to drowsiness. Papi and the uncles play dominoes. The grandparents rest and play with their memories. The kids jump and play with laughter. And Mami and the aunts walk around the balcony and from there they recite the four dominical lines: "What a pretty view we have." "Look how much the flowers have grown." "Boys, don't run with sticks in your hands because if you fall down you can stab yourself." And, "Girls, don't go roaming around, one never knows where there are hoodlums." If only once they would make a mistake and say something like "Boy, don't run with the flowers," "You may go roaming around," and "Look how the hoodlums have grown"; but no. Nothing breaks Sunday's plan. Only the color and my house.

I wait until they are all occupied with something so that no one will call me and no one will follow me. Without their noticing I leave through the gate. I go toward the stream through a muddy path, and I hop across the rocks. Through the neighbor's banana grove, up the hill, and then back into our farm over the highest mountain. Turn left to the bamboo forest. And where they form an arch, there begins the path that leads to my house. Up here voices are barely heard. And once I go through the arch, nothing is heard except the sounds of the mountain. The gigantic bamboos sway in the breeze and the sun's rays move, searching the earth although the trees barely let them through. It is a humid path, like the nave of an old church. And at the end, where an altar would be, is my house. It doesn't have doors or windows, so the trees and the flowers and the green lizards and the tiny orange spiders live in it. It doesn't have a roof, either, and at this time in the afternoon an enormous ray of light rushes in and illuminates the staircase that opens to both sides of the second floor. I run my fingers through the trees I know, I see which flowers have been born and which have died, and I sit on the balcony, which has no view of the city, only of the forest.

★   ★   ★

I recline against the walls of gray, dark stone that have been there as long as the gigantic trees that surround them. It's my house. The thing that is most mine. The only thing that is mine. A fantastic family had to live here, I believe. A family with children, uncles, and grandparents. And parents worried about their children. And a kitchen smelling of rice with chicken. And a daughter that used to sit here. As I do. Looking at the trees and feeling the presence of this, her house. And perhaps one day she saw a man and a woman in a corner of the yard, hidden in a clearing among the bamboos, making love. Peasants from the mountains or cousins from the house. There, they stayed for so long that when the sun was going down, the soft light reflected from the bamboos blended with them and made them appear green, as I saw them, as she saw them. I must beware of myself, of my house. I look beyond the arch, outside, and I see that time goes by and I must return before it is late. And it is already late and tomorrow is Monday and then the week goes by. And it is Saturday. And they are unloading his books from the car. My brothers are delighted and they run with his clothes and his radio and they throw everything in the living room and they go out again. When he arrives on the balcony, Mami kisses him and Papi hugs him. He is my oldest cousin, sort of the family favorite. As kids we used to play together here. He is coming to stay with us while his parents travel through Spain looking for more relatives than the ones we already have.

"Hello, José Julián," I say from the door.

"Hello, sweetie, we have not seen each other in a long time," he says, and smiles. I think that it's me who brought him here. And we look at each other for a few more seconds than one is supposed to.

"Aren't you going to kiss your cousin, child? Isn't she shy!" says Mami.

Yes, yes, Mami, I say in my mind. I come close. I kiss his extremely soft cheek. Like all the men in the family, José Julián is almost beardless.

"Oh José, they tell me that you are very good in math," says Mami with the voice of a mother worried about her daughter's grades. "See if you can help this child because her math—"

"Don't worry, Aunt, I'm going to make her study an hour each day including Saturdays and Sundays, and you will see how she learns," and he smiles and looks at me.

I don't find it funny at all and I look at him in silence. No, it wasn't for this that I brought you here. I look at him and I realize that we had seen each other many times before but we had never looked at each other. I'll help you, I say to him: and, *Okay,* he says. We walk to the garage.

"Why do you look at me like that?"

"No, I'm not looking at you, it's the spirit of an eighteen-year-old girl who died who looks at you."

"Oh! And where does she come from?"

"From my house, she is from my house."

"From your house? I did not know that it was bewitched. Listen, Aunt," he yells. "No one had said anything to me."

"What are you talking about?"

"About the spirit."

"Ah, that again. It is your cousins' fault; they took her to a spiritualist. You know that I don't want anything to do with superstitions. . . ."

"No, Aunt, don't worry, it's the same as having a guardian angel next to you."

He's already beginning to bother Mami, who is an arch Catholic since she has to be so for Papi and for herself. But Mami laughs. Papi says that José Julián was born under a lucky star because everyone loves him.

"Thanks for defending me," I say, "on behalf of the spirit."

"Ah, if it is for the spirit, no problem, I'm always at its service."

He smiles again. And as he takes out the last suitcase from the trunk, Saturday begins to die. And we stay still looking at each other. At each other. At each other.

★ ★ ★

And since he arrived, he is always with us. And every night he tells us jokes, and talks to us about what happens at the university, and about the parties he sometimes goes to.

—Last night I had to escort a girl who was going to make her debut. I'm fed up with this, but Mami had promised it to her mother years ago, and I had to go.

Papi lowers the newspaper, smiles with one of those smiles that only men with pencil mustaches can make so that their mouths sparkle with suspicion, and he asks, "Did you have a good time? I understand that she's very cute."

"Yes, of course, Uncle Felipe. The entire family is very cute. She is a little elephant, the brothers are two big elephants, and together with mama and papa elephant they are very beautiful, if you are also an elephant. She was so huge that I swear to you that her fat sprouted from her plunging neckline and I didn't know how to hold her to dance."

"My man, that's what comes from grabbing forbidden flesh," answers Papi wisely.

"Felipe, please!"

Mami is very correct, very correct, but she also smiles. I think that I like my immediate family, although I have serious doubts about the rest.

And then comes Saturday, Sunday. The mass, the food, the view, the games. But today, also, José Julián. I sit on a rock to stare at him. He has climbed a mango tree. Maybe the family bores him. Listen, I say to him softly, do you want to get out of here and go for a walk? Fine, he answers. Since he moved south with his parents he doesn't come every Sunday with the rest of the family. The family bores you, I know, just like it does me. No, it's just that we don't have much in common. You and I do. You and I do. I think that I would like to show you my house, José Julián, you will like it.

"Come," I say to him. "Let's go for a walk."

★ ★ ★

And he asks no questions, he just walks next to me. Along the muddy path, across the stream, by the plantain grove, to the left toward the bamboos. We walk without talking.

"We have arrived," I say all of a sudden.

"Here?"

"Yes, I live here."

"Here on top of a mountain."

"No, in the house."

José Julián, would you like to see it? And I hold his hand. We walk by the row of bamboos until we find the arch and through it we enter into the green vortex. The farther we walk, the greener the forest turns. Violent green, on one side, and soft green, yellowish green, and forgotten green. Nothing is heard now from the outside world and above us the bamboos sing. The dead leaves also sing when we step on them. And the house awaits. We walk up to the balcony. It is my house, I dream about it very often, I explain to him, but it can't be explained. What do you think? Silence. Are you here? José Julián, tell me how you like my house; José Julián looks at the walls. Limbo must be like this—he says, finally breaking the silence for the first time since we left the country house.

"How, without doors or windows?"

"No, gray, without white or black."

We sit under the trees, and on the stairs and on the balcony.

"Once there was a family here just like us."

"Ah, yes! And what happened to them?"

"I don't know. They are around, I believe."

"Ah, so this is your bewitched house."

Why bother? It seems that he doesn't understand either.

"Listen, don't feel bad, I like your house, but it's so hidden."

"You would like it to be like the family house, with a view."

"Here the light is different, it looks unreal."

★ ★ ★

But it isn't, it doesn't matter what it appears to be. And it has a view, can't you see? You can see trees and in between them the sky.

"Every Sunday I look at the sky through here and that way I know if it is a blue and green or a gray and green Sunday."

—Yes, I see.

He says he does, but he sees nothing. I thought you were going to understand.

"I had no idea that there was an abandoned house around."

It's not abandoned, I live here.

"No one else knows about this abandoned house?"

Yes, of course, all of us who live in it.

"It must be a little dangerous for you to walk alone around these places."

Ah, he worries about me.

"No, it is not dangerous," I say finally.

"You have never met anyone here," he doesn't ask, he states.

"Once, yes."

"Whom?"

"No one."

"How?"

"No one I know. They didn't see me."

"What were they doing here? Who were they?"

"Do you want to know? They were a man and a woman. There among the bamboos, they were making love; I had never seen anything like that."

"But who would come all the way here for that? They must have been hicks from around here."

"No, I don't know. They were green."

"Green? Ah, of course, Martians."

No, those words don't belong here, I'm going to wipe them off your lips. They were a man and a woman from this house.

"They were making love," I insist. "And maybe someone like me also saw them."

"Or imagined it."

"Saw them."

And we return to the family house. I don't tell him not to say anything about my house because I know that he won't.

On Monday night Mami gives us the news. We are going to have a little sister. "A little brother," say the twins. "No, sister, to be two and two." "Let's put it to a vote and let the majority win," suggests Papi. "It will be what God wills," says Mami, who always leaves it all to God to end the discussion. "José Julián, I want you to be the godfather," she says. "No, he can't be anyone's godfather because he's a heretic like me," says Papi before he answers. "Yes, I would like to be the godfather, Aunt, I would like it a lot, maybe I'll reform."

The next day we go with Mami to buy baby articles. My brothers want to buy a mechanical bear for the baby. "No, no, the baby will not be able to use that for a long time," says Mami. We run into one of Mami's friends. When Mami gives her the news she smiles from ear to ear and congratulates her.

"But how was that? Did you count the days wrong?" she says, and smiles inwardly, as in a vacuum.

"If God sends them, I take them," answers Mami ceremoniously. God and I. I and God. Mami and God. Mami and Papi. I can't imagine Mami and Papi making love. "José Julián, can you imagine your parents making love?" He laughs. "No, I can't" "Ah! then, I'm not the only one?" "No, I think that everyone finds it difficult to imagine their parents making it." "Unless, maybe, they have seen them," I tell him. "Or if they have made it," he answers. Suddenly I look at him, and although I don't want to, I turn red. I would like to know if he has made it. Almost certainly, no university guy walks around a virgin, I guess. There are so many things I would like to ask him. "Do you want to ask me something?" he says to me. "Yes, do you think it is bad?" "What's bad?" "To make love." "No, never." "Never? and if one is not married?" "Never." "Mami says it is." "And what do you think?" "The Church says it's bad, and you are a heretic." "And what do you think?" he repeats again. "I used to believe so." "You used to?" "I don't know." "Look, don't believe everything they teach you. The world is not bad and good, or reality and fiction, or white and black only, what's more almost everything is gray." "As in limbo," I say, and I look at him. "As your house," he answers, and he looks at me.

And today is Sunday and we return to the house and we always run holding hands. His hands. I open them. I touch them. I look at them. I touch each one of his fingers and I kiss the center of his hand. And he does the same and he kisses mine. Since I brought you here, I tell him, I want to give you something. I'm going to give you half of my house. But I will do it in writing. In case someone dies.

Or in case someone leaves. Ah, yes, it's late already, we must leave. Or in case someone leaves.

When we arrive home we write the document. TITLE OF PROPERTY, date: Every Sunday. In a sane and doubtful state of mind, by the present I admit, say and repeat that the house called Abandoned House, which will be alluded to throughout this document as Our House, from now on is gray, and ours, instead of mine. . . . And then we sign it and bury it next to a feeble oak where no one looks.

And this Sunday we don't go to the country house. In the last few months Grandpa has been sick and we take turns staying with him in the city. Today is our turn, and Mami is going to prepare a great dinner on the terrace of my grandparents' house. They send me to San Juan for sweet

Majorcan buns. It is something like communion. The entire family is supposed to eat them together, and every Sunday, when we don't go to the country, we eat them. I take José Julián. It is a gray and green day, a sad Sunday, as we walk through old San Juan's almost deserted streets. Streets that belong to no one, streets that belong to all. We go to the Parque de las Palomas. We sit on a bench to look at the sea. On the other side of the bay are the mountains, and in them, our house. Both of us think the same. And I know it without asking him. We have been together for so long that we can almost read each other's mind. Sometimes we walk holding hands, when no relative or no acquaintance is around. Not because it is bad, but so that they won't misunderstand, says José Julián. From the park we hear the water beating slowly below, beside the city. We lean out to look at it. The foam jumps and licks the cracks of the old walls, cracks open to the hot sun for so many years. The park around us is deserted. I'm going to kiss José Julián on his beardless cheek, but since we think at the same time, at the same second, he turns his face toward me and we kiss. Below, to the rhythm of a lament, the sea kisses San Juan and moves away. Kisses and moves away. Kisses. And it gets late.

Somehow he must leave as he arrived; he must leave because his parents return from Spain. Time has gone by. Today is the last Sunday in a long time that we'll go together to our house. After lunch, we begin to walk out the gate of the country house. "What a crush this one has on José Julián," says Aunt Pura, delighted to see me talking with someone from the family. *Families, I think, never realize.*

"Be very careful by the stream. Bring strawberries if you find them. Come back early. Don't walk around the hills at night. Bring torch ginger if you see any in bloom," and a thousand and more things that we don't hear; they are heard in the distance. Family errands like always when one leaves on a trip.

Today the sun gives light without heat. And the green doesn't shine. Once we enter the path, we hold hands and we walk slowly. "You return to live with your parents and you'll never come to our house." " 'Never' doesn't exist, that was invented by men, who also invented 'always,' " he says, and he squeezes my hand. "If you already live here, you belong here, so you will not be able to leave." "This house was very pretty in its time." "Don't you think it is pretty now?" "We don't have much time." "I know," I tell him. "Outside there is time, not here." "I know," he answers. "Have you been waiting for me for a long time?" "Yes, years," I say. "From here they can see us from the house, let's go to that clearing among the bamboos." We walk softly like if we weren't there. We have looked at each other for so long a time. And later we don't see each other. And we spin around all over the mountain, all over the grass and leaves with moss and flowers and very fine spiderwebs that we break unintentionally, we spin around. And we spin in the air, and I spin around. And my pink dress floats where we left it next to some trees that face the sky. And I don't see his eyes looking at me. And he floats in the air in something that I don't know is my body, that is his, but it's the same. "José Julián," I say, and what, I answer to myself. "No, nothing," I say "that it's our house." It doesn't have doors nor windows, and is open to everything, and to a kiss, and I don't understand where I end and where he begins and his hands tremble next to my thighs that tremble together with the flowers that tremble together with the loose green leaves, green of the paths, paths that extend up to the sky between the trees that move, and like that with them, we move, or they move with us, they move their leaves, they move their branches and they breathe together; together the two of us breathe and the mountain breathes under us and the free wind breathes and touches us with trembling fingers and we tremble and it continues its route. And we don't move anymore.

I want to think. I want to be able to understand what's happening to me. I want to be able to run everything through my memory like a movie, but I can't. Back home, they have taken Mami to the hospital; it seems that my sister is going to be born two months early. I know that it will be a girl because my brothers and I took a family poll, and the decisive vote, Grandpa's, was in favor of a sister for me, and Grandpa is sure. He is fine again. No one in my family ever dies. They are only born, or they are created or invented. I have to stay home with the twins. How silly, I should be next to Mami now. This Sunday the night arrived very softly and brought by her hand a useless drizzle, a half rain, like a woman lying alone in a bed. It doesn't make sense. I look at my body. There is an air of death in it, here lying alone. My feet pointing toward the ceiling. My muscles still. My mind aware. My muscles inert. All seem to spell END. This Sunday.

My little sister is dressed in white. Her enormous eyes are open, although I don't think she can see yet. Today is Sunday and they are going to baptize her. The priest takes her in his arms and tells the Devil something about not getting close to her. If the Devil could answer, I think he would tell the priest a few rude words. Maybe we should give her three baths with flowers in the water, it occurs to me, but I guess not; she must be baptized so she will not end up in Limbo. The family has come from all over the island for the baptism. And then we have gone to the country house for a big family reunion. In the midst of so many people it is easy for me to escape. And I come to my house where time doesn't exist, to live. If I estimate in hours, I don't know how long I have been here. It gets dark and I start to run. Today there is a strong wind and the noise it makes is a little scary, besides that, I don't see anything along the path. I guess that all of them will be worried, but they know that every Sunday I like to go for a walk alone, to walk, to see the mountain. I can hear their voices and I see the light in the house.

"Look at her; here she comes at last. For God's sake! Why do you have to go roaming alone around the forest at this time?" I don't come, they take me, I don't belong to God, or anyone, I don't walk alone, but with my house, I answer, but I don't say it.

"Come, come and eat something, you have been walking alone for more than five hours and the entire family is waiting to greet you," says Mami. I pay attention to her. I go into one of the bedrooms; on the bed my little sister, minuscule, sleeps. It doesn't seem possible.

★ ★ ★

I have been imagining for months that I have a sister, and now she is here, for real. I go out to the balcony and I start to greet cousins and relatives. Aunt Pura brings a young man by the arm.

"I'll bet you don't remember him," she says enthusiastically.

I look at him.

"It's your cousin José Julián. Years ago when you were children, you used to play and you used to go for walks to the mountains, don't you remember?"

It's my oldest cousin, something like the family's favorite. Years ago when we were kids, we used to play together, and we used to go for walks to the mountains. I remember.

"Hello, José Julián," I say to him.

"Hello, sweetie, we have not seen each other in a long time," he says, and smiles.

"And guess what," continues Aunt Pura. "He and your aunt and uncle are moving again to San Juan, after such a long time. Now the entire family will come again every Sunday." Every Sunday. The entire family will come again. The insects buzz around the light bulbs. The night takes possession of everything. The *coquí* marks time with its singing. I have noticed it in a fraction of a second, while I look at José Julián.

"Aren't you going to kiss your cousin? Isn't she shy?"

I come close to him. I kiss his extremely soft cheek. Outside of us the family celebrates. You are going to come every Sunday, I think. And we stay still looking at each other. At each other. At each other.

SOFIA

Yvonne V. Sapia

*Yvonne V. Sapia has been the recipient of fellowships from the National En-
dowment for the Arts and the Florida Arts Council, and the prestigious Morse
Poetry Prize. She has published two collections of poetry,* The Fertile Crescent
(1983) and Valentino's Hair *(1987), and a novel,* Valentino's Hair *(1991),
which she has adapted into a screenplay. Her novel in progress,* Dimaggia
Dream, *is based on her experiences in Miami. Sapia, who was born in 1946 in
New York City, now lives and teaches in rural north Florida.*

*Valentino's Hair, set in the Bronx, New York, during the 1950s, explores
the evolving relationship between an old Puerto Rican barber and his lame son
Lupe. In "Sofia," Lupe's eccentric grandmother clarifies the merits of spiritualism
and magic, as well as their limits.*

LUPE'S GRANDMOTHER SOFIA LOOKS LIKE AN OLD GYPSY WOMAN.
She wears long, colorful, flared dresses. A silver crucifix hangs from a
thick silver chain around her neck. Her disheveled gray hair is covered
by a scarf, and on Wednesday nights when she attends the Hallelujah
Church, a storefront down the street, she wears a white scarf and carries
the tambourine she brought with her from the Island many years before.
And she practices magic.

Lupe climbs the long road of stairs to Sofia's apartment on the top
floor. He stops at the fourth floor to catch his breath before he makes
the last push up, up to where his grandmother lives in her different world.

On Sofia's door are the crookedly placed numbers announcing #646. Pasted on the door are a decal of the island of Puerto Rico, its shape floating above the numbers, and a small poster, cut out from a calendar, of a black saint. Below the saint's image the tops of the letters of February can be still seen. Lupe gives his secret knock.

"*Muchacho*, what are you doing here?" Sofia's voice blares out in Spanish. She opens the door and is looking for Mishu, her black cat. "Have you seen Mishu? Oh, well, never mind," she continues without hesitation as she ushers Lupe in. "Your mother just called and asked if you were here. Do you know something? She didn't believe me when I said you weren't here. I think she thinks I want to steal you away. And maybe I should, the way she ignores a smart boy like you. Put those books down and I'll get you some Kool-Aid."

Sofia's apartment is a festive yet odd place. The hallway is lined with family photographs of the dead. There is a yellowed photograph of Severo, the candy maker, Lupe's grandfather, which was taken before Lupe was born. The picture is in a round frame. Severo stares seriously at the world as he stands next to his candy wagon. He has his straw hat pressed against his chest, and he looks sunburned and tired. On the side of the wagon it reads, *Severo's Dulce de la Isla, cinco y diez centavos.*

Next to Severo's picture are pictures of their dead children, for three of Sofia and Severo's twelve children have died. All three photographs are in the squarish frames that can be bought at Woolworth's or Kresge's.

One frame holds the photograph of a soldier, a son who was killed in World War II. The second frame holds the badly damaged photograph of a little girl around the age of ten years old. She is staring out but covering her eyes with her left hand; there is a strong sun blinding her. Her right hand is being held by a very young Sofia, who looks basically the same as the old Sofia except for her young skin and dark hair. And this young Sofia is not wearing the thick bifocals the old Sofia in the kitchen is wearing. There are several blotches on this old photograph, as if it has been accidentally used as a coaster. This photograph is of Estrella, Sofia's first child. The little girl drowned shortly after the photograph was taken. It is often said by the family that Sofia communicates spiritually with Estrella. The last frame holds Uncle Armando's photograph. Lupe was three years old when Uncle Armando died, but Lupe remembers Antonia was so distraught over his death that she tried to jump out of a second-story window at the funeral home. Fortunately, his father, Nieves, the barber, was there to drag her from the frame. Uncle Armando died of a heart attack while in the arms of another man. The family prayed for Armando's soul. Others pitied his wife. Sofia forgave him.

Once past the pictures of the dead in the hallway, Lupe steps into Sofia's large and airy kitchen, the brightest of all the rooms in the apartment. *El Gallo,* Sofia's rooster, is chained to a leg of her old stove. He is a large cock with black, brown, and white feathers, and he crows loudly with the rising and setting of the sun. The neighbors never complain. Another cry in the city air makes little difference.

The Kool-Aid is very sweet and cold, and Lupe sits sipping his drink and watching *El Gallo* drop two little turds on the floor and proceed to smash them with his large feet, as he paces back and forth. Sofia immediately grabs him and wipes his feet and the floor. "You bad bird," she mutters. "You are a bad little boy."

One wall of Sofia's kitchen is covered with shelves. Large containers for dry beans and rice occupy many of the shelves. But the top shelves have jars of various sizes, each jar labeled and marked by Sofia's script. Every jar houses something different. Some jars contain spices for cooking. Other jars contain medicinal herbs: *el ojo de Dios, fuego rojo, mala pierna, llerba buena.* A few jars, most of them small, have unexpected items: feathers, nail clippings, eyelashes, teeth, and hair.

Lupe once thought his eccentric grandmother was a scientist like the scientists in the movies on television. But his grandmother isn't a scientist. She is a *bruja.* Or so Lupe is told by his cousins. Sofia takes his small palm and begins to read his fortune. "Oh, my boy, my boy, what a sad life it is for some of us. No one deserves such a sad life. It breaks my heart not to be able to help you."

"What do you see, Sofia?" he asks.

"Death, my boy," she answers, "but I see death everywhere. Everywhere."

The kettle on the stove begins to whistle, and Lupe hears Sofia on the phone in the living room. She is arguing with Lupe's mother. Lupe can tell. Sofia's voice is so loud it flusters *El Gallo.*

"Antonia, I'll make sure he gets to school in the morning. He won't be late," Sofia responds. "*Muchacha,* you worry too much. Listen, you didn't get that from me. Worry, worry. Your son will be all right. We're going to eat soon. *Cuidate. Sí. Adiós,*" and then Sofia hangs up. Lupe knows he will stay with Sofia tonight.

After Sofia gets off the phone, Lupe helps Sofia with preparing the evening meal. Sofia and Lupe wash the black beans and cut up peppers, onions, tomatoes, garlic, and herbs to cook with the beans. While Sofia begins cooking the vegetables and herbs in a large saucepan, Lupe slices open the plantains and removes the peels. Along with the beans and fried plantains, Sofia also prepares rice, a large omelet, and a salad of lettuce and blanched eggplant covered with vinegar, oil, and fresh parsley. All this will be followed by *tazitas* of strong and sweet black coffee.

El Gallo crows loudly, and the sky is almost dark. Miriam, Sofia's youngest daughter, drags herself in just before dinner. Miriam is only twenty years old, but she looks older. "Hello, Lupe," Miriam says. "Ma, I got an awful headache. I'm going to lay down in my room." Miriam disappears into the hallway. Miriam's room is very cluttered with boxes. The small sunken bed is in the center of the room surrounded by the chaos of the assorted boxes. Lupe is never sure whether she is moving in or moving out. A lamp without a shade lights the room, and the walls have peeling paint. Miriam stays with her mother because she has no other place to go.

Sofia's room is a striking contrast. She calls her room *El Cuarto de los Santos.* Sofia's soft double bed, covered by a frilly pink quilt, is in the far corner, and the walls are painted pink, except for the ceiling, which is white. A small dresser with an oval mirror is on the opposite wall from the bed. And all around the room, on shelves, nailed to the walls, on the floor, are statues of various saints Sofia worships and admires. Saint Francis of Assisi sits in a prominent place on her dresser. Candles are placed before each saint, and at night before Sofia goes to bed, she lights a candle for each saint and recites a short prayer. Lupe counts the saints and decides there must be twenty different prayers each night. From these nightly prayers, Sofia Ramirez seeks strength and sanity and salvation. Lupe thinks the world is fortunate that this old lady prays for it each night.

After dinner that evening, Lupe and Miriam help Sofia clear the table and wash the dishes. The leftovers are put in the refrigerator once *El Gallo* gets his share. Lupe cannot resist asking his grandmother about her room of saints.

"*Muchacho,* they are like friends you go to for comfort. And they always provide comfort. You are your father's comfort. Yes, you believe me or don't believe me. Why does a person need comfort? Why? Let me show you why."

Sofia reaches into the cabinet and takes out some red balloons, and she begins filling one with water in the kitchen sink.

"Oh, not again, Ma." Miriam gasps.

Sofia shushes her and walks over to the kitchen window. Below, the street is active with cars and shoppers. She calls Lupe to the window.

"You are twelve years old, and by now you should know that you're going along in life, right, day to day, right, and suddenly out of the blue something happens you didn't expect. Bang! Your daughter drowns. Bang! Somebody robs you. . . . Bang!" And she tosses the water balloon out the window and holds Lupe back from leaning out to watch the balloon take its wobbly but heavy drop to the shoppers below on the sidewalk. "And then somebody drops a water balloon on you," she says as she begins to cackle so loudly she startles *El Gallo,* who proceeds to drop a small turd. Then she stops laughing and grows very serious.

They listen to the commotion below. Many voices are shouting obscenities up to the building. But within seconds the protest dies away into the drumming of automobiles. "So you have to watch out for waterballoons," Lupe says.

"And that, my grandson, is why I have my saints," she answers. "They comfort me when things are bad, when I feel bad, when the unexpected leaves me alone without help, *sin remedio.*"

"I hope I help comfort you, Sofia," Lupe says as he holds her hand tightly and brings the old woman's hand to his lips and kisses it, pressing the baby-soft loose skin of the back of her hand to his cheek for a very long moment.

Miriam watches Lupe carefully and with curiosity. The kettle begins to whistle, and Miriam removes the kettle from the burner. Sofia takes a jar off the shelf—*llerba buena*—and makes a very pungent tea for the three of them.

"Sofia, would you teach me about your magic? My father says you are a . . . a *bruja*. A good *bruja*. Would you show me?" Lupe asks. Gesturing toward the jars with nervous hands, he stands by the shelves in the kitchen.

Sofia turns from her teakettle. She walks over to Lupe and adjusts her bifocals.

"Ma," Miriam says with caution in her voice. "She hides the recipes for her potions from us, Lupe."

"Shhh," Sofia says to her youngest daughter.

"Ma, you know you won't tell him about these things, so don't play with Lupe like that. Lupe, she wouldn't tell me either about that shit," Miriam says.

"It is not shit." Sofia raises her voice slightly. "It is not shit."

"I'm sorry, Ma," Miriam recants.

"Why do you want to know about this?" she asks Lupe. She places her hand on his shoulder.

"I worry about my father," Lupe begins, eyes cast down to the cracked linoleum floor. "He limps now. He limps more than I do. He gets so tired. His strength is going. Is there some magic you have to make him younger?"

"I am so sorry, Lupe," Sofia tells him with sympathy. "I have no magic to make Nieves younger. Or to make you older, although you don't seem to need that. Lupe, I don't have the medicine to make me younger. If I did, wouldn't I use it? I'm an old lady. Wouldn't I use it if I had such a magical potion? Your father actually has more magic than I could ever have. But magic doesn't make a person young. Maybe it's something else, but it isn't our magic. Drink the tea," Sofia says, motioning Lupe and Miriam to the table.

The tea makes Lupe feel light and sleepy, and when the three of them finish, Sofia prepares the couch in the living room for Lupe.

During the night Miriam comes to his bedside in the room, unlit except for the headlights' glare. She stands by him for a long time. His eyes open, and she takes his hand and slips his hand under her nightshirt. He feels her rounded belly. It is enlarged like a small melon.

"I'm going to have a baby, Lupe," Miriam whispers, her voice beginning to sound with fear. She holds his hand there, and he senses a life brooding under his warm palm. As Miriam drops down to her knees, Lupe's fingers touch her small breasts. For a moment he envies the lips of cloth. Miriam is whimpering, "Please don't hate me for this, but I have to talk to someone. I don't know who the father is. Isn't that terrible of me, Lupe? I don't know who he is. Please don't hate me."

"I would never hate you, Miriam. You're my aunt. Does Sofia know?" Lupe's face is almost touching hers.

"Yes. But she won't help me. She told me she won't use her medicine to destroy a baby."

Lupe puts his arms out and hugs her, and Miriam rises and crawls in with him, her small body fitting along the very edge of the couch. She wraps Lupe's arm over her, his hand near her heart, and she and Lupe sleep like infants in the smooth dark mouth of the night.

PART III

SURVIVAL ON THE STREETS

KIPLING AND I

Jesús Colón

Jesús Colón was born in Cayey, Puerto Rico, in 1901. At the age of sixteen he left the Island as a stowaway on the S.S. Carolina and settled in New York City. Even as he survived over the years by working on ships and in factories, as dockworker, dishwasher, postal worker, and labor organizer, Colón remained involved and active in literary endeavors and community politics. He was a regular contributor to numerous Socialist newspapers and magazines published in Puerto Rico and in New York. He served for many years as the head of the Hispanic Section of the International Workers Order, and ran as the American Labor Party candidate for the New York State Senate and later for the New York City Council.

In 1955, Colón became a regular columnist for the Daily Worker, *a publication of the Communist party. He published a collection of essays and reminiscences, originally written for the* Daily Worker, *in* A Puerto Rican in New York and Other Sketches *(1961, 1982). He died in New York at the age of seventy-three. The posthumously published* The Way It Was and Other Writings *(1993) assembles selections from the Jesús Colón Archives housed at the Center for Puerto Rican Studies at Hunter College. In "Kipling and I" Colón recalls doing away with a source of inspiration for the practical benefits of survival.*

SOMETIMES I PASS DEBEVOISE PLACE AT THE CORNER OF WILLOUGHBY Street. . . . I look at the old wooden house, gray and ancient, the house where I used to live some forty years ago. . . .

My room was on the second floor at the corner. On hot summer nights I would sit at the window reading by the electric light from the streetlamp, which was almost at a level with the windowsill.

It was nice to come home late during the winter, look for some scrap of old newspaper, some bits of wood and a few chunks of coal, and start a sparkling fire in the chunky four-legged coal stove. I would be rewarded with an intimate warmth as little by little the pygmy stove became alive puffing out its sides, hot and red, like the crimson cheeks of a Santa Claus.

My few books were in a soap box nailed to the wall. But my most prized possession in those days was a poem I had bought in a five-and-ten-cent store on Fulton Street. (I wonder what has become of these poems, maxims, and sayings of wise men that they used to sell at the five-and-ten-cent stores?) The poem was printed on gold paper and mounted in a gilded frame ready to be hung in a conspicuous place in the house. I bought one of those fancy silken picture cords finishing in a rosette to match the color of the frame.

I was seventeen. This poem to me then seemed to summarize the wisdom of all the sages that ever lived in one poetical nutshell. It was what I was looking for, something to guide myself by, a way of life, a compendium of the wise, the true, and the beautiful. All I had to do was to live according to the counsel of the poem and follow its instructions and I would be a perfect man—the useful, the good, the true human being. I was very happy that day, forty years ago.

The poem had to have the most prominent place in the room. Where could I hang it? I decided that the best place for the poem was on the wall right by the entrance to the room. No one coming in and out would miss it. Perhaps someone would be interested enough to read it and drink the profound waters of its message. . . .

Every morning as I prepared to leave, I stood in front of the poem and read it over and over again, sometimes half a dozen times. I let the sonorous music of the verse carry me away. I brought with me a handwritten copy as I stepped out every morning looking for work, repeating verses and stanzas from memory until the whole poem came to be part of me. Other days my lips kept repeating a single verse of the poem at intervals throughout the day.

In the subways I loved to compete with the shrill noises of the many wheels below by chanting the lines of the poem. People stared at me moving my lips as though I were in a trance. I looked back with pity. They were not so fortunate as I, who had as a guide to direct my life a great poem to make me wise, useful, and happy.

And I chanted:

> *If you can keep your head when all about you*
> *Are losing theirs and blaming it on you . . .*
>
> *If you can wait and not be tired by waiting*
> *Or being hated don't give way to hating . . .*
>
> *If you can make one heap of all your winnings*
> *And risk it on a turn of pitch and toss . . .*
> *And lose and start again at your beginnings . . .*

"If," by Kipling, was the poem. At seventeen, my evening prayer and my first morning thought. I repeated it every day with the resolution to live up to the very last line of that poem.

I would visit the government employment office on Jay Street. The conversations among the Puerto Ricans on the large wooden benches in the employment office were always on the same subject. How to find a decent place to live. How they would not rent to Negroes or Puerto Ricans. How Negroes and Puerto Ricans were given the pink slips first at work.

From the employment office I would call door to door at the piers, factories, and storage houses in the streets under the Brooklyn and Manhattan bridges. "Sorry, nothing today." It seemed to me that that "today" was a continuation and combination of all the yesterdays, todays, and tomorrows.

From the factories I would go to the restaurants looking for a job as a porter or dishwasher. At least I would eat and be warm in a kitchen.

"Sorry" . . . "Sorry" . . .

Sometimes I was hired at ten dollars a week, ten hours a day including Sundays and holidays. One day off during the week. My work was that of three men: dishwasher, porter, busboy. And to clear the sidewalk of snow and slush "when you have nothing else to do." I was to be appropriately humble and grateful not only to the owner but to everybody else in the place.

If I rebelled at insults or at a pointed innuendo or just the inhuman amount of work, I was unceremoniously thrown out and told to come "next week for your pay." "Next week" meant weeks of calling for the paltry dollars owed me. The owners relished this "next week."

I clung to my poem as to a faith. Like a potent amulet, my precious poem was clenched in the fist of my right hand inside my secondhand overcoat. Again and again I declaimed aloud a few precious lines when discouragement and disillusionment threatened to overwhelm me.

> *If you can force your heart and nerve and sinew*
> *To serve your turn long after you are gone . . .*

The weeks of unemployment and hard knocks turned into months. I continued to find two or three days of work here and there. And I continued to be thrown out when I rebelled at the ill treatment, overwork, and insults. I kept pounding the streets looking for a place where they would treat me half decently, where my devotion to work and faith in Kipling's poem would be appreciated. I remember the worn-out shoes I bought in a secondhand store on Myrtle Avenue at the corner of Adams Street. The round holes in the soles that I tried to cover with pieces of carton were no match for the frigid knives of the unrelenting snow.

One night I returned late after a long day of looking for work. I was hungry. My room was dark and cold. I wanted to warm my numb body. I lit a match and began looking for some scraps of wood and a piece of paper to start a fire. I searched all over the floor. No wood, no paper. As I stood up, the glimmering flicker of the dying match was reflected in the glass surface of the framed poem. I unhooked the poem from the wall. I reflected for a minute, a minute that felt like an eternity. I took the frame apart, placing the square glass upon the small table. I tore the gold paper on which the poem was printed, threw its pieces inside the stove, and placing the small bits of wood from the frame on top of the paper, I lit it, adding soft and hard coal as the fire began to gain strength and brightness.

I watched how the lines of the poem withered into ashes inside the small stove.

FROM *A PERFECT SILENCE*

Alba Ambert

Alba Ambert was born in Puerto Rico and brought up in the South Bronx, New York. Ambert, who has a B.A. in Philosophy from the University of Puerto Rico, is trained as a psycholinguist with master's and doctoral degrees from Harvard University. In addition to numerous scholarly books and articles, Ambert has published four collections of poetry in both English and Spanish, and two novels: Porque hay silencio *(1989), which received an award from the Institute of Puerto Rican Literature, and* A Perfect Silence *(1995), which received the Carey McWilliams Award. Ambert is currently Senior Research Scholar at Richmond College, the American International University in London, England, where she lectures and continues to advance her writing of fiction.*

A Perfect Silence *builds on Ambert's firsthand experience with the world of poverty and alienation, as well as the power of hope. In this excerpt from the novel, Blanca displays her resiliency amid a cruel environment that leaves her no recourse other than her imagination and the charity of the welfare system.*

PUBLIC SCHOOL 9 WAS A RED-BRICK STRUCTURE BUILT AT THE TURN of the century. It loomed on 138th Street across from the Puerto Rico Theater like a huge armory vigilantly surveilling students, teachers, and staff who scuttled in and out its wide staircase. P.S. 9 did not inspire teachers to draw out the best in their pupils. Teachers never expected the children—who were mostly Puerto Rican and black, with a smattering of Irish and Italians too poor to have fled the ghetto—to occupy the ivy-scented halls of distant universities or mark history with distinguished feats. Teachers felt gratified beyond their expectations when girls turned twelve without "getting themselves pregnant," and boys managed to elude reform school. Their biggest success consisted in steering the little lambs into a trade that would keep them off the public dole, such as auto mechanics or sewing.

Teachers and principal lingered at the shore, their backs turned to the island of isolation in which the children lived. From the periphery, they looked away and refused to learn the language of the dispossessed. Teachers were often overheard in the lounge by the girls who cleaned up after them. They expressed shock that little girls would have their earlobes pierced, a savage tribal custom that, they thought, had to be some form of child abuse. They criticized when children were absent from school to care for younger siblings if a mother had to run errands, or if they had to translate for a sick relative in the hospital. They accused children of cheating when they copied from each other's homework. When the children explained that they were only helping out a friend, they were doubly punished for lying as well as cheating. And their diet was atrocious, teachers said, eating disgusting food like black-blood sausages and boiled green bananas.

The children of P.S. 9 were, at best, no more than question marks. If the children were hungry, suffered abuse, needed assistance to realize their potential, their silent appeals for help fell on stone hearts. Most teachers were at P.S. 9 not because they wanted to be, but because inexperience or limited pedagogical abilities did not allow them access to a more desirable school district.

There were exceptions. Mrs. Kalfus, a second-grade teacher, once kissed Blanca's swollen cheek when she had a toothache. Years later Blanca, who forgot much of her disrupted childhood, remembered that kiss. In the fifth grade, Mrs. Wasserman kept a collection of children's books in the classroom. These were precious books about princesses who slept under flowery canopies and were always loved by handsome princes. There was a book about a girl who owned a black horse and galloped gloriously on the sandy beaches of a place called New England, and about two-story white houses inhabited by happy people and dogs and cats and canaries and lots of dolls. That school year Blanca read the books in Mrs. Wasserman's collection over and over again until they were etched in her memory. She transformed the stories into dreams of possible worlds. Because Blanca was a manipulator of symbols, she took the only symbols at her disposal and dreamed them possible. She hid them in a quiet nook of her mind, and from there they gave her light and comfort.

Blanca read in two languages. She had taught herself to read in Spanish after a cousin arrived from Puerto Rico and brought with her a book. The young woman recognized Blanca's hunger for words and offered the book to her like a sacrament. Blanca avidly spread its pages, but could not read it because it was written in Spanish. Hungrily, she pored over the first book she ever owned. She searched through its pages and scrutinized the drawings. Then she went back to the first page, the first sentence, the first word, the title. Familiar letters, letters she knew, words that she knew also, but did not know she knew. Oh, the pain, the pain of those intractable symbols. She wanted to possess them, drink them, devour them. Her hunger for those words did not wane. She held the book tightly, the words wiggled and swam and titillated. Then she split the words like ripe pomegranates and spilled the letters like seeds. She gently gathered the seeds into their shells one by one, again and again, over and over, until each word burst in her mind like a blossom. The world was never the same after that.

Blanca read with desperate thirst in her two languages. If there were no books at her disposal, she read labels on olive jars and tomato sauce cans. She read street signs and cigarette packets. She stood for hours in front of the newspaper stand and gulped words until intoxicated. The attendant always knew she was there. He would shoo her away like a fly. And like a fly, she zoomed back for her honey. One day he asked her name. She said Blanca. And he said that's a pretty name; it means white, doesn't it? She said yes, how do you know? And he said oh, I know many things, which surprised Blanca because he was blind.

When does conscious life begin? Is it born from the astonishment we feel when we discover that deception lies everywhere? Or is it the smell of another's distinctive sweat, or when destiny marches on, echoing cruelties? Is it born from lost pride or the humiliation of a slap? Or is it when we realize that gods mock and sneer? Could it begin with the explosion of a perfect silence?

Blanca's conscious life began when she lay on her cot and her rum-colored eyes shone with imaginary scenes. It was when Blanca discovered fantasies and daydreams. She was an Amazon galloping on a white horse, or a princess sleeping amid veils of tulle. In her fantasies, Blanca was a ballerina, a movie star, a cabaret singer, a championship horseback rider, a modern sculptor, a teacher who stunned students with her beauty and wisdom. Once she discovered the magic of fantasy, there were many occasions during the day and night when Blanca fled to a private, secure world where she found silence. A world without grandmothers or fathers or fake parents or beatings or desertions or betrayals. Even when night terrors preyed and she woke up trembling, she floated away to green meadows and strolled by clear streams until a sweet sleep claimed her.

The children were filing out to the lunchroom, and Blanca lagged at the end of the line.

Mrs. Wasserman narrowed her eyes. "Why are you limping, Blanca?"

"My shoes broke, Mrs. Wasserman, and the tacks are sticking into my feet."

"Are you still living with your father and stepmother?"

"No, Mrs. Wasserman."

"Who do you live with now?"

"Some people my father knows."

"I thought so. Your stepmother always sent you to school with clean and freshly ironed clothes."

When Blanca did not respond, the teacher sent her off to lunch. The next day, when the dismissal bell rang, she asked Blanca to stay for a few minutes. Mrs. Wasserman brought out a big box from the closet and placed it on her desk. She opened it and took out a pair of black patent leather shoes with wide buckles, socks of the whitest hue, a heavy dark blue coat, and two beautiful dresses, one woolen and the other corduroy.

From the bottom of the box, Mrs. Wasserman brought out a white brassiere of simple cotton with a label that read 28AA. She smiled. "It's time you wore one of these. You're growing quickly."

The basement seemed unusually quiet and still when Blanca came up to the door carrying her treasured box from school. Genara was always in the apartment waiting for her children to come home. Blanca was accustomed to Genara's silence when she unlocked the door for her every afternoon and Blanca put her books away and went out again. Rafael's wife hardly spoke to her. Blanca was an added burden, another mouth to feed, another bother. She already had six children, why take on the responsibility of another? But Rafael insisted on taking in the orphan who always made a mess at the table with her books and papers, she fumed to friends and relatives.

"Look, woman, her pa gives me good money, and we don't spend a dime on her. We hardly feed her, for Chrissake. In school she gets breakfast and lunch, and if we give her a bite of something left over from dinner, that's it. If I ask her pa for extra money for clothing, he dishes it out. And it's money that goes straight into my pocket, because he don't even ask how she's doing. And you know he don't come to see her. So in this little business, I'm the winner. Shit, don't complain no more, I'm sick of your naggin'," he emphasized with his *caudillo* voice.

Genara's dislike was obvious, and Blanca spoke to her only when absolutely necessary. She tried to stay out of her way as much as possible. She was terrified of Rafael. She spent time out of school roaming the streets like a stray cat, in friends' apartments, and looking for something to do in the neighborhood park with its swings and slides and bunches of teenagers who hid behind the guardhouse to pet, drink, and shoot dice and heroin. She returned to the basement as late as possible to finish her homework and sleep. Sometimes, Miriam and Rebeca played with her, but Genara disapproved of time spent with the orphan, as she called Blanca. The four boys had their own interests in the streets. To them, Blanca was another piece of furniture in the crowded apartment.

Genara had seen the light and received the spirit in her soul. She was a member of the Pentecostal Church of the Seventh Day and went out every evening to attend services. She returned about ten, exalted by the brothers and sisters who had spoken in tongues. Frequently, she took her reluctant children to services, hoping that they, too, would be blessed with a pledge of salvation. Since she was not interested in running into Blanca in the afterlife, the girl was not invited. Blanca was left behind, without a key to get into the apartment, to roam the dingy streets, pacifying hunger pangs and the bitter cold with constant movement. She never returned when she knew the man was in the apartment alone.

But that afternoon, when Blanca came from school with her treasure trove, it was Rafael, and not Genara, who opened the door.

The girl stared at the brick skirt of a building through the narrow half-window. Dumped on the bed like an empty sack, she concentrated hard on the uneven rectangular lines drawn on the soot-blackened wall. She could see a red curve, the beginning or the end, she was not sure, of a letter scrawled in the night by a disgruntled neighbor wishing to preserve his immortality. The letter bobbed as she did. At times it became a blur. She followed the red curve intently with stark wide-open eyes, head twisted to the side. In the depths of her self-inflicted daze, she knew this lonely pain would always be with her.

She walked very slowly to school, as though holding a large ball between her legs. Mrs. Wasserman's eyes almost burst in anger. She called the school authorities, who called the medical authorities, who called the police authorities. The swift rescue climaxed in social-services offices and court. The neglectful father apologized.

"I'm a widower. I gotta work and had no one to take care of her. I didn't know what was going on. I swear on the sacred Bible, I didn't know."

Blanca was taken to live with Conchita, her new guardian, inspected and licensed by the city to care for children in crises. She took antibiotics provided by the city for a stubborn infection and wore clothes provided by the city. Blanca, whose life was continually regimented by municipal fiat, perceived that an omnipotent, omnipresent, and omniscient being must surely reside in the mayor's office, sitting in front of a great city map and pushing pins with colored heads. One of those little heads, red maybe because it was her favorite color, represented Blanca. She felt calmer knowing she was taken care of by this faceless, amorphous being.

It was a long time before she removed her heavy blue coat.

THE CHAMP

Pedro Juan Soto

Pedro Juan Soto, born in Cataño, Puerto Rico, in 1928, spent his youth in New York City, where he received his college and graduate education, and returned to the Island in 1955. He has published two collections of short stories, Spiks *(1956), which was translated in 1974, and* Un decir (de la volencia) *(1976). He has also published several novels:* Usmail *(1958);* Ardiente suelo, fría estación *(1961), translated in 1973 as* Hot Land, Cold Season; El francotirador *(1969);* Temporada de duendes *(1970); and* Un oscuro pueblo sonriente *(1982). In 1990 he published* Palabras a vuelo. *Soto has a Ph.D. from the University of Toulouse, France, and taught at the University of Puerto Rico.*

Puruco, the adolescent protagonist of "The Champ," tries to establish himself as a big man among the barrio's machos, only to be reminded he still has some growing up to do.

THE CUE MADE A LAST SWING OVER THE GREEN FELT, HIT THE CUE ball, and cracked it against the fifteen ball. The stubby, yellowish hands remained motionless until the ball went *clop* into the pocket, and then raised the cue until it was diagonally in front of the acned, fatuous countenance: the tight little Vaselined curl fell tidily over the forehead, the ear clipped a cigarette, the glance was oblique and mocking, and the mustache's scarce fuzz had been accentuated with pencil.

"Wha' happen, man?" said the sharp voice. "That was a champ shot, hey?"

Then he started to laugh. His squat, greasy body became a cheerfully quaking blob inside the tight jeans and the sweaty T-shirt.

He contemplated Gavilán—the eyes, too wise, didn't look so wise now; the three-day beard tried to camouflage the face's ill temper, but didn't make it; the long-ashed cigarette kept the lips shut tight, obscene words wading in back of them—and enjoyed the feat he had perpetrated. He had beaten him in two straight games. Gavilán had been six months in jail, sure, but that didn't matter now. What mattered was that he had lost two games with him, whom these victories placed in a privileged position. They placed him above the others, over the best players in the neighborhood and over the ones who belittled him for being nothing but a sixteen-year-old, nothing but a "baby." Now nobody could cut him out of his spot in Harlem. He was the new one, the successor to Gavilán and other individuals worthy of respect. He was the same as . . . no. He was better, on account of his youth: He had more time and opportunities to surpass all their feats.

He felt like running out into the street and shouting, "I won two straight games from Gavilán! Speak out now! C'mon, say something now!" He didn't do it. He only chalked his cue and told himself it wasn't worth the trouble. It was sunny out, but it was Saturday and the neighbors would be at the marketplace at this hour of the morning. He would have no more audience than snot-nosed kids and disinterested grannies. Anyway, a little humility suited champs well.

He picked up the quarter Gavilán threw on the felt and exchanged a conceited smile with the scorekeeper and the three spectators.

"Collect yours," he told the scorekeeper, hoping that some spectator would move to the other pool tables to spread the news, to comment how he—Puruco, the too-fat kid with the pimply face and the comic voice—had made a fool of the great Gavilán. It seemed, however, that they were waiting for another show.

He put away his fifteen cents and said to Gavilán, who was wiping his sweaty face, "Play another?"

"Let's," Gavilán said, taking from the rack another cue that he would chalk meticulously.

The scorer took down the triangular rack and shaped up the balls for the next round.

Puruco broke, and immediately began to whistle and pace around the table with a springy walk, almost on the tips of his sneakers.

Gavilán came up to the cue ball with his characteristic heaviness, and centered it, but didn't hit it yet. He simply raised his very shaggy head, his body still bent over the cue and the felt, and said, "Hey, quit the whistle."

"Okay, man," Puruco said, and juggled his cue until he heard Gavilán's shot and the balls went running around and clashed again. None of them went home.

"Ay, bendito," Puruco laughed. "Got this man like dead."

He hit number one, which went in and left number two lined up for the left pocket. Number two also dropped in. He could not stop from smiling toward the corners of the parlor. He seemed to invite the spiders, the flies, and the numbers bookies dispersed among the bystanders at the other pool tables to take a look at this.

He carefully studied the position of each ball. He wanted to win this other set, too, to take advantage of his recent reading of Willie Hoppe's book, and all that month-after-month practicing when he had been the butt of his opponents. Last year he was just a little pisspot; now the real life was beginning for him, the life of a champ. Once he beat Gavilán, he would lick Mamerto and Bimbo.

"Make way for Puruco!" the cool men would say. And he would make it with the owners of the pool parlors, gather good connections. He'd be bodyguard to some, and buddy-buddy to others. Cigarettes and beer for free he would have. And women, not the scared, stupid chicks who went no farther than some squeezing at the movies. From there, right into fame: big man in the neighborhood, the one and only guy for any job—the numbers, the narco racket, the dame from Riverside Drive slumming in the neighborhood, this gang's rumble with that one to settle manly things.

With a grunt, he missed ball three and cursed. Gavilán was right behind him when he turned.

"Watch out puttin' foofoo on me!" he said, ruffling up.

And Gavilán:

"Ah, stop that."

"No. Don't give me that, man, just 'cause yuh losin'?"

Gavilán did not answer. He centered the cue ball through the smoke that wrinkled his features, and pocketed two balls in opposite sides.

"See?" Puruco said, and he crossed his fingers to protect himself.

"Shaddup yuh mouth!"

Gavilán tried to ricochet the five in, but failed. Puruco studied the position of his ball and settled for the farthest but surest pocket. While aiming, he realized that he would have to uncross his fingers. He looked at Gavilán suspiciously and crossed his legs to shoot. He missed.

When he looked up, Gavilán was smiling and sucking his upper gums to spit his pyorrhea. Now he had no doubt that he was the victim of a spell.

"No foolin', man. Play it clean." Gavilán gazed at him with surprise, stepping on the cigarette distractedly.

"What's the matter?"

"No," Puruco said. "Don't you go on with that *bilongo*!"

"Hey!" Gavilán laughed. "This one t'inks a lot about witches."

He put the cue behind his back, feinted once, and pocketed the ball easily. He pocketed again in the next shot, and in the next. Puruco began to get nervous. Either Gavilán was recovering his ability or else that voodoo spell was pushing his cue. If he didn't get to raise his score, Gavilán would win this set.

Chalking his cue, he touched wood three times and awaited his turn. Gavilán missed his fifth shot. Then Puruco eyed the distance. He hit, putting in the eight. He pulled a combination shot to pocket the eleven with the nine. The nine went home later. He caromed the twelve in, and then missed the ten. Gavilán also missed it. Finally Puruco managed to send it in, but for ball thirteen he almost ripped the felt. He added the score in his head. About eight more to call it quits—he could relax a little.

The cigarette went from behind his ear to his lips. When he lit it, turning his back to the table so that the fan would not blow out the match, he saw the sly smile of the scorekeeper. He turned around rapidly and caught Gavilán right in the act: feet lifted off the floor, body leaning against the table rim to make an easy shot. Before he could speak, Gavilán had pocketed the ball.

"Hey, man!"

"Wha' happen?" Gavilán said calmly, eyeing the next shot.

"Don't you pull that on me, boy! You can't beat me that way."

Gavilán raised an eyebrow at him, and bit the inside of his mouth while making a snout.

"Wha's hurtin' you?" he said.

"No, like that no!" Puruco jerked his arms open and almost hit the scorekeeper with his cue. He threw the cigarette down violently and said to the onlookers, "You seen it, right?"

"See wha'?" said Gavilán, unmoved.

"Nothin', that dirty play," squealed Puruco. "T'ink I'm stupid?"

"Aw, man." Gavilán laughed. "Don't you go askin' me, maybe I tell you."

Puruco struck the table rim with the cue.

"With me you gotta play fair. You ain't satisfied with puttin' a spell on me first, but after you put me on with cheatin'."

"Who cheatin'?" Gavilán said. He left the cue on the table and, smiling, moved closer to Puruco. "You say I'm cheatin'?"

"No," Puruco said, changing his tone, babying his voice, wavering on his feet. "But that's no way to play, man. They seen you."

Gavilán turned to the others.

"I been cheatin'?"

Only the scorekeeper shook his head. The others said nothing and looked away.

"But like he's lyin' on the table, man," Puruco said.

Gavilán clutched the T-shirt as if by chance, baring the pudgy back as he pulled him over.

"Me, nobody call me a cheatin' man."

The playing had stopped at all the other pool tables. The rest of the people watched from a distance. Nothing was heard but the buzz of the fan and the flies, and the screaming of children in the street.

"You t'ink a pile of crap like you gonna call me a cheater?" Gavilán said, forcing his fist against Puruco's chest, ripping the shirt. "I let you win two tables so you have somethin' to put on, and now you think you king. Get outta here, jerk," he said between his teeth. "When you grow up we'll see ya."

The push threw Puruco against the plaster wall, where his back smashed flat. The crash filled the silence with holes. Somebody laughed, tittering. Somebody said, "He a bragger."

"An' get outta here before I kick you for good," Gavilán said.

"'Kay man," Puruco stammered, dropping the cue.

Out he went without daring to raise his eyes, hearing cues clicking again on the tables, and some giggles. On the street, he felt like crying, but held it in. That was for sissies. The blow didn't hurt; that other thing—"When you grow up we'll see ya"—hurt more. He was a full-grown man. If they beat him, if they killed him, let them do it paying no mind at all to his being a sixteen-year-old. He was a man already. He could do a lot of damage, plenty of damage, and he could also survive it.

He crossed over to the other sidewalk, furiously kicked a beer can, his hands, from inside the pockets, pinching his body nailed to the cross of adolescence.

Two sets he had let him win, Gavilán said. Dirty lie. He knew he would lose every one of them to him, from now on, to the new champ. He had pulled the voodoo stuff on account of that, on account of that the cheating, the blow on account of that. Oh, but those three other men would spread the news of Gavilán's fall. After that, Mamerto and Bimbo. Nobody could stop him now. The neighborhood, the whole world, would be his.

When the barrel hoop got trapped between his legs, he kicked it aside. He gave a slap to the kid who came to pick it up.

"Careful, man, or I knock yuh eye out," he growled.

And he went on walking, unconcerned with the mother who cursed him and ran toward the tearful kid. Lips held tight, he inhaled deeply. At his passing, he could see confetti falling and cheers pouring from the closed and deserted windows.

He was a champ. He was on the lookout only for harm.

STOOPBALL

Edward Rivera

Edward Rivera was born in Orocovia, Puerto Rico, in 1944 and came to New York City at the age of seven. He attended parochial and public schools in El Barrio (Spanish Harlem) and then received his B.A. in English from City College. Rivera holds an M.F.A. from Columbia University and currently teaches English at City College of New York. His major work is Family Installments: Memories of Growing Up Hispanic *(1982), a compelling chronicle of the Malánguez family that is based on Rivera's own childhood experiences.*

Through the alternately compassionate and humorous narration of Santos Malánguez, Family Installments *traces his family's history, from the mountains of Puerto Rico to New York City and back to the Island. In "Stoopball," Santos recalls his and his brother's romantic misfortunes.*

JUDGE DEGETAU'S THREE DAUGHTERS WERE THE BEST-LOOKING girls on our block. My brother, Tego, went out with Norma, the middle one, for almost a year, and almost married her. I had a crush on Delia, the youngest of the three. "She's what I want," I'd say to myself. But I didn't think I stood a chance. She was too good-looking and too choosy for someone like me, so I didn't make a play. Tego said I was too shy for my own good. He wasn't shy, and he didn't think Norma was too good-looking, or too good anything, for him. He was more self-confident around girls. But in the end it didn't get him Norma, or her him.

Delia looked a lot like the oldest sister, Amparo. When Amparo was nineteen, she appeared on the cover of *Picadillo,* a popular men's magazine, a Latin *Playboy,* a *tetas* publication that sold well. Even women bought it. It carried articles on all kinds of interesting topics, including hints on what the ideal young woman was supposed to look, act, and think like, even what she should eat, and what she was supposed to do with herself when she hit thirty and started sliding downhill. It also published advice for men: what, for example, a man, young or getting on, single or "domesticated," could do to get his hands and teeth on an ideal young woman of the *Picadillo* variety; how to hold on to her once he had her eating out of his hand; and how a *Picadillo* playboy could free himself from an over-thirty woman who was sliding downhill fast or, as one of the magazine's columnists put it, "when her beauty span is played out."

The *Picadillo* issue that displayed Amparo on the cover sold out fast. Tego stashed his copy inside the bottom drawer of the four-drawer dresser we shared. I looked at it five or six times every day for weeks. Then Mami found it and threw it out. When I got back from school that day, the garbage truck had driven off with it, and none of the newsstands I visited had any copies left. I was angry over that loss, but there was nothing I could tell Mami. I had to play it dumb. That's what she did.

Looking at Amparo on that cover had been like looking at Delia a couple of years older. They had the same face and build. The only significant difference in their looks was that Delia had a chipped front tooth, one of the upper incisors.

Amparo was smiling at the photographer. She had hazel eyes and long light-brown hair. She was reclining in a bikini on a fake beach. Maybe the sand was real; maybe it was only extra-fine sawdust. But the solid-blue sea and sky behind her, and the sunlight spotlighted on certain parts of her—those were man-made *fakerías.* Her body looked wet, too, like the physiques of weight lifters in body-building magazines. Some kind of oil was supposed to account for that shiny look. One of my friends on the block, a barbell fanatic, said they sprayed them with Mazola. Whatever it was, Amparo looked well done. Tego could have done worse with his thirty-five cents. I should have told Mami that after she junked Amparo.

"You know what you threw out, Mami?"

"Trash."

"That thing cost Tego thirty-five cents."

"You'd better not tell that to your father. He has a lot of debts."

That's how she would have answered me, with her *gorge* going up. So I kept it to myself.

A lot of good-looking and ugly guys, and men too old to be called guys, made plays for Amparo, but there was no way they could get their hands or paws on "Miss Picadillo," our new nickname for her. (Before that, it was "Miss Tetas," because she had big ones.) She knew she was something special, and her father, El Judge, was a choosy man. And what did those "jung buns" and "old buns," as he called them and every other male in our neighborhood—what did they have to offer his Amparo? A Home Relief life on Willis Avenue? Half a dozen kids and sagging breasts by the time she reached thirty? Summers at Orchard Beach and City Island? Sunday picnics near the baseball diamonds and mulch pile of Central Park? An early grave in a run-down cemetery? In other words, what the buns had to offer his Amparo was nothing, *nada*. And *nada* was what they were going to get from Amparo and the judge.

So they played it smart: She married the Cuban freelancer who had taken her cheesecake for *Picadillo,* and the *gusano* got her a glamorous position as a steno-typist in that publication. He was a well-dressed, striking-looking man from Mother Cabrini Boulevard up near the Cloisters. Tego told me his dark hair and mustache were taken care of by Orlando of Miami Beach on Amsterdam Avenue, and that his fingernails were trimmed by Orlando's sister, Sarita. Whenever I saw him he was walking fast with his camera, in a big hurry, as though his day wasn't long enough.

Right after he and Amparo got married, they moved out to Corona in Queens; and after that we saw them around only when they came to visit her family on certain holidays (Thanksgiving, Fourth of July) and Good Friday. On Good Friday she always wore black; he always wore white ducks and Cuban heels, and he had a black Leica with telephoto lens looped around his neck. It looked to me like the biggest medal in the world. Jealous or not (and envious, too), some of us had to admit that they made a fine-looking couple, the kind that put others to shame in dance halls.

"So what, Santos?" Tego said when I told him something wasn't fair about the whole thing. "Some people have it made. Others have to ride the subway." He was the one who filled me in on most of the gossip about Amparo and the photographer.

Tego took his love affair with Norma seriously, I thought, but I don't think El Judge did; and it was the judge who wore the *pantalones* in his apartment. We—his friends and I—were sure he'd marry Norma after they both finished high school. Even Mami and Papi thought so, though they weren't exactly crazy over the prospect. They wouldn't do a thing to stop it, but they weren't looking forward to it, either. They considered the Degetaus a snobbish family who thought they had been condemned by God and circumstances to live on our block. In all the time he was going out with Norma, Tego never brought her home. I concluded that she didn't want to visit us. "I'll bring her up one of these days," he used to tell me. But he never did.

I was sure he was serious about her because he spent most of his spare time up at her house dancing to LPs of Tito Puente, Tito Rodríguez, Machito and his sister Graciela, and other salsa types. He said those were some of her favorites, and he kept their records stored alphabetically in our bedroom. He housed them in a shellacked cabinet he'd made in Chelsea Vocational.

"You can play them anytime you want, Santos. But don't mess them up."

"I don't want to play them." I preferred listening to the kind of music Papi played on his guitar in our dining room: Puerto Rican hillbilly, the le-lo-lai stuff, which meant I was a hopeless case, out of it.

Tego was the dancer in the house. He used to practice new and standard steps by himself, or with Mami's broom, in our living room, while I'd be sitting in our bedroom doing homework or playing stoopball outside with my friends the Turbine Tots, or flying a kite on a rooftop. He practiced five or six times a week, and I could tell when he was going to Norma's house because he always took a stack of records with him.

But it didn't work out between them, and when I asked him why, he told me to mind my own business. That was his first reaction. Then he reconsidered. I knew he would; he didn't want to hurt my feelings.

"She just wasn't my type, Santos. That's all." Some answer.

"So how come you used to spend so much time up in El Judge's house?"

"Why? She was a good dancing partner." But he sounded depressed when he said it. He'd been seeing her almost every day or night for a year, and all of a sudden she wasn't his type. What had happened, I was sure, was that El Judge didn't think my brother was fit to be his son-in-law, so he ordered his daughter to drop him. This happened after Tego quit Chelsea and went to work in a luncheonette in the garment district.

El Judge was a guard for Bowery Savings. We called him Judge because he liked to tell gullible kids that he was "a justice in the Appellative Division of the U.S. Supreme Court." He was also very proud, and contemptuous of other Puerto Ricans. He wanted his three daughters to marry men who could take them out of our neighborhood into a "good" one. Men like that freelancer with his Leica medal. One of the things I heard him say on his stoop, after his oldest daughter's marriage, was that *"los cucubanos"*—the fireflies—"they put our people to the shame. They are more esmart, that is why. Very ambishows."

"And what does that make you, Judge?" the Tots' center fielder asked him.

"A very esmart judge," I said. I think I hated him.

He was a short man, he was going bald, and he had a froggy mouth. I also thought he was built like a walrus, round and hipless, and I began referring to him as "Your Honor, El Walrus," or simply "El Walrus." My friends on the Tots picked those nicknames up. They didn't like him any more than I did. Tego didn't think it was so funny, though.

"You're just being nasty, Santos."

"Maybe. But he asked for it."

"You're just playing his game."

"Why do you like him so much?"

"Who said I did? I just want to get a good night's sleep."

"Me too, but you keep sticking your feet in my face." I slept at the foot of our bed; he slept at the head, and he did kick my face a lot in his sleep. Sometimes I kicked him back, and we'd have a short kicking fight in the dark. Sometimes we ended up laughing ourselves to sleep, and sometimes we didn't talk to each other for days because of those foot fights.

"When I get a job," he used to say, "I'm going to get us a huge bed so you can stop complaining."

"No, you won't," I said. And I was right. He couldn't afford one.

His Honor El Walrus had married a very attractive woman (it was her the three sisters took after), and I couldn't understand why she had picked him.

"How come Mrs. Degetau married that walrus, Tego?"

"How should I know? Women have weird heads."

"She does, anyway."

"She did. They've been married going on twenty-two years."

"That's a long time to be a walrus's wife."

"He's a good supporter. You should see their apartment."

"Yeah, he's a peeping Tom, too."

"Who told you that?"

"I saw him. I was up on the roof with some of the Tots one night. He was looking down at windows."

"So what? Maybe he was just checking up."

"On what?"

"Crooks. Burglars. What else?"

"Women."

"So what were you and your friends doing up there that time of night?"

"Checking things out."

"Don't talk, then. You're another one."

"I'll tell you something, Tego. Just keep it to yourself."

"Go ahead."

"He was checking out his own apartment."

"El Judge?"

"His own house."

"So what? It's his house. He's the one that pays the rent."

"What's the rent got to do with it? He was looking down at Amparo and the *Picadillo* man. I don't have to fill in the details. Her room door was locked, and her light was on."

"You must have had a good front seat."

"El Walrus had a better one. They must have thought he was down on the stoop putting down people."

"And I think you're putting me on, Santos. Don't kid around like that."

"Forget it, then." How could he?

"Stay off the roofs at night."

"Don't get the wrong idea, Tego."

"What idea?"

"About Norma. We never saw her from up there."

"I know you didn't. You can't, that's why. Her room's on the other side of the building."

"That ain't why."

"You're telling *me* where her room is?"

"I wasn't talking about her room."

"So what the hell were you talking about, then?"

"I don't know."

"Don't go up there at night. I'll see you later." He was on his way to their house.

That topic never came up again, but for a while after that he gave me some extra kicks in the head. I don't think he was always asleep when he did. I complained about it. He apologized and said he'd been having "a couple of nightmares lately." One night I had to sleep on the floor, and when I looked in the mirror next morning, there was some blood caked in one of my nostrils.

"You see what you did, Tego? Just take a good look."

"I did that?"

"Yeah, *in your sleep*."

"Hey, I'm sorry, man. I'll sleep on the floor tonight, all right?"

"No, you keep the bed. I like the floor. It's good for my back."

"I told you I'm sorry. You think I did that on purpose? To my own brother?"

"No. You were sleeping."

My way of rubbing it in. He had a delicate conscience.

"Why your brother quit the school?" El Judge asked me one day out in left field.

"He said Chelsea stunk. Didn't he tell you?"

He shook his head and smacked his lips. I imagined tusks and whiskers on his face. "No good now," he said. "Now he is a bun too."

"Yeah, well. This block's full of buns, Judge. They're all over the place."

"No more future for Tego now."

"Nope. He's had it."

"That is correct. Now he is a jung bun too."

"Maybe. But maybe you shouldn't call him that, Your Honor."

"And why not?"

"Because I'm his brother."

"So you are a jung bun too?"

"Sure. I got it made."

Right there I came close to asking him what he was doing up on the roof the night I was on another roof with my friends looking down at his Amparo and her *gusano* in her bedroom—with the door latched. It was none of my business; I just wanted to hit him where it hurt. But just then the opposing team's man-at-the-plate hit a blooper out to left, and I caught it to retire the side. When I returned to my position, he was gone.

Left field was my permanent position on the Turbine Tots' stoopball team; it took in El Judge's stoop. Sometimes, while I was out there leaning on a railing, waiting for something to field, he'd be sitting on a neatly spread-out hanky on the top step of his stoop, looking at every-thing and passing judgment on the people and dogs who lived on our block. The sight of two dogs sniffing each other up or humping away was something most of us ignored or laughed at; but to the judge it was "a spectacle immoral," and he'd say that the two animals "should be sended away or gasséd to dead."

One afternoon a pair of them had just finished copulating and were trying to come unstuck. The male had dismounted and was attempting to get to Madison Avenue; the female was headed for Fifth. Neither was getting anywhere. After a while they came loose and trotted off in different directions. Next day they'd be at it again. No one could care less, except the Judge. He said they should get the hot-water treatment: Somebody should pour a pot of hot water "in the place where they are stuckéd."

"Why don't *you* do it, Judge?" I suggested. "Run upstairs and bring the pot of hot water. I'll hold them for you."

"That is not my job," he said.

"He only finds them guilty, Santos," our center fielder said.

El Walrus agreed. "Correct."

"Ask him about Amparo and the *gusano,* Santos."

The judge heard that, got up, and disappeared in a hurry.

And yet, this bank guard who didn't see much difference between humans and dogs was a responsible family man. Tego himself told me so, and Tego wasn't the kind who went around exaggerating, as he said I did.

"I wish I had the Judge's job, Santos," he told me after he'd quit Chelsea and was in a position to know what a lousy job was like.

"A bank dick?"

"Why not?"

"They all get it in the end. One day some hard-up junkie or something walks inside the bank with a stickup note, and the potbellied old dick has to draw his piece to protect the bread in the vault. Most of them don't know how to pull a trigger, so they get it in the gut or head and their widows collect the pension."

"Who told you that bullshit?" he asked.

"Mami. She read it to me from *El Diario* while I was having dinner. It happens all the time."

"It doesn't happen all the time. And even if it did, it's still worth it. They make better bread than a short-order cook."

"Why don't you get a better job?"

"Where? Doing what?"

"I don't know. Anything."

"Stay in school, Santos. Don't make my mistake."

"You know who you sound like?"

"Papi?"

"You must be getting old already."

"He's not always wrong, you know. Sometimes he knows what he's talking about."

"Oh, I don't know about that."

"That's why you should stick it out in school."

"You wanna cut the sermon short now? I already heard it from the Judge."

El Judge went to Sunday Mass. He attended the ten-thirty with Mrs. Degetau. They never missed it. His daughters went to the eleven-thirty. He trusted them to do that by themselves. Maybe he shouldn't have. One Sunday morning, close to eleven-thirty, I was walking with Tego down Fifth Avenue. We were headed for a big play-off game in the Central Park baseball diamonds, and we spotted Norma and Delia walking inside the Vanderbilt Garden; they were in a hurry.

"I thought they were supposed to be in church," I said. "Did they lose their faith too?"

"I don't think so, Santos. Sometimes they just lose their sense of direction and end up in there."

"For what, to pick flowers for the altar?"

"No, that's against the law. They just look at them. They have some nice flowers in there."

"So they're playing hooky from Mass, eh?"

"It looks like."

"If the Judge catches them, their ass is cooked."

"He won't catch them," said Tego. "He trusts them. Why don't you go in there and say something to Delia?"

"Like what?"

"Anything you want, as long as it ain't nasty."

148

"She's never said boo to me. Why should I be nasty?"

"I know. You're supposed to say it first."

"What should I tell her? You know all about this stuff."

"I just told you. The first thing that comes to your head. She ain't stupid."

"I know she's not. I am."

"Forget it, then."

I couldn't. We walked to the diamonds in silence, and when we got there, I had a hard time keeping my mind on an interesting game. He didn't, even though he had more reason to be distracted by the play-offs. His team had been eliminated a few weeks before, and he had been the starting pitcher in the fatal game between the Orocovis Shipping Co. Pirates and the Muñoz Meat Market Matadors. He had given up a bar-rage of hits, a slew of walks, and five runs before Millo the manager, all pissed off, walked up to the mound, spitting tobacco juice left and right, and asked him what the hell was the matter with his stuff.

"You're our ace hurler, Tego," he said, still spitting. (Tego told me what he'd said afterwards; the spitting I saw for myself.)

"I just ain't got it today, Millo." He had just split up with Norma, and he couldn't concentrate on his delivery. His curves were high and outside, his fastballs went into the dirt in front of home plate, and his breaking balls were extra-base handouts. So he told Millo to yank him out of the game. Millo clawed the mound with his cleats, shoved both hands in his back pockets, and nodded at the bullpen, a roped-off area next to the cuchifrito and beer vendors.

"He said he made up his mind to pull me out ten batters ago," Tego told me, "and send me to the bush leagues, whatever the hell that means. He gets nasty when things are going bad for the team."

"You should have hit him one."

"Yeah, sure. That's how you cure everything, right, Santos? You hit 'em one. Maybe you should get those fists of yours insured before you break your knuckles on somebody's teeth."

"I was just talking. Norma really got to you, eh?"

"I told you she wasn't my type, dammit."

"Is that what El Judge told you? I'd like to hang him by the—"

"You better go play with your friends, Santos. I'm losing my cool."

"Don't let it get you, Tego. Fight it. See you later."

"Yeah, no hurry." He was like that on and off for about a month; then he met Amalia, a pieceworker, and got over it.

Delia was going out with two Conquistadores and a Wizard at the same time. The two Conquistadores wore glossy black jackets that displayed the name of their "action club" in white letters on the back. The Wizard's jacket was a Day-Glo-orange job with black lettering. The initials V.W.C. were printed over his heart. That made him the Vice War Counselor, the one who subbed for the regular W.C. when that officer couldn't attend a war council.

I never saw Delia coming home by herself; one of those three was always with her. As far as I knew, they never overlapped, so she must have had the situation under control. They walked with her as far as the stoop; then they'd sit there, chewing the rag between two old pillars. She smiled and laughed a lot. I used to wonder if maybe she wasn't overdoing it, just to show off her terrific chipped tooth; she can't be all that happy. Maybe she is. And her nonstop gum-chewing could have been a case of nerves, but maybe it wasn't. She had been a tomboy in grammar school; now she was a very successful flirt, from the looks of it. And she went in for "action-club" types, goons, like those three.

After five or ten minutes of talk (which I never got close enough to overhear), she'd yawn or frown, or give the air in front of her a sad, glazy-eyed stare, flick a look at her wristwatch, give the Wizard or Conquistador a see-you-later smile, and disappear inside the building. I never saw her take any of them upstairs with her. El Judge, if he knew of their existence (I think he did), wouldn't have been hospitable; she was still too young to be bringing boys home, and she'd never be old enough to bring home a bun, jung or not.

But going out with them was something else. Almost every weekend, before Tego and Norma broke up, Delia and one of the Conquistadores or the Wizard accompanied them. They went to dance halls like the Palladium and the Taft, or to one of the three movie houses on Eighty-sixth Street—German Town, we used to call that street—where you could see first-run flicks fresh from Hollywood, if you had that kind of money. Tego, before he left Chelsea, had worked as an ice boy, delivering blocks of it in buckets to those neighborhood merchants who hadn't caught up with refrigeration; and with what he made from that part-time job he could afford to take Norma to high-class places like the Taft, the RKO 86th, and the Loew's Orpheum. Whatever good times they had, or how good they had them, I knew nothing about; I guessed at them. He didn't give me the details. I pictured them swinging to the salsa in those jam-packed ballrooms everybody talked about, and passing popcorn around in the German Town flicks.

"Why don't you make a play for Delia, Santos?"

I was sitting on the edge of our bed scribbling the first draft of a composition on mouth-to-mouth resuscitation for my swimming instructor at Franklin. It was a penalty he had imposed on me because I couldn't float. I could do everything else well enough to pass, but I couldn't float without treading water, which the instructor said was cheating. He finally gave up and told me my bones were too heavy, and the composition he'd assigned me was meant to compensate for my deficiency. "Maybe you should go in for wrestling, Malánguez," he had told me, and I had pretended to take him seriously.

"Why should I make a play for her, Tego?"

"For one thing, she likes you. And for another thing, she's a good-looking girl, which you shouldn't pass up."

"Did she tell you she likes me?"

"She wouldn't come right out and say that to a guy, Santos. But she told it to Norma, and Norma squealed."

"What else?"

"She said she likes the way you play stoopball. In my opinion, you're some kind of show-off on the outfield. You make easy catches look impossible, but maybe she likes that, which I think is a big hint."

"I've never caught her looking at me showing off on the field."

"They got sneaky ways of taking in an outfielder, Santos. The time to look you straight in the eyes comes later, after they get to know you. I'm talking about *her* type, though. The others are another story. Types like Delia have to protect themselves from *Picadillo* types like you. At first, anyway. Otherwise, you'll think she's an easy lay."

"Who said I thought she was?"

"That's not the point, Santos. Stop playing stoopball with me."

"I'm not. What's the point? Tell me."

"Forget it."

"No. What's the point?"

"I forget. Do what you want. I can't help you."

Maybe he thought we were all born with the same making-out talent. He had it, so he couldn't see why everyone else didn't. That's how it looked to me.

He said he couldn't help me, but I think he tried. I think he talked to Delia about me. He probably told her she'd have to make the first move, "because Santos is a shy guy. He's nice, though, even if he's my brother."

I was covering left field; she looked me in the eye and asked me if I was "Tego's kid brother." She was playing it as dumb as she could, which I appreciated. I felt nervous, but I controlled myself enough to play it straight.

"When your hands are shaking and your heart's going like crazy," Tego had told me, "play it straight. Don't even try to make a joke. It'll flop."

So I played it straight. "Yeah, he's my brother."

She was smiling, and chewing her Chiclet; I stared at her chipped tooth.

"You ever go out, Santos?"

"To where?"

"Anywhere. Dancing, the movies. Things like that."

"Sure. Some of the—sometimes." Her eyes, as I put it to myself later, were "very hazel," and there were smile wrinkles at the eye-corners of her nose.

"That's nice," she said, and waited for me to go on from there; but my mind had gone blank. *Nice* was a word I had trouble dealing with, anyway. Brother Fish back in the seventh grade took off points for *nice* whenever it showed up in our compositions. "It's an open-ended word, boys. Doesn't mean anything, doesn't lead anywhere. Be more specific."

All this lasted two minutes at most. She checked the time on her wrist, shut her mouth without letting up on the chewing, and lost or took back her smile. Then her eyes got glazy, and a line drive caromed off my shoulder. The opposition's man-at-the-plate had caught me napping out there, and all I could do was watch the rubber ball bounce toward third, a manhole cover. The Tots' third baseman one-handed it at the same time that the runner on second was sliding into the bag. It would have been a putout, but a careless driver in a Chevrolet coupé came along just then and almost creamed the runner, who was saved from a permanent putout only because he overslid the bag. And I got chewed out by my teammates.

"Santos, goddammit," screamed the third baseman, "either you're gonna play left or you're gonna bullshit with the broads!" The second baseman nodded and said I couldn't have it both ways.

"Who said I did?" I said, just to say something face-saving. In my shoes, Tego would have told them to find a sub for him, and spent the time talking to Delia on the stoop. But I didn't even have the time of day to offer her; she had her own watch.

She was still there when I turned around. "That could have happened to anybody, Santos." Maybe so, but so what? It had happened to *me*. In her opinion, she said, I was "a very good stoopball player." I thanked her; she smiled; I couldn't. She said she'd see me around sometime, then turned and climbed up the steps of her stoop.

She saw me around sometime, all right. She saw me lots of times, whenever she was coming or going and I was out there manning left field. Usually the Wizards' V.W.C. or one of the Conquistadores was waiting for her on the stoop, taking in our stoopball game. Sometimes, coming and going, she said hi or hello, and sometimes she said nothing, depending on her mood. I always returned her one-word greeting, and the smile that went with it; and her companion of the day always looked me up and down with a threat in his eye. That was it; I'd had my chance.

One day, chasing a fly ball backwards, I crashed into one of the Conquistadores. He was sitting on the spot where El Judge alias Walrus liked to sit, and I knocked him on his back. I forgot about the ball and started to help him back up; he slapped my hand away and told me to watch it.

"Watch what?" I said. "The ball? It's down the basement. It went down there for a ground-rule double."

He didn't like that, and started removing his Conquistadores jacket. I backed up a couple of steps and waited for him to hang his garment up on the picket fence. He was wearing polished shoes with pointy tips, tassels, and leather soles; I was in sneakers, which gave me the advantage. I'd keep moving around him and tire him out, then move in on him. But the Tots stepped in and yanked me away. The center fielder wanted to know whether I was crazy or something. He said I had to have flipped to be messing with one of the Conquistadores, who outnumbered us about nine to one and who specialized in warfare.

"I don't care," I said. "He started it."

"So what, Santos?" the third baseman said.

And the second baseman: "He started it, and he's gonna finish it, too."

And the first baseman: "You better apologize to him. If he goes to get his boys, we're gonna be in for a wasting, and then what difference does it make who started it."

So I walked up to the Conquistador, who was waiting for me, and told him I was sorry, though I didn't know for what. "The guys said to tell you I'm sorry," I said. "They don't wanna mess with your boys, and I don't blame them. I don't either." I held out my hand and asked him if he wanted to shake.

"Go shove your handshake," he said.

I nodded and walked off while he removed his jacket from the picket. A couple of minutes later, while waiting for my turn at the plate, I saw him and Delia walking toward Madison. They were going somewhere in a hurry.

I think it was sometime in her high-school senior year that she got involved with Cisco Barcelo, the third baseman of the Orocovis Shipping Co. Pirates. Cisco was tall, wiry, and fast on his feet; he also had a neat Emiliano Zapata mustache and a missing front tooth on the right side of his upper jaw from a hot grounder that had taken a bad hop on wet grounds. He couldn't afford to replace the knocked-out tooth (and never would, I thought, because he was another high-school casualty. I think

Tego's entire team was a high-school casualty). He was one of several Orocovis Pirates who had tried out for the Yankees' and Mets' farm clubs, but he didn't make it. Tego said he hadn't come anywhere near making it. We all thought it was too bad, because we'd always wanted one of the guys from the block to make it to the majors, and of all the guys on the block, Cisco had stood the best chance of playing in Shea or Yankee Stadium, or wherever. We would have settled for Philadelphia.

El Judge must have gone into mourning when Delia told him she was going to marry Cisco. Tego said he didn't think Mrs. Degetau would mind Cisco for a son-in-law. "He's a nice guy, even if he ain't going nowhere." But the Judge was less interested in nice guys than in successful ones. I pictured him pulling his hair and asking her, "*Porqué, mija? Why? Why this jung bun? Why you did not find a photographer, like Amparo?*" And she: "Because he's a nice guy, Papá, and he's cute and he knows how to give a girl a nice time, too."

If anybody had bothered to ask my opinion, I would have said it served El Judge right. After what he'd pulled on Tego, he deserved a bun with a missing tooth in his family, somebody to offset the *gusano*. The judge had gotten his at last. Maybe God had given it to him. Maybe "circumstances" had.

"How come Delia married Cisco, Tego?" We were in the dark; he had just kicked me awake.

"I don't know why. Go back to sleep."

"Maybe she liked the hole in his teeth."

"What's bugging you now, Santos? You had your chance."

"I don't think he's her kind."

"That's not up to you to say."

"A lot of guys had the hots for her."

"Yeah, except you."

"To tell you the truth, I did too."

"So what stopped you?"

"I don't know. How many girls with a smile like that you think have a chipped tooth?"

"Twenty million. Maybe thirty. You talk like she was born with that broken tooth."

"I don't care how she got it."

"She liked you, too. But all you did was play stoopball."

"Yeah, well, that's under the bridge now."

"I told you, Santos, don't let 'em come to *you*."

"Okay, but stop kicking me in the face."

"Next time, you make the play. It's the only way. Take it from me. Now let's go to sleep."

"Not if you keep kicking me in the face."

"I'm not kicking your face."

"Who the hell is, then?"

"Nobody. It's all in your head. See you in the morning."

He had to open up the luncheonette early. He had to start cooking breakfast by seven for those workers who didn't make it at home. One of them was a seamstress, his future wife.

FROM *CARLITO'S WAY*

Edwin Torres

Edwin Torres was born and raised in New York City, where he became the first Puerto Rican to serve as assistant district attorney and was appointed a New York State Supreme Court justice in 1979. Inspired by his memories of growing up in Spanish Harlem, Torres wrote Carlito's Way *(1975), and the sequel,* After Hours *(1979). The two novels were turned into a screenplay, and the movie* Carlito's Way *was released in 1993. Torres's detective novel,* Q & A *(1977), has also been made into a movie.*

Carlito's Way is the story of a Puerto Rican street fighter and small-time hustler who rises to a position of power in New York City's heroin business. This excerpt from Carlito's Way *sets the scene.*

I CAME ON THE SCENE IN THE 1930S. ME AND MY MOMS. BRIGANTE Sr. had long since split back to Puerto Rico. Seem like we was in every furnished room in Spanish Harlem. Kind of hazy some of it now, but I can remember her draggin' me by the hand from place to place—the clinic on 106th Street, the Home Relief on 105th Street, the Pentecostal church on 107th Street. That was home base, the church. Kids used to call me a "hallelujah"—break my chops. My mom was in there every night bangin' on a tambourine with the rest of them. Sometimes they'd get a special *reverendo* who'd really turn them on. That's when the believers, *feligreses,* would start hoppin' and jumpin'—then they'd be faintin' on the floor and they'd wrap them in white sheets. I remember I didn't go for this part. I was close to my mom, it was just me and her.

I was comin' into my teens in the 1940s when they laid her out at Gonzalez's Funeral Home on 109th Street. Looked like she was into one of her faints, like she'd be all right. Wasn't like that. I ain't sayin' my way would have been any different if she'd been around. That's all you hear in the Joint—aw, man, I didn't have a chance. Bullshit. I was already a mean li'l fucker while my mom was alive, but I always respected women because of her.

Anyway, the court put me on to this jive uncle who come out of nowhere up in the Bronx. I got promoted from the basement to the sub-basement. No good. I cut out. Back down to Harlem. Sleepin' on the roof. Stayin' with friends. Then the juvenile people put me in the Heckscher Home near 104th Street. But I was always takin' off on them. I was still in my teens. World War II was over but they was warrin' in the streets. Kiddie gangs was goin' strong. The Puerto Ricans was boxed in. Irish on the south, Italians to the east, blacks to the north and west. Wasn't none of that brotherhood jive in them days. Git that Po'Rican! We was catchin' hell.

The crazy part is me comin' up rumblin' against these groups as a kid—it should end up that the only two cats that was ever in my corner was Earl Bassey, a black dude, and Rocco Fabrizi, a wal-yo. Unbelievable. But I'm jumpin' ahead.

Lemme tell you about them rumbles. The wops said no spics could go east of Park Avenue. But there was only one swimming pool and that was the Jefferson on 112th Street off the East River. Like, man, you had to wade through Park, Lexington, Third, Second, First, Pleasant. Wall-to-wall guineas. The older guys be standing around in front of the stoops and stores, evil-eyeing us, everybody in his undershirt; the kids would be up on the roof with the garbage cans and in the basements with the bats and bicycle chains. Mostly busted heads, black eyes in those days. First into the street was always me, loved a swingout. That's when I first saw Rocco Fabrizi. He was running with a wop gang, the Redwings. One day we went down to the pool with about twenty or thirty P.R. guys—a hell of a rumble—and right up front is this guy, Rocco, swinging a stickball bat. Stuck in my mind, tough kid. We took a beating—their turf, too many guys. A while later we get the word that this Rocco is sneaking up on a roof with a Latin chick named Carmen—fine head—near Madison Avenue and 107th Street. The balls. He caught some beatin', but he stood up; the Lopez brothers wanted to throw him off the roof but I said enough. He remembered.

The spooks said no Ricans could go west of Fifth Avenue. So if they caught you in Central Park, shame on you. The Copiens, the Socialistics, the Bachelors, the Comanches—all bad motherfuckers—these were the gangs that started using hardware. Then the rumbles got mean—like if the Copiens caught you, you knew they were going to stick you. Then the zip guns came out, metal tubes with door latches as firing pins set off by rubber bands—if the pin hit the .22 on the primer and the piece was held close to your head, you were in trouble. Lucky for a lot of diddy boppers it wasn't often. I once got caught by the Copiens in Central Park by the lake near 106th Street. Me and this black kid duked it out after he said, "Let me hold a quarter." I said, "Let yo' mammy hold it." We got it on, I was kicking him on the ground when his boys arrived on bikes—my blood was up; I said, "I'll take any one of you motherfuckers." "No, motherfucker, we gonna kill yo' ass," and they started pulling the rubber bands on the zip guns. So like I quit the scene, they chased me all the way to 110th Street. That was the last chase on me like that. I always carried a piece from then on. I wasn't about to take no shit. You step up, I'm gonna knock you down.

Summers were hotter in them days. No air-conditioning—the asphalt could burn your sneakers. Took the bus up to Highbridge Pool in Washington Heights. The Irish jumped us in the locker room—we fought with the metal baskets. Know what the pool guard said? "You don't belong up here." No sooner we was on the bus back, we had to bail out the windows on to Amsterdam Avenue, a mob of micks was comin' through the door after us.

That same summer I got hit in the head with a roller skate by some spade in Central Park by the boats near 110th Street. Another time I got my neck all scraped up from a bicycle chain some eye-talian wrapped around me. We caught it from everybody. Don't get me wrong, we gave good as we got—but you remember your own lumps better. We was tryin' to melt into the pot but they wouldn't even let us in the swimming pool. *Hijos de puta.*

Irregardless, I was never a race man. Us P.R.'s are like that—maybe 'cause we come in so many shades. We always had a stray wop or Jew-boy and plenty of spades with our gangs. Anyway, I figure them beatings get you ready for later on—when you gotta get the money.

But the clubs wasn't always fightin'. There was a lot of stickball play-ing—we had the Devils, the CBCs, the Home Reliefers (dig it), the Turbens (that's the way they spelled it), the Viceroys, the Zeniths, the Falcons, the Tropical Gents, the Royal Knights, the Boca Chica—these all claimed to be S.A.C.—social and athletic club—ha.

Pimping was popular. Tony Navarro, the Cruz brothers, Bobby Rol-dan, all had whores. We looked up to these guys—big cars, always a ringside table at the Palladium; always clean, none of that zoot-suit shit—wingtip shoes, conservative-cut clothes. Imagine lookin' up to a pimp! Later on we wouldn't let one of them scumbag motherfuckers stand near us at the bar.

About that time *motherfucker* came into style—it came down from black Harlem in a game called "the dozens." Two cats would meet on the street and start playin' the dozens; one guy would say, "Ashes to ashes, dust to dust, your mother has a pussy like a Greyhound bus," and the other guy come back with, "The dozens ain't my game but the way I fuck your mother is a goddamn shame!" Rough on the mothers. From then on everything was motherfucker.

Mostly we stood around corners on Madison Avenue. Just like Mid-dletown, U.S.A.—ha. The schools, Patrick Henry, Cooper—forget about it. No YMCA, no Boys' Club, no gym, raunchy houses, scummy streets. If you inclined to plea-cop, them streets contributed to the de-linquency of a whole lot of minors. But who wants to hear that shit? Only plea I ever copped cost me three years in the slams. A man got to stand up. Take his shot.

Like when the junk started arrivin' about this time. And where did the wops first arrive it? Right on ol' 107th Street between Lexington and Third. A punk-ass kid I was, but I looked it over. I'm gonna ride the horse, or the horse gonna ride me? That was the question on a lot of them corners, 'cause the junk was still a new scene in the forties. All the losers went for the spike and the dynamite high behind it. Only a skag high ain't but good the first few times out, then you hooked, all they gotta do is reel you in, by the crotch now, and squeeze till you cough up another five dollars for a bag. I seen the horse play with them junkies like a cat with a rubber mouse.

Age fourteen, I saw that. I said, uh-uh. Them's the humped—I'm goin' with the humpers. The dealers had the pussy, the clothes, and the cars. That's what I wanted, in that order. The dope fiends had the sores, the scabs, the O.D.'s. Maybe that's what they wanted. Must be crazy—couldn't see it then, can't see it now.

I was thinkin' myself, among other things, half a pug in them days. I didn't really know the science of the game, but I was heavy-handed, with a lot of snap in my shoulder, so when I tagged a stud, he was hurtin'. So now I'm gonna go in the Gloves, this must have been 'round '48 or '49. With a little trainin' everybody said Carlito was a natural. I was gonna fight for the Police Athletic League. Ha. And who was the man there? Moran of the Twenty-third Precinct, my sworn enemy. "What, this fuckin' troublemaker on my squad?" So I ended up fightin' unattached. My trainin' was drinkin' wine and smokin' pot. One time I ran around the 106th Street lake in the park—finished up puffin' on a joint. Some program for a contender. Irregardless, I kicked some ass down in Sunnyside and Ridgewood, including a bad spook from the Salem-Crescent A.C. But then they busted my jaw in a street fight on 105th Street and I had to drop out of the tournament. What a laugh on Moran if I had gone all the way to Chicago. Him with his squad breakin' their ass runnin' around the reservoir every day.

Anyway, I'm too good-lookin' to be a pug. I'm gonna be a pimp. I'm runnin' 'round with these fly broads from 111th Street and Fifth Avenue. That's where all the whores were trickin' in them days. Whores galores. But I could take a knock-around broad but so long. I didn't go for that scene too tough. Pimp got to hate women. That sure wasn't me.

There was some nice chicks around but their mothers wouldn't let them out the house. 'Specially with *delincuentes* like me waitin' on the stoop. Them was not "free sex" days. Leave it to me to come up at the wrong time. The good girls held on to their cherry. And it was a big

deal. If a broad dropped her drawers, right away she lost her rating—
even to the scrounge who copped them; "I ain't gonna marry no broad
what lost her cherry!"

I used to get laid in Central Park, but you had to have a long switchblade ready 'cause always some degenerate motherfucker would be
sneakin' up on you and your girl from behind the bushes. I didn't mind
a guy lee-gating (peeping), I used to do it myself, but these pre-verts
would want to gang-bang your broad. I chased more than one around
that park at night. One guy tried to hit me with a wooden Keep Off
The Grass sign, which he pulled out the ground while he was running
from my sticker. He missed, I didn't. Many a piece I missed out on,
gettin' interrupted by this element.

I was a big pussy-hound. Ain't changed much either.

Was a big movie fan too. Knock-around kids was always in the movie
house. No TV in them days. The Fox Star on 107th Street and Lexington
Avenue was our show. There was some bad guinea racketeers in there.
You had to go with a gang, 'cause if the wops caught you alone on the
balcony, you was a flyin' Po'Rican. I remember once they had a singin'
contest on the stage on a Saturday. They was givin' ten dollars to the
winner. I was there with a whole mob of guys smokin' pot in the balcony. I ran up on stage and sang "Bei Mir Bist Du Schön," which I sang
as "My Dear Mr. Shane." I couldn't sing worth a damn, but you rated
on applause and my people made the most racket. I won. Then I did
"Playmate" and the dirty version of "La Cucaracha," which was my best
number—they couldn't get me off the stage.

I was into being a musician too. This was 'cause I noticed they was
gettin' all the fine women. Some ugly clown be shakin' maracas or a
cowbell in front of a band and all the chippies be saying, oh, he's showbiz!
Jive-ass bitches. Showbiz is the guy giving enemas to the elephants in
the circus. Anyway, I got me a big conga drum out of the pawnshop
and thought I was Chano Pozo, the great Cuban conga player used to
work the skins for Dizzy Gillespie. Chano was the greatest. Bad too, big
stud, used to be strongarm for the politicals in Havana. Came to Harlem,
was bad there too. Somebody forgot how bad and blew him away. But
he had some tough hands while he was around. My hands couldn't keep

no beat, I was not about to be no great *conguero*. So be it. I'll get me that trim some other way.

Used to play at block parties—everybody in Harlem be there, dancin', drinkin', smokin', 'n fightin'. Had one on 107th Street, Copiens or Dragons came around—forget who—anyway, they started shooting pistols. My friend, Tato—"Carlito, they got me"—fell on his back under the lamppost. *Coño, Tato, he's dead!* No way, cap hit him on his belt buckle—didn't have a scratch. Just like in the movies. After that, I used to throw myself on the ground—"Tato, they got me!" I was a big ball-breaker as a kid.

But don't get me wrong, I used to do a lotta good things too. Although later on they never showed up in any of my probation reports. Like God forbid somebody abuse a buddy of mine. I'd travel for blocks to duke with a cat that would try to gorilla a friend—I tangle-assed with Sabu from 104th Street and Flash from 110th Street, bad motherfuckers in the first degree, and it wasn't even my beef. "This ain't witchoo, Carlito"— "Never mind, take to the street." That's the kind of guy I was. But sometimes could backfire on you. Like m'man Políto—went up to 113th Street to straighten a kid out for somebody. Políto told me he was a stringbean black kid. Skinny arms and legs. Políto was a regular li'l buzz saw. He said shee-it, I'll tear 'im up. Políto say that spook kid like to bust him everyway but loose. Later on he found out the kid was Sandy Saddler.

One time I had to rumble a deaf-mute guy. On me like white-on-rice. Couldn't get off on this guy. Whipped me. I had respect for the handicapped after that.

A lot of Hollywood names in Harlem at the time. We had Tarzans and Sabus and Cheyennes. I remember a guy used to call himself Nai-yoka—like from Pago Pago. We had Cochise and we had Apache. Sometimes a name could cause a problem. Like Cheyenne from the Bronx would come down with ten or twelve guys to see Cheyenne from Harlem—"Who said your name was Cheyenne?"—"Not me, my name is Jacinto Quinones." I seen that one. Then you had a pimp name of Red Conk on account of he conked his hair red (hair was straight in them days one way or the other—Dixie Peach or Sulfur 8). We had a white guy named Negro, and we had a black guy named Indio. We had a lot of Louies—Louie the Jew (crazy Jew got killed in a stickup, spoke better Spanish than me), Louie Lump-Lump (had a funny-shaped head), Louie Push-Push (used to run fast). We had Tobacco, Chuleta, Machete, Frankie *La Cagona* (Frankie the Shitter).

How'd I exist on the street? Sometimes legit—like delivery boy on an ice truck, or a grocery, or a dry cleaner's. But mostly hustlin', thievin', break and entry—shootin' pool was my main stick. I used to catch merchant marines for a hundred, hundred-fifty dollars playin' nineball—this when I was fourteen or fifteen years old—always had good wrists. Then there was boostin' in department stores—and there was dice, cards, writin' numbers (single action) for Jakie Cooperman, one of the few Jew bookies left around. We had a little scare with Jakie once. Jakie used to book out of a candy store on 108th Street and Fifth Avenue—he was a degenerate gambler himself. Me and some other kids were hangin' around one night. This big black car pulled up with four rays of sunshine—older wops from the East 107th Street mob out of the Fox Star. Two stayed in the car, two came into the candy store. Skinny guy, Nino, he had half a button, cool head, he'd talk to you. The other guy, Buck, was a terror—looked like a buffalo, only bigger—and he used to carry a softball bat—was the bouncer at the Fox Star. God forbid he should catch you sneakin' in the side door. Buck stands by the door, Nino walks up to the counter and pulls an empty bag out of his coat (the two of them was wearin' black coats and black hats with the brim turned up—wops got this Al Capone shit down to a science). Anyway, the bag was a cement bag. Nino gives the bag to Moe, owner of the store—"This is for Jakie." Moe shit a milk shake right there. Then Nino turned to me and the rest of the kids—"Anybody here seen Jakie around?" No, not us, never happen. They split. We was shook up. Seems Jakie was into the shylocks for fifty thou. The wops said he ran away to the coast on them, but Jakie himself would have given you five hundred to one he was planted on Long Island. Wops was already leery about goin' up to black Harlem. Not Buck (really Buccia)—he'd jump out of a car on 116th Street and Lenox Avenue bat in hand—"C'mere"—spook would run—one shot—lay 'im out. Buck didn't give a fuck. He went up in the mob later on. Stayed mean.

There was other guys like Buck around. *Abusadores,* we called them—abusers or ballbreakers. Uptown Harlem had one named Jenks, or Jinx. Bad nigger. Big—didn't fit through no door, 'cept sideways. Take everybody off. Take your money, your welfare check, your watch, your dope—take a wheelchair, glass eye. Mean. When he was outta jail, people stayed home. Jinx had a pretty long run, then he tried to run a game on a friend of mine. Shakedown. So much per week 'cause I'm bad. My buddy was hardnose, so he had to deal with Jinx. Shot him in the legs—kept coming. Shot him in the chest—kept coming. Finally stopped Jinx with a bullet through his head. All this time Jinx was chasing him around the bar. My friend had to do time for this. Judge said, "Victim was unarmed"—that motherfucker was armed when he was unarmed. Some judges will say, "Why didn't you go to the police?" The fuckin' police only want to know you as one of two "de's"—de deceased or de defendant. In between—"Don't bother me, I got lotta paperwork." If the judge took time to check out a "victim" like Jinx he'd give the defendant the Distinguished Bronze Cross, first degree. And if His Honor had to live in the same tenement with a Jinx or a Buck, he'd put the contract out hisself. Buck and Jinx—some neighbors we had.

Another source of likelihood for me was a first-class Murphy game I used to run up on 111th Street with the tricks looking for whores. Me and m'partner Colorado used pencil and paper (that would impress the johns)—"Okay, write it down, eh, Chico? These two gentlemen, ten dollars a piece—that's twenty dollars. No rough stuff or fancy fuckin', boys; Lolita is only sixteen and just startin' out. I'll hold the money." Colorado would go upstairs, then he'd call down, "Lolita wants to see the money and the list first, Pancho." Wait right here, boys, she's very shy—I'll call you from upstairs. You could come back an hour later and they'd still be waiting with their hard-on. Lo-leeta, Lo-leeta, they'd be yodelin' in the canyon. Sometimes me and Colorado would fall down on the roof from laughing.

Them roofs was busy for us. Flyin' pigeons, flyin' kites, flyin' dope. Somebody was always jumpin' off the roof too. Usually some Rican who couldn't cut it on the street. But the street got him anyway—unless he jumped in the backyard.

Anyway, I was a busy li'l snot in them days.

JOHNNY UNITED

Jack Agüeros

Jack Agüeros was born in New York City in 1934. He has published poetry, plays, and children's stories, and has written for television, notably for Sesame Street *and* WNBC-TV. *For almost ten years he was director of the Museo del Barrio in East Harlem, the only Puerto Rican museum in the United States. His book* Dominoes and Other Stories from the Puerto Rican *(1993) has been widely adopted for use in public schools, and named to the New York Public Library's 1994 list of Recommended Books for the Teen Age. His new book of poetry,* Sonnets from the Puerto Rican, *is forthcoming.*

Set in East Harlem during the 1940s, "Johnny United" sheds light on the neighborhood's changing demographics, through the stickball games between the Italian and Puerto Rican kids. Johnny, the story's frustrated stickball hero, finds himself looking for a way out of a life dictated by his stepfather's miserliness.

I

JOHNNY UNITED WORKED IN HIS STEPFATHER'S *BODEGA* ON LEXINGton Avenue and 109th Street. He had worked Monday through Friday from as soon as he got out of Galvani Junior High School, which was around three-fifteen, to nine at night. He worked thirteen hours on Saturdays. Sundays he worked from eight A.M. to noon. Delivering groceries, unloading trucks, and loading basements and stacking cans and moving hundred-pound sacks of rice, beans, and coffee had made Johnny United muscular. In high school, Benjamin Franklin High School, he looked older than the other students, older than his sixteen years, because of his size. He worked a little less now from Monday to Friday, because Franklin was on 116th Street and Pleasant Avenue, and it took much longer to walk back home from school.

Johnny United never complained.

He didn't mind the hard work. He regretted that it was all for his stingy stepfather. Not all. Some was for his mother.

Early Sunday morning was Johnny United's favorite time. Especially in the summer. Although he was working he was already relishing the afternoon game to come. And Sundays was a light day anyway. The work consisted only of working behind the counter, taking care of the occasional customer buying a bottle of milk and a loaf of sliced bread. Nobody bought much on Sundays and nobody delivered anything at all on Sundays. Sometimes families would stop in to get soda to take to the beach, or ask him for things he didn't have, like sand buckets for the kids.

Over on 107th Street there was a convergence of stickball players from some of the near blocks of Spanish Harlem and Italian Harlem. Early in the morning some of the players would be out on the block moving the few parked cars that had been left overnight. Old Dodges and DeSotos, Fords and a few Pontiacs. Usually not more than six cars were in the whole block on a Sunday morning, and usually the ball players knew the owners of at least three.

The car owners were so used to the routine of reparking their cars that they frequently parked on Saturday night around the corner on Lexington in front of the Star Theater, or else they threw their car keys out the window so the players could move the cars.

Johnny United was not too poor to have a bicycle, but he did not have a bicycle, and his stingy stepfather, who had a booming business on a well-traveled corner just one block from the subway, didn't own a car. The few people in the neighborhood who could afford a car took off early on a summer Sunday, packed their families into their four doors, and took off for exotic places like Jones Beach or South Beach early in the morning, some lucky neighborhood kid riding the running board all the way down the block to the corner of Park Avenue, then running back up the block to tell everybody how exciting it had been.

The day didn't always start with stickball. Some of the older Italians liked to play a game called punchball. The pitcher used the same Spaulding Hi-Bounce as in stickball, and threw it in the same one hop to the plate—the batter stood over the manhole cover and punched the ball with his fist. The best hitter in punchball was a tall, sandy-haired Italian called Don, who lived in the same block as Johnny United. Everybody liked to watch him bat; he never missed a pitch that he went after. Johnny United never saw him play stickball, but Don often backed the Italian teams in the big-money games.

On Friday Johnny United had taken the route back home from school that took him past his old junior high. Not for sentimental reasons, but because the broom factory was near the school. There he purchased two new broomsticks—he didn't like to take the sticks from old brooms because he believed that the two nails that were used to attach the wire and corn bristles weakened the stick and made it an inferior bat for stickball. He sneaked the broomsticks into the *bodega*'s basement and put them next to where he had the tape.

Sunday when he was alone in the store, he meticulously wrapped the lower part of the broom stick in Johnson & Johnson's Red Cross adhesive tape. The narrow white tape in a spiral made a bright contrast on the dark blue and dark green bats. And although he worked slowly, like a doctor bandaging a patient, he couldn't wait to get to 107th Street. Johnny United sanded the unpainted last six inches of the stick—the part where the bristles would have been attached. After the sanding, the stick was now a real stickball bat. Next he oiled his glove, and fussed with the leather thongs that kept it together. He had never seen one come loose, or rip, but nevertheless he checked all the knots to be sure they were secure.

He loved Sundays, because there was no stepfather. Just the old toothless man who worked the counter in exchange for food. Johnny United's stepfather didn't believe in paying salaries. He believed in equations though—I did this for you equals you do this for me. Even Johnny United's mother never got any cash. When Johnny United asked his mother why he couldn't get paid—just a little—and why she never had any money either—she just said, "You have everything and I have everything. You have your own room, and no beatings. Give thanks to your stepfather. When you are older you will understand what it means to have everything. Be grateful, he doesn't beat you or me, and doesn't drink. We're never short of food, or short of anything."

Except money. Which you needed to buy tape, broom handles, and which you needed to bet on your games, bet on your own team. Take a girl out for a malted.

II

On 107th Street, the teams were starting to form. Don had chosen his favorite captain, Chops, who was also a third baseman. And Terry, who always backed the Puerto Rican team, had picked Lefty to be his captain. Lefty had lost one joint on each of two fingers of his left hand. A policeman had taken a bat away from kids playing stickball and thrown it down the manhole. As soon as the cop was out of sight, the kids picked up the manhole cover and one of them went down into the sewer and brought back the bat. But when they were dropping the heavy iron cover back on the open hole, it slipped from somebody's hand and pinched Lefty's two fingers, severing the first joints. Lefty, who had already recovered from infantile paralysis and walked with a limp, taught himself to pitch right-handed, just as easily as he had taught himself to ride a bike with a withered left leg. He batted lefty, and it seemed impossible to imagine him as a better hitter. And even with the lame leg he was still faster than a lot of other players.

The captains started picking players, eight to a side, as stickball was played without a catcher. A catcher was unnecessary since there was no calling of balls and strikes—each player had latitude as to how many pitches he could take before swinging. There was no rule as to how many pitches he could let go by, but impatient players waiting their turn at bat, would jeer the batter if he was taking too long. So would spectators, so that jeering was just as effective as counting balls and strikes.

And captains would skip over players who were known to stand up there and wait and wait—it was a sign of a poor player.

Just as in the boxing matches, there were prelims—fights where beginners would dance around, warming up the crowd for the main bout. Even the Golden Gloves followed this routine, with the skinniest kids going first, their stick arms out of proportion to the stuffed glove. And while Johnny United taped, sanded, and oiled, the younger stickball players played warm-up games, getting a chance to show their stuff—light betting, two dollars a man, but while everything was a prelim, the games were played with a lot of heart, as if each game was a big-league World Series game.

Terry was talking to Lefty while they watched a prelim.

"Is Johnny United going to be here on time?"

"Ain't he always?"

"The big game is gonna cost me two hundred bucks if you lose, Lefty. I ain't gonna put no two hundred bucks on youse if Johnny United ain't playing."

"So let me go over to the store and talk to him. I'll be back in a flash. Put Jackie in to pinch-hit."

"Jackie? That kid can't do nothing right."

"So what? Let 'im play, we're way ahead. Le'me go."

Lefty walked the two blocks quickly to 109th Street and whistled from the sidewalk. None of Johnny United's friends ever entered the *bodega*. It was a message for the stepfather.

"I can't go yet, but I'll be there for sure. I got two new beauties." Johnny United ducked back in the store and showed them to Lefty.

"You gotta come—it's gonna be a two-hundred-dollar game! No lie!"

"Twenty-five dollars a man?" asked Johnny United, wiping his palms on his trouser legs. That's the highest we ever played for."

"Twenty-five a man. Hurry up. I gotta get back."

"Lefty, can you lend me some money?"

"How much?"

"Twenty-five or fifty."

"Crazy?"

"Come on, man, I'll pay you back."

"I ain't got twenty-five bucks—whatchu need it for?"

"I'm going to run away from home."

"You gonna run away from home with my twenty-five bucks? Whatchu think, I'm stupid? See ya. Hurry up, we ain't got a lot of time."

III

In the last half of the ninth inning the Puerto Ricans were losing 2–1. There was a man on second and Johnny United came to bat. He took his dark blue beauty and looked at it as if he had never seen it before. He shook it to feel its weight and swung it with one hand. On the very first pitch he ran into the ball with his well-known skip step and brought his broomstick square across the center of the Spaulding, and the ball took off on a low trajectory that carried it across Lexington and halfway toward Third Avenue. It was a spectacular drive—nobody had ever hit a ball that far before. The outfielders were used to backing up ten to fifteen feet when Johnny United came to bat, but he still put it over their heads.

The man on second easily scored, tying the game and sending the onlookers on the stoops and the ones who stood on the sidewalk's edge into a roar and applause, and Johnny United rounded second going faster than a thoroughbred in the home stretch. And then a child of four or five broke from the crowd and ran into the street between third base and home plate, right in the path of Johnny United coming down as fast and as hard as a human being was able to run.

There was nothing Johnny United could do to avoid the collision. He was both running and looking back over his left shoulder to see where the ball was, trying to gauge whether he had time to get all the way to home plate, or if he should stop at third. When he saw the child in his way, he did the only thing he could think of doing—tried to leap over the child—but it was too late. He kicked the child about midbody and both went down against the hot tar, *thunk*. Even in his falling, Johnny United was trying to twist, trying not to fall on top of the child, trying to convert his momentum into a force that would get him to home plate.

Johnny United was tagged out one and one-half feet in front of home plate.

Everyone was in an uproar—"He's safe, he's out, we won, you gotta do it over, *afangoul,* why didn't you kill him, pay up the money, fuck you, he's gotta do it over, *ougotz* you won, we ain't gonna do it over, *ougotz, ougotz,* it's a home run, fuck you, we won 3–2, *afangoul, maricon, maricon, tu madre, strunso!*"

Johnny United was looking at the kid, who had a welt on his rib cage. The father was saying it was the kid's fault and apologizing to Johnny United. Friction burns and tar were all over Johnny United's legs and arms, but he had no major wounds, no broken bones.

In the commotion and yelling of the spectators and the teams, only the gamblers looked cool. The teams were falling into another mood. Only Lefty and Chops yelled at each other now. Chops had a father who was always in a black Cadillac. Louie Bananas, the fantastic outfielder who had made the long throw to home, had found his father shot to death in a parked car on Second Avenue.

The Puerto Ricans had heard of the Black Hand, and all the silent terror that it implied, but the fight now would have to be on the street. Spider, the kid who played second base, would have one, maybe two, switchblade knives on him, and Lefty himself would likely have a gun in his gym bag. A real gun, not a homemade or a zip gun.

As the teams sized each other up, a quiet fell, and everyone turned to Don and Terry. The players were keyed to look for the first punch, and then mayhem would start. But Don and Terry were talking quietly.

Terry said, "The game is definitely tied."

Don said, "I don't want no fight on the block."

Terry said, "Me neither. Let me talk to my captain."

When Terry came over, the team crowded around him. Johnny United was crying and saying, "I shoulda creamed that kid, I coulda gone right through him but I didn't have the heart. *Coño,* I didn't do it."

Terry said calmly, "You did right, Johnny. You coulda killed that kid. The kid is worth more than the game, worth more than the money. I know money. I know death, believe me. You think about that father.

You're a hero, Johnny—you hit the longest ball ever—who's gonna take that away from you? You did a good thing—who's gonna take that away from you? Those are dollars you'll never lose. Come on, let's figure out what to do."

Danny, who was an up-and-coming good ballplayer said, "Look Terry, let Johnny go back to third—he made that base safe, so why not? Next batter is Lefty and then me. I know we'll bring Johnny United home. We'll get him in, I mean it, Terry."

Privately Terry didn't like that arrangement. The pressure on Lefty and Danny to get a hit would be too much and the odds were they would blow it. Don would go for it because he would calculate the odds the same way, but maybe not. Now the whole game would pivot on one batter, on one strikeout, on one hit—like a winner take all—like a sudden death. Terry liked long shots, but he didn't like this one. He also never wanted to let his team down, his kids down. He never wanted anyone to think he was cheap, either.

"Okay," said Terry, "let's offer it."

Don looked down at his loafers. Didn't like it. Figured the odds were for Terry. Fucking Lefty with no fingers and a bum foot, and you still had to be scared of him. And after Lefty was still Danny. Fucking Danny, you never knew what he could do. He was up-and-coming, the kid was gonna be murder by next year. And Don knew that if he didn't accept, everyone would know he was scared of Lefty. And Danny. Fucking Danny, who last year could barely make a team.

So Don said, "He can go back to third, but you gotta give one out."

"No good, the man made third safe, where do you get off we gotta give an out?"

"That's what we give. Don't forget we tagged him out altogether. Kid or no kid, we tagged him out."

"But the game is tied, right?"

"Right, tied," answered Don.

"Then let's call the greatest game of the year off—nobody loses."

Don looked down the very sharp crease in his slacks to his loafers, each of which had a very shiny penny. He might have been trying to calculate the offer on his toes. Then he looked up and asked, "Terry, how come you always put your money behind the Puerto Ricans?"

"I always go for long shots, Don. And they haven't done bad by me. Your boys never tromped them. They're winners, my kids."

"They don't play bad," conceded Don. "If they played bad we wouldn't want their money. Your money either. Could you tell them Puerto Ricans that they don't scare us, that they don't run the neighborhood yet?"

"Don, I'll bet you that next year will be the last of these games, and in three years there won't be any Italians on this block, and in five years there won't be any Italians in the neighborhood at all. So who's afraid of who? Don, you better look around. Our people are throwing in the chips and getting out of here. Angelo is selling the diner, Little Max is giving up the record store. You know what I'm talking about. Our people are getting the hell out of East Harlem."

"Terry, I tell you what I regret. I regret that kid Johnny United ain't Italian. You sure he ain't got some Italian blood in him?"

"You live in his block—ask his mother," said Terry, laughing.

IV

Johnny United said to Lefty, "Today's my day for running."

Lefty said to Johnny United, "We showed them Italians. What a fucking shot you hit. You put it in the second manhole of the next block."

"Lefty, you lend me the twenty-five bucks, I'll pay you back."

"Hey, I'm talking about the game. You would have been home a half hour before the throw came in—even with that arm Louie Bananas' got."

"I'm talking about twenty-five bucks."

"Where you going with twenty-five bucks? I don't think it's enough to run away with. My father pisses me off too. You need more. But here's eight dollars—it's all I got. Whatchu gonna do?"

"I don't know, Lefty. First I'm gonna run away. I'm a man. Then I'm gonna do something. Keep your eight bucks. I'll see you next Sunday, but don't tell nobody."

Johnny United opened the store and went to his hiding place. He removed all the money he had saved from tips for delivering groceries. And money he had saved from his winnings, since Terry always gave the team members a couple of bucks when they won. He also went to the place where his stingy stepfather hid his money, and he carefully counted out twenty-five dollars. And then he ran away from home.

PART IV

ONCE ON THIS ISLAND

There Is a Little Colored Boy in the Bottom of the Water

José Luis González

Translated by Lysander Kemp

José Luis González was born in 1926 in Santo Domingo of a Dominican mother and Puerto Rican father, and at the age of four came to Puerto Rico, where he was educated and began his writing career. The themes of his many works focus on the social and political problems that affect the workers and the poor of Puerto Rico. In 1953 González immigrated to Mexico as an act of protest against American colonialism and in turn was barred from entering the United States and Puerto Rico until 1971. He has published short story collections that include En la sombra *(1943),* El hombre en la calle *(1948), and* En Nueva York y otras desgracias *(1973); and the novels* Paisa *(1950),* La llegada *(1980), and* Balada de otro tiempo *(1978), which was translated in 1987. González lives in Mexico, where he has been a professor of literature and continues to write about life in Puerto Rico.*

"There Is a Little Colored Boy in the Bottom of the Water" shows how innocent children are lost on the margins of society without basic necessities like a safe place to play.

THE FIRST TIME THE LITTLE BABY MACARÍN SAW THE OTHER LITTLE colored boy at the bottom of the water was early in the morning, the third or fourth day after they had moved, when he crawled to the door of the new house, leaned over, and looked down at the still surface below.

His father, who had just awakened on the pile of empty sacks stretched on the floor, next to the half-naked and still-sleeping woman, shouted at the boy:

"Hey! . . . git youself down an' inside! Restless li'l baastad!"

And Macarín, who had not yet learned to understand words, but understood shouting, crawled inside again and stayed quiet in a corner sucking one small finger, for he was hungry.

The man raised himself on his elbows. He looked at the woman who slept beside him and shook her lazily by one arm. The woman woke up startled, looking at the man with fear in her eyes. The man laughed. Every morning it was the same: the woman woke up with that frightened face, which made him want to laugh, but without malice. The first time he'd seen that frightened face on the woman was the night they had lain together for the first time. Perhaps this was why it seemed attractive to him to see her come up out of sleep like that every morning.

The man sat upright on the empty sacks.

"Good," he said to her then. "Make the coffee."

"There's none left."

"Oh?"

"No, there's none left. It ran out yesterday."

The man started to ask, "Why didn't you buy more?" but stopped himself when he saw that the woman was beginning to make that other face, a face that did not please him, the one she put on only when he asked questions like that. The first time he had seen that particular look on the woman's face was the night he'd come home drunk, wanting her, and got on top of her, but the drunkenness kept him from doing anything. Perhaps for that reason it did not please him to see that face on the woman.

"Mean to say we ran out yesterday?"

"Mm-hmm."

The woman got to her feet and began putting her dress on over her head. The man, still seated on the empty sacks, shifted his glance and looked at the holes in his undershirt for a while.

Macarín, already bored by the uninteresting taste of his finger, decided to cry. The man looked at him and asked the woman:

"There's nuthin' for the kid either?"

"Yes. . . . I got some guanábana leaves. Goin' to make him some broth in a little bit."

"How many days he go he don't have milk?"

"Milk?" the woman asked, and there was a little unconscious fear in her voice. "Not since day before yesterday."

The man stood up and put on his trousers. He went to the door and looked out. He said to the woman:

"Tide's high. Have to go in the boat today."

Then he glanced upward to the bridge and the highway. Automobiles, buses, and trucks passed in an endless file. And the man smiled, noticing that from almost every vehicle someone looked with surprise at the hut sitting in the center of that arm of the sea: the caño, on whose quaggy edges the slum had been growing for years. Whoever they were, they began to stare at the hut, generally when they came to the middle of the bridge, then kept on looking, turning their heads slowly until whatever vehicle it was took the curve there up ahead.

The man smiled. And then he muttered: "Shitheads!"

In a little while he got into the boat and rowed to shore. From the boat's stern a long mooring line was made fast to the door of the house, so that whoever stayed in the house could draw the boat back to the door again. Between the house and the shore there was also a small bridge, which now, at high tide, was covered.

Once ashore, the man walked up to the highway. He felt better when the traffic noise drowned out the crying of the small Negro boy in the hut.

The second time little Macarín saw the other little colored boy at the bottom of the water was a little after midday, when he crawled to the door of the hut again and leaned out and looked down below. This time, the little boy at the bottom of the water favored Macarín with a smile. Macarín had smiled first and now he took the other's smile as an answer to his own. Then he went like that with his little hand, and from the bottom of the water the other little boy waved back. A laugh broke from Macarín, and it seemed to him that there came from below the sound of another laugh. At that moment his mother called him, because the second broth of guanábana leaves was finally ready.

Two women, two of the lucky ones who lived on dry land, on the hardened mud alongside the inlet, were swapping opinions:

"You have to see it to believe it. If they'd told me about it, I'd have said it was a lie."

"It's necessity, lady. Even me, for instance, I even had my little bit of land. . . . Who'd've said I'd have to end up here?"

"Well, we were one of the first, there were almost no people here then and you grabbed the driest spot, see? But those who are coming now, well, they're stuck, they have to throw themselves into the water, like they say. But still . . . those people, where the devil could they have come from?"

"I was told that over there, by Isla Verde, they're organizing and have got rid of a whole heap of Negro riffraff. They're probably part of that."

"By all the saints . . . ! And have you seen what a cute little colored boy they have? The woman came over yesterday to see if I had some leaves of anything to make a drink, and I gave her a few guanábana leaves I had left over."

"Ai, hoy Mary . . . !"

At sunset the man was tired. His back hurt. But he walked along feeling the coins at the bottom of his pocket, making them tink against one another, guessing from the touch which was a copper real, which ten centavos, which one peseta. Fine . . . today he'd had luck: the white man who'd driven by the dock to pick up his merchandise from New York. Then the worker who'd lent him his cart for the whole afternoon because he had to go chasing to find a midwife for his woman, who was dropping one more poor wretch into the world. Sí, señor. I'll get it going. Tomorrow's another day.

The man slipped into a grocery store and bought coffee and rice and kidney beans and some small tins of evaporated milk. He thought of Macarín and quickened his pace. He had come from San Juan on foot so as not to spend the copper for the bus.

The third time that little Macarín saw the other little colored boy at the bottom of the water was at sunset, a little before his father came home. This time Macarín started smiling before he peered over, and was surprised to see that the other little boy had also been smiling down below. Again he waved his small hand and again the other one answered him. Then Macarín felt a sudden warmth and an inexpressible love for the other little colored boy.

And he went to look for him.

LILIANE'S SUNDAY

Ana Lydia Vega

Translated by Lizabeth Paravisini-Gebert

Ana Lydia Vega was born in Santurce, Puerto Rico, in 1946, and obtained a Ph.D. in Comparative Literature at the University of Provence. She has published four collections of short stories, Virgenes y mártires *(1981),* Encancaranublado y otros cuentos de naufragio, *winner of the Casa de las Américas Award in 1982,* Pasión de historia y otras historias de pasión *(1987), and* Falsas cronicas del sur *(1991). Vega teaches French at the University of Puerto Rico.*

In "Liliane's Sunday" Vega artfully re-creates from multiple perspectives the 1937 Ponce Massacre, an ambush perpetrated by the United States against a Puerto Rican nationalist demonstration.

> Out of respect for myself, I will not interrupt the silence of the dead. And I will keep my tale free of names in all references to those who were the main actors in the Ponce Massacre; because most of them have already stepped beyond the frontiers of life, and my remembering their deeds seems to me to be enough sorrow for those few still alive, awaiting their turn to depart and slipping away like shadows fleeing their past.
>
> —RAFAEL PÉREZ-MARCHAND, *Historical Reminiscence on the Ponce Massacre*

EACH TIME THE MEMORY OF THAT DAY REAWAKENS IN ME, I RELIVE the unchangeable ritual that marked the beginning and end of all the weeks of my childhood.

Every Sunday we went to *La Concordia,* my grandfather's farm in the Real Abajo district of Ponce. In the backseat of the square Packard my three sisters, my brother, and I fought over the windows. No sooner had we left Hostos Avenue behind to drive across the city to the Juana Díaz detour than we went through a thousand contortions before settling down, while Mother scolded us because of the commotion and Father watched us, amused, in the rearview mirror.

I liked going around the Plaza de las Delicias, watching the young girls showing off their new dresses and the ladies entering and leaving the cathedral with their veils and fans. But I preferred crossing it on foot with Father on those afternoons when he allowed me to accompany him to the barbershop; on those days we always stopped at Eusebio's cart to buy the best vanilla ice cream I have tasted in my life.

That Sunday we left a bit later than usual. The night before, Father had taken us against Mother's wishes to the Teatro la Perla to see a zarzuela: The *Chaste Suzanna* was, according to her, "too strong" for our tender ears. We had gone to bed well past ten, which in my house was considered not only a risk to the children's fragile health but a real abuse of trust.

We had a light breakfast in anticipation of Mamina's chicken with rice in the country. While Mother laid on my bed the pink pinafore with its little lace collar, I did my exercises with Father in the lean-to in the yard. At eleven we were on our way, asking in unison to stop at the square for ice cones. People walked by with their holy palm branches in their hands, which made us redouble our entreaties and tripled our longing. But with the pretext of our delay there was to be no stopping and certainly no ice cones. Through the rearview mirror, Father gave me a wink of consolation, which didn't amuse me one bit.

As we drove past the Pila Clinic, we saw a large number of policemen walking on the street and, naturally, we asked if there was to be a parade. "The nationalists are coming," Mother said, quickly changing the topic. And that was the end of that.

★ ★ ★

Angel was coming from El Tuque. He had spent the entire morning at the beach gathering shells to make bracelets and necklaces for the girls. He had found many pretty ones, rimmed in pink and violet. He was carrying them in the basket on his bicycle, in a paper sack pressed between the coffee jug and the tin bowl.

He was eager to catch a glimpse of those nationalists who had announced their meeting with such fanfare. He didn't much like those sorts of things, but, after all, there was nothing better to do to kill death-bound time on a Sunday afternoon in Ponce.

He tried to make his way into town up Marina Street. The policemen, who had placed barricades on several intersections, would not let him through. He made an attempt at Aurora Street, but almost before he reached the first corner they made him go back. Then he hit on a master plan. He left the bicycle leaning against a tree in front of the Asilo de Damas, and putting the bag of seashells between his chest and undershirt, limped across the street to ask the guard with the long carbine pacing nervously up and down the entrance to the Alvarado Garage to let him through to the Pila Clinic to tend to his twisted ankle. The guard threw him a malicious glance and, shrugging his shoulders, allowed him through.

The road was paved, a rare thing in the 1930s, and the flamboyan trees growing all along it must have been scandalously red to have remained etched in my memory for such a long time. That day, by dint of arguments and shoves, I had earned the fiercely sought-after window. As we neared Coto Laurel, I could comfortably watch the furious geese of *La Constanza*.

Father was singing old ballads and *danzas*, with Mother providing the chorus. We contorted our faces in incredible grimaces, trying to repress our laughter, which burst without warning, the more clamorous the more we tried to suffocate it.

From the balcony of the Amy family home, on a second floor on Aurora Street, the view was perfect: the ideal spot from which to take sensational photos. In any case, it was pointless to look for another: there was not a single balcony that was not crammed.

Carlos climbed the steps two by two. He had the pleasant surprise of finding the door open. As he made his way to the balcony across the living room crowded with the curious, he noticed with growing ill temper that the best spots were already occupied. If he had not had to park the car so far away, if the walk had not been so long . . . But the police had cordoned off the neighboring streets and not even his press pass from *El Imparcial* had been enough to get him the necessary dispensation.

He took a cigarette out of his jacket pocket and lighted it with the last match he had left. Between puffs of smoke he began to study the faces around him, hoping to recognize some friend who would help him further his cause. On the first row, the ladies had placed stools on which to rest their buttocks, a noble and considerate gesture that allowed those on the second row to enjoy the panorama. There, between two men discussing the merits and demerits of Governor Winship, was final proof of the fact that, on that day, luck was definitely not with him.

We were still far from the curve with the pumpkins when I began to feel that vague anxiety that always gripped me when I anticipated its approach. Mother had diagnosed carsickness but the sensation was not the same. It resembled more the queasiness that gripped my stomach when, playing hide and seek, I was about to be found.

The spot of my dread finally appeared, with its wooden crosses, mementos to the victims of the highway. Knowing my vulnerable point, Father left "Happy Days" unfinished to intone, in a deliberately lugubrious voice, "Don't Bring Me Flowers." I surreptitiously reached for Lolín's hand, which I did not let go of until the irresistible attractions of the road captured my eyes again.

Climbing the fence that separated the hospital from the convent was not an easy task. The privet hedge bordering it presented an additional obstacle. The nuns, moreover, were looking out their windows. But, thank

God, too absorbed in what was going on on the other side. Angel concentrated, dug his fingers as hooks on the wall and, hoisting up his torso, accomplished the jump that brought him down on all fours on holy ground.

The removal of a neighbor by hammock to an unknown place, which could be none but the hospital or cemetery, forced my father to slow down his speed while the cortege passed by. I remember that we could only glimpse, at one end of the hammock, a pair of skinny yellowish feet sticking out. As she hurriedly rolled up the windows to protect us from mysterious viruses floating in the air, Mother explained to us that water was probably to blame and that that was precisely why it had to be boiled for ten minutes by the clock before we dared drink it.

The Inabón river now bordered the road. Lent had revealed the intimacy of its rocky bed and dried its wide and foamy pools. Father stopped so I could toss out the window the garden pebbles I had brought in my pocket to measure the depth of the water.

Crafty Conde had arrived early, had sneaked between the ladies by dint of gallantries, and was already happily shooting with his camera over the crowd on the sidewalk awaiting the beginning of the parade. *El Mundo* had its front-page photo more than assured. Carlos was biting his tongue with rage.

Just then a young girl, small and round, with lips as red as the hearts sprinkling the ruffles of her skirt, said very near to him, forcing him to lower his eyes:

"Are you a professional photographer or an amateur?"

The question stunned Carlos, who had been, in view of his present predicament, pondering that very same question. Fortunately, his masculine pride replied for him and the girl was suitably impressed.

We were not very far from the farm, when the startling spectacle of what seemed to me a house moving by itself across the fields made me exclaim, in alarm, that the earth was shaking. Father's burst of laughter dislodged his spectacles, and Mother had to replace them on the bridge of his nose. It is not an earthquake, he said when he recovered his voice, it's simply a move.

Fascinated, we followed the house's progress, as it was pushed, riding on rollers, by more than twenty men. I wanted to know why, instead of moving the furniture to another house, they chose to go through the trouble of moving the house. But I didn't dare ask, afraid of being ridiculed and provoking my sisters' eternal mocking laughter.

Once in the yard, Angel meant to go out quite nonchalantly by way of the alley that separated the convent of the Sisters of Mercy from that of the Sisters of Joseph and take a peek out the gate, armed with the genial excuse of being nothing less than the Lord Bishop's messenger. But a nun who had been keeping her eye on him from the moment she saw him climbing the fence yelled out the window. Luckily, with the din coming from the street, he could pretend not to have heard.

The big iron gate with the *hacienda*'s name emerged through the breadfruit trees. As we drove past the payment shack, we saw the overseer's raised hand and noisily returned his greeting. The Packard found its habitual spot under the shadow of a carob tree.

Mamina and Papiño were anxiously awaiting us on the immense porch of the wooden house. Why were we so late? Had that thing in Ponce already started? Was there a lot of traffic? The questions alternated with the kisses and embraces. In the kitchen, Ursula was giving the final touches to the gigantic *mofongo* reigning supreme on a tray by the fire.

My brother left with my father to converse with the sharecroppers, who had come out to greet us. Ursula and Grandmother started to take the dishes and silverware to the table on the *bohío*, the palm-thatched hut in the middle of the grapefruit grove. Accustomed to Corsican gastronomic rites, Mother would have preferred to have her lunch comfortably inside the house. But we would not accept another dining room but that of the *bohío*. My sisters went to the swings. I lost myself amid the coffee bushes, sniffing and exploring the aromatic mysteries of the berries. And I so truly lost myself that when it came time to sit to table, Mamina had to come looking for me.

The conversation did not end there. The girl offered him a sip of her raspberry ice cone, red as the mark of her lips on the white ice she was sucking. Pleasantly surprised, Carlos accepted, and the ice cone bridged the space between the two youths, whose hands lightly touched.

Suddenly, the irritating click of his rival's camera worked like an alarm clock waking him from his nirvana. Carlos remembered the sacred mission that had brought him with such difficulties from San Juan.

"Why don't we find another spot?" the girl then said, her face slightly blushing from the reflection of the ice cone. Carlos, who couldn't have hoped for anything better, bowed to her desire as if it had been an order and joined the compact mass vainly craning their necks to catch a glimpse of the street. When he realized she had not followed him, he looked behind him and saw her standing, with arms akimbo and the expression of an impatient bride, at the end of the living room. Confused, Carlos thought she was signaling him to return. He attempted to justify himself, pointing a finger at the camera. But she shook her head insistently, and, torn between pleasure and duty, he stood still for a few seconds, undecided, before retracing his steps, as fast as he could, toward the girl.

Without a word, she conducted him to the entrance door, from which she pointed, with quite a mischievous smile, to another closed door. Making sure that only Carlos and no one else accompanied her, she took out of her pocket a ring of keys and put the smallest one in the keyhole.

Atop a staircase, a slice of blue sky crowned his confidence. Closing the door behind them, they ran triumphantly to the roof.

After lunch, no matter what and come what may, the grandparents always took a siesta. Father let himself down in the hammock on the veranda with a sigh of satisfaction. Mother lay down, with a novel she had had the wise precaution to bring, on the sofa in the living room.

Lolín took advantage of the adults' withdrawal to search at her ease in the small odds-and-ends room. From there she returned with an album full of old unglued photographs, which unleashed a fury of sneezes that almost betrayed her. Carmen and Lina grabbed hold of it and devoted themselves, to my great boredom, to perusing it.

The sky was so perfectly blue and the afternoon so dazzlingly white that I couldn't resist the primitive call of the animals. I approached the chicken coop with great caution and full of bad intentions to steal the eggs. But the ruckus of the guinea hens immediately defeated my plans.

Then I slipped toward the pens where the rabbits grew and multiplied biblically. And I spent a lot of time pestering them, sticking them with a lemon-tree branch and hiding their food. I chased the goats, tried to milk the cows, and I didn't ride the horses because crafty Papiño had locked them in the stable. Emboldened, I carried my audacity to the barrel of landcrabs. With a long stick with a curved hook used to knock down loquats, I lifted them one by one to bring near my eyes the bluish threat of their claws and then dropping them, from that height, on the resigned carapaces of their companions.

When, due to an excess of repetition, I grew tired of doing mischief, a gluttony for fruit beckoned me to climb trees. Soon, the ground was carpeted with the last oranges and grapefruits of the season. The mangoes, still green, climbed grudgingly off the branches. But it was the guavas that accomplished their revenge. Not only were they all full of worms, but the thorns of a lemon-tree bodyguard they had next to them left my fingers as if I had spent the morning grating plantains.

Angel had already reached the gate and was in the very act of sliding the latch to glide discreetly onto the sidewalk when he was surprised by a clarion call that made him stop dead in his tracks. Immediately, the martial chords of *La Borinqueña* imposed themselves by beat of cymbals and trumpets. Making sure no one was watching, Angel considered for a moment removing his hat as a sign of respect. A guard's frowning gaze, nailed on the musicians, forced him to reconsider. The nationalist cadets clutched their black berets against their chests while their lips formed the words of the banned anthem.

★   ★   ★

The aroma of the coffee Ursula was brewing wafted over the farm announcing the proximity of the midafternoon snack. Although the fruits had turned my intestines inside out, the image of the sweet buns, meekly lined up on the kitchen table, made me start on my way back.

Amid a melancholic ballad, my father's powerful tenor hovered in the still air:

> There's no heart like mine
> suffering without complaint
> a heart that suffers in silence
> a heart that suffers in silence
> is not found everywhere.

It was his favorite song, the one he asked me to sing to him when he returned tired from the courthouse at seven o'clock at night and dropped himself on the wicker rocker. I paused on the narrow space that separated the storeroom from the mill and, projecting as far as I could my weak girlish falsetto, I replied with the responding couplet:

> I had a little dove
> which was my amusement
> it flew out of my little cage
> it flew out of my little cage
> though I had always treated her well.

Father applauded and yelled enthusiastic bravos from the veranda. At that moment, not knowing yet why, my eyes welled with tears and my chest tightened up.

★   ★   ★

Carlos felt his ill humor dissolve away, and a smile tickled the corners of his mouth. The girl had sat on the edge of the white wall, posing coquettish, her legs crossed, inviting a photograph. With his usual skill, he pressed the shutter release to please his guardian angel and, with the pretext of seeking an angle, moved near her.

La Borinqueña rose to the sky on the wings of the breeze. Shy or maybe just curious, who knows, the girl turned her head and evaded the kiss destined for her lips. He saw the nationalists standing at attention with their wooden rifles; he saw, behind them, the women dressed in white. And he saw also the line of Thompson machine guns, like a dark frontier between life and death, like a frozen river.

"Look at that, it's an ambush," he said, tracing a broad circle with his raised finger.

Carlos spread his legs, squared his body, and took a step forward to take his first photograph. A voice gave the order to march. Two sharp detonations were heard. A piteous chorus of cries and moans took possession of the air.

Before the buzz of a bullet forced them to throw themselves on the ground, Carlos was able to press the shutter and imprison in the exorbitant eye of his lens that scene of horror he would never be able to tear from his memory.

Wounded on the head, Angel barely had time to crawl to the tall grass of the patio. His pierced cap covered his face. A long line of split seashells extended from his last hiding place to the convent gates.

Mamina was calling me. The sudden irruption of a butterfly of all colors had distracted me, prolonging my return. It was then that the black car with a policeman at the wheel and the police insignia on the rear bumper entered the gate, like a huge scarab of ill omen. The insistent croak of his claxon made my mother drop the steaming cup of coffee and run down the steps.

★   ★   ★

A veil of gray smoke was floating over Ponce when the black car parked at the intersection of Marina and Aurora. It must have been six o'clock of an afternoon prematurely darkened. The few people on the streets walked hurriedly with heads bent. The long carbines kept watch over the streets. Only the ambulances mocked with their shrill sirens the stillness of the beleaguered city.

The Prosecutor had to lean against the door that was held open to remain on his feet as he faced the overwhelming smell of death that rose from the stained cobblestones. The muffled buzzing that filled his ears drowned the words of the Colonel, whose thin hands moved gracelessly accompanying his high-strung description of the "attempt." When the Prosecutor was finally able to formulate, with a wisp of a voice, something as simple as "What happened?" or maybe a hopeless "Were there any deaths?" and embark on the macabre tour through the entrails of a bad dream, his bewildered eyes discovered, in the bluish light of Ponce's twilight, the words painted in red on the white pediment wall of the convent:

LONG LIVE THE REPUBLIC
DOWN WITH THE ASSASSINS

The Prosecutor had the foreboding that those words, traced with the waning strength of a dying hand soaked in blood, had the power to turn his life upside down, a life that never again would run its course as placidly as his day at the countryside every Sunday.

BLACK SUN

Emilio Díaz Valcárcel

Translated by C. Virginia Matters

Emilio Díaz Valcárcel was born in Trujillo Alto, Puerto Rico, in 1929 and has lived in New York and Spain. He has published Figuraciones en el mes de marzo *(1972), translated in 1979 as* Schemes in the Month of March, *and* Harlem todos los días *(1978), recently translated as* Hot Soles in Harlem *(1993). Díaz Valcárcel has been a Guggenheim Fellow and a fellowship recipient of the Institute of Puerto Rican Culture. He served in the Korean War, wrote educational film scripts for fourteen years, founded and edited the literary review* Cupey, *and has had a long academic career that includes teaching at the University of Puerto Rico.*

"Black Sun" celebrates the sounds of Africa while critiquing how Puerto Rican society, despite its long interracial history, continually uplifts those who are fairer over those with the strongest physical ties to Africa.

BLACK BERNABÉ QUIRINDONGO FELT THE BLOOD BOIL IN HIS VEINS whenever he heard his kind of music. Seated at the door of his wooden shack, surrounded by the other closely-packed-together huts of the tiny Negro colony of the town, he would spend hours and hours searching for meaning to the sounds. At the edge of the plot of land a dozen black faces crowded around, eyes burning, hands like knotted vines pounding against their knees, to help out Bernabé Quirindongo, whose fingers beat futilely against the flimsy wall partition, against the floor; not once was there a rich, full sound like the one ringing in his head. Luciana

Quiles, leaning out from the window of her shack, had been watching the boy since he was very small; from the beginning she understood the rhythm that tortured him; the little black boy had been born a drummer.

Mama Romualda, sweltering over her little stove, fanning the flames with a greasy piece of cardboard, grew sad thinking about her black son's harmonic frustrations. She sold chitterlings that even the daintiest and blondest little girls of the town licked their lips over. In an old tin can she would drop the coins, one by one. Black Bernabé Quirindongo, black good-for-nothing to the people, wanted a hide on which to unload his rhythm; he pestered his mama demanding the marvelous skin of a bongo for his fingers.

"Pa-coo-pah," moved his lips, "pa-coo-pah," but the wooden wall, or the floorboards, or the garbage can produced only a disappointing noise under his miraculous fingertips. The black faces, huddled together at the edge of the lot, beat their palms together. Neighbor Luciana Quiles, seventy years old, granddaughter of slaves, caught up by a dizziness that shook her bony body, led the group with her cattle bell of a voice.

In the silent late afternoons the coconut groves atop the little rise turned into metallic shadows, the horizon burned red, and Bernabé Quirindongo's soul was filled with a noisy peace, expressible only through the slow roll of the skins. In the mornings the sun ripened on the tips of the pines, nailing daggers of light within the shack, and Bernabé Quirindongo ("Pa-coo-pah," his lips moved) would have described it all with a joyous drumroll. Thunder volleys burned the silence above the shack, scared away the peace of the whites, rolled on until quenched in the brambles on the other side of the river, and Bernabé Quirindongo, better than anyone else, could have reproduced their sonorous mystery by vibrating his sausagelike fingers. But Bernabé Quirindongo, black good-for-nothing, who beat the air in search of a nonexistent bongo, had to pour out his soul through his lips.

"Pa-coo-pah," he murmured.

When Bernabé Quirindongo was sent to the little town hospital because of a hernia, his mama Romualda Quirindongo got drunk and began to beg, her eyes swimming in tears. Of each dollar collected, she drank half. It was a sight that amused even the most refined whites. The

Negress went up and down the streets, staggering along in her faded rags, and her enormous breasts wobbled as if they, too, were drunk; she pleaded, whined, begged. Later, alone, she counted the money.

Actually, it was never known whether or not the Negro was being cured of a hernia. The truth is that one morning, after all his mama's pleas and collecting, he appeared at the door of the shack with a new bongo. Luciana Quiles herself, who understood about such things, yanked off the price tag. Bernabé attacked the skins, and his thick lips followed the cadence and emitted sounds of a bongo being beaten: "R-roc ko-to, ta—coo-pah." His eyes, fixed in a faraway gaze, seemed to be aflame. His noise bothered no one: his mama's last husband, the red-skinned man who appeared one morning stretched out in the tall grass of the abandoned dairy farm, had left for the center of the island, cursing the coast.

Bernabé had never known his father. Luciana Quiles was suspicious of a Jamaican who landed, twenty years back, when the tiny colony had only half a dozen tumbled-down hovels, to work on the bridges. For all purposes, Romualda was the boy's papa and mama. Last Three Kings' Day, while Bernabé was tuning his instrument and the admiring black faces began to crowd together outside the plot, Romualda gave him a nail clipper.

"This is so you don't break the skin," she told him. Old Luciana Quiles hugged her. *Coc, ko-ro, pa-coo,* said the bongo on that memorable date.

Romualda had many arguments with the people. Her son was no idiot, he had simply turned out to be a musician; let them look around all over town for anyone—anyone, mind you!—who could match his harmony. The young boys gathered around him with guiros and maracas, trying to pick up a rhythm. Bernabé Quirindongo didn't even look at them, and his eyes, glowing, stared over their shoulders. When his fingers were drumming, not even his own mama nor the neighbor Luciana Quiles merited a glance. He was complete concentration. All ears. A casually shouted word was enough to set the skins to releasing their harmonies together with the murmuring lips. "Ramón!" *R-roco-to bem-bon.* When lightning tore up the horizon above the guava bushes, he would wait motionless, ear ready, until the deafening roar of the thunder reached him. His fingers then came to life. The black faces ran through the rain to listen to the miracle. *Bo-roam boam,* and his eyes turned loose for a moment while his magical hearing registered the noisy cadence.

"Thass a black saint," neighbor Luciana Quiles would say. "He gonna die through the ears."

Romualda felt proud of her boy and encouraged him. She passed her greasy hand over her son's bent head. There was a somewhat ancestral vengeance in those drumbeats. Her black boy was redeeming her from something she couldn't understand. She felt light, agile; some indefinable weight dropped from her whenever she listened to the percussion in the doorway of her shack.

One morning, without Bernabé Quirindongo's seeing her, the lightest of the daughters arrived. She had silky hair and yellow eyes. Mariana brought a six-month-old mulatto in her arms and stated it very clearly, so all the neighborhood could hear: the baby, born in one of San Juan's slums, would not be taken away from her by anyone. She let them know his name: Milton, Milton Quirindongo, and she kept watching the people just in case anyone said something. She would raise him even though he had no father. For him, the best blankets in the world, the tenderest looks, the best bottles, the softest bed, the best scraps of food. Bernabé didn't even bother to look at his nephew, busy as he was. Black Romualda, enthused by the milky color of her grandson, changed the course of her affection. She felt her knees go soft when her grandson bawled. She sold her pork cracklings in a hurry, neglected the seasoning of her fried delicacies, forgot to give her customers the change. The memory of her husband disappeared like a mongoose into a bush. Nobody else existed for her.

And Bernabé Quirindongo, with his dauntless face, his eyes aflame, searched for the meaning to the sounds. The baby cried: "Gwa, pa coopah." "I've dropped the frying pan," his mama said. *Tan, tan ta-ran,* he answered, moving his lips, purple and cracked by silence. The black faces crowded about the plot, eyes and teeth white, hands restless, surrounding his cadence. Luciana Quiles quaked in a trance; an atavistic wriggling shook her parchmentlike flesh. "Bernabé! . . ." *Merecum-bay.* The sounds leaped forth crazily. "Mariana!" *Baram barambana.*

Mariana worked in the afternoons. She went to wash dishes in the house of the richest man in town. From there she brought pieces of chicken, dainty tidbits wrapped in newspaper for her little mulatto. Romualda stayed in the kiosk, sweltering over the stove, blowing on the live coals. Her bloodshot eyes became tender when she looked at her grandson, and now words no longer sounded in the house. There were no words in the house, but the bongo was new, although grease had stained it almost blue.

One day Bernabé's little nephew woke up with a fever. Luciana Quiles and her half-dozen darkies came running: she brought a concoction of herbs. Then came a pale man, dressed in white and wearing a strange rubber necklace. The Negro, in the door of the shack, waited with his fingers ready on the skins. Only the indistinct murmur from the pale man and the women in the bedroom.

"Doctor," begged a voice. "Doctor," Bernabé repeated, and for the first time he felt helpless at not being able to translate the word on his instrument.

"He won't die?" asked the same voice. *Rrrrr,* sounded the skins in vain, lifelessly. Suddenly he felt an indefinable anguish descend upon him, covering him.

He spent some time trying to attract the neighbors, already weary of his efforts. Luciana Quiles looked at him with a furrowed brow, a bad omen. Thunder made him fall into a sort of trance: from that came his best music. But the sickness of the baby had Mariana so worried that, in an outburst of hopeless rage, she broke the skin of the bongo.

"While he's sick, don't make any noise in this house," she said, and pushed the sharp heel of her shoe through the skins that, upon breaking, produced a dissonant noise (*pru-oh, pru-ah*), hurting the Negro's ears.

Without a bongo, Bernabé Quirindongo felt fenced in by the silence. The afternoons became heavy and insufferable. The black faces turned away, presenting only the disdainful backs of their heads. His fingers beat unsuccessfully on the walls, the stone that served as a doorstep, his knees, the stool. Romualda didn't want to replace the skins. Everything she earned she spent on her grandson, who was getting better as the days went by. The neighbors all came to the shack, passing Bernabé by without even looking at him, and peered tenderly at the color of the little mulatto. Bernabé spent his time hunting for new resonant surfaces that could take the place of his instrument. His lips moved in desperation: "Ta ta ta." But it was not the same. He had already lost two good thunderstorms with long, fiery lightning flashes, as well as a large number of words for which he could have found rhythmic synonyms. An inexpressible sensation of confusion began to mount up in his head. He beat upon whatever came within reach: a washbasin, the bare beams of the house; he would stand on the stool and anxiously pummel the tin roofing, which only gave forth a hopeless *toom toom*. The back of a chair offered him an immense possibility; he went at it, but as he beat it with his convulsive fingers he noted that the sound came out opaque, dissipated, from the termite-damaged wood. He had to content himself with an inferior quality, while a series of impulses in disordered flight made him move his fingers incessantly. At times he seemed to beat the skins of an invisible bongo, and his gaze remained fixed beyond the pines and the bamboo fences. "Pa-coo-pah," he murmured; sweat streamed from his armpits.

A rumor swept the town: it began like a superstitious whisper in the Negro colony, broke out at last, and leaped from mouth to mouth through all the municipality, filling the eight streets.

"Bernabé Quirindongo isn't playing anymore."

"Bernabé Quirindongo, black good-for-nothing."

"Bernabé Quirindongo, crazy Negro beating the air."

"Bernabé Quirindongo, widower of a bongo."

Romualda was still blind and deaf to her son's need.

"Mustn't make no noise," she would say, putting her finger to her lips.

Mariana watched him, scowling.

So Bernabé Quirindongo lived isolated in an ominous territory of silence. An infinite number of noises, lost for lack of a skin, assaulted his memory.

One afternoon, looking at the roof in search of a board or something suitable to release his intolerable tension, he noticed that the sky had become stern. There were black clouds that for a moment seemed to split apart into two islands: a streak of lightning had lashed the air above the long necks of the pines. The sky was like an immense black skin. He tuned his ear, eagerly. The thunder rolled through the valley, full and round, magnificent. His fingers moved nervously. "Boo-room boom," his lips articulated. The rain scourged the earth abruptly, like an enormous ejection of spittle. *Tic-tic-ticky* vibrated the drops on the tin. The pines bent in slow reverence. *Boom, ba-room,* a thunder clap said to him petulantly. A sharp-pointed heel, gleaming, slashed the skin of the sky. Bernabé Quirindongo, good-for-nothing. "Bernabé!" shouted the voices brought by the rain. "Quirindongo," let loose a thunderbolt. "Bernabé Merecumbé!" cried a gust of wind as it swept across the wall.

Bernabé Quirindongo felt that the marvelous rhythm of nature was enclosing him in a monstrous bongo. His fingers beat frenetically upon the partition wall. Mariana could not scold him: She was working in the town. Mama was taking care of the kiosk. *Boom,* the thunder mocked. *Tic-tic-ticky,* laughed the rain, which leaned against the wall. *Toc-toc-toc,* said a drop that hammered solemnly into a tin can. "Where's your skin, your bongo bo-rom-bom?" a furious voice asked him. Without a bongo, black Bernabé Quirindongo was lost. The voices harassed him in the little living room.

The window, opening abruptly, let out a roar of laughter. *Toc-toc-boom-tic-ticky.*

He threw himself against the floor and pounded on it until his fingertips hurt. But his fingers could not drag from the boards the world of unbelievable sounds that beat in his brain. *Boom, ba-room, ticky-tic-toc, ko-toh.* From the bedroom the baby's voice called him quietly.

"Waaaaaayyyyy, Bernabé."

His heavy lips trembled: "Waayyyy, merecoom-bay." *Ba-room,* challenged the sky. "Black Bernabé Cumbé Quirindongo Dongo doesn't have a rawskin bongo, borom-bon," they whispered in his ear. *Toc-toc-ticky.*

"Waaaayyyyyy!" his nephew called again.

The branch of a tree slapped against the back of the house: *tac, tac, tac.* The wind whistled its mockery of the powerless fingers.

"Waaayyyyy," the baby called for a third time.

Bernabé Quirindongo went to his nephew and looked at him seriously, thoughtfully. The baby twisted among the blankets, shaking his little fists. "Waaayyyy, merecum-bay. Where's your skin, good-for-nothing?" they said in his ear. *Boom ba-room.* The smooth forehead, the young skin . . .

Ta coo-pah, sounded the gifted fingers on the skin of the forehead.

Boom, ba-room, they beat on the chest.

The thunder challenged him, *boom, ba-room.* "Ha!" laughed the window.

Black Bernabé Quirindongo was sweating, drawing out rhythm from his new skin. The tension was fading: he had unloaded a great part of his rhythm and felt there was still much more to be expressed. While the thunder continued to roll, calling him, while sonorous words hummed in his ear, he would have marvelous sounds with which to parry them. *Ta coo-pah, boom.*

Until Mariana's fingernails seized him furiously and threw him to the floor. *Goo-whop!* creaked the floor without the slightest acoustics. Mariana's shouts were terrible: There was no resonant quality in them. The black faces squeezed about the entrance of the shack, with Luciana Quiles at the fore, shaking her fists in the midst of the flashing half-light, beneath the persistent rain; they wanted to kill Bernabé Quirindongo, black good-for-nothing, bereft of his bongo.

Mariana kicked him unrhythmically.

Romualda and a policeman arrived: *tuc, tuc,* beat the nightstick on the Negro's head, with the fortunate timing of a pair of sticks in a dance band.

Mama Romualda was shouting very unpleasantly, way out of tune.

The policeman grabbed Bernabé and carried him off through the rain.

Pa-coom, ba-room, the sky shouted at him.

"Pa coo-pah, pa coo-pah," he went off saying.

THE GIFT

Rosario Ferré

Rosario Ferré was born in Ponce, Puerto Rico, in 1938. She founded and edited Zona de carga y descarga, *an important literary magazine devoted to innovative Puerto Rican literature. She is the author of* The House on the Lagoon *(1995),* The Youngest Doll *(1991),* Sweet Diamond Dust *(1989), and* Sonatinas *(1989), among many other works. Her novel,* Eccentric Neighborhoods, *is forthcoming. A frequent lecturer in the United States, she lives in Puerto Rico.*

In "The Gift," two schoolmates insist on maintaining their friendship despite the elitist and racist barriers Puerto Rican aristocracy sets up between them.

NO ONE EXPECTED MERCEDITAS CÁCERES, ON THE DAY CARLOTTA Rodriguez was expelled from the Sacred Heart, to hang her silk sash from the doorknob, drop her medal of the Congregation of the Angels in the alms box, and walk out through the school's portico arm in arm with her friend, head held high and without deigning once to look back, with that gesture of paramount disdain so commonplace in those of her social class. Next to her through the half-light of the entrance hallway went Carlotta, her huge body gently swaying forward like a tame heifer's, her thick mask of makeup running down her cheeks in furrows, hopelessly staining her white blouse and the starched collar of her uniform with its varicolored tears.

At that moment Merceditas was giving up, in the name of friendship, ten, perhaps twenty crowns of roses that already shimmered like snowy rings at the bottom of the wardrobe where the nuns kept the prizes to be awarded on graduation day, while Carlotta went in pursuit of hers, that astonishing fan of golden peacock's feathers that was very soon to gird her forehead like a crown. There at the school's hallway she left behind, amid the rustling of blue pleated skirts and starched white shirts, the many honors she had so arduously worked for during her three and a half years at the academy, the ribbons and medals that now would never shine on her breast, while Carlotta went in quest of hers, of the bottles of cheap perfume and of the flowered handkerchiefs, of the earrings and bangles in gift boxes of garish velvet, which were to be so lovingly presented to her by the members of her retinue on her coronation day. Followed by her silver parade floats, she would walk a few days later down Ponce de León Avenue (as she would also do months later down the principal thoroughfares of Rio de Janeiro, New Orleans, and even Surinam), outfitted in her eighteen-karat gold robe and revealing, on the diamond-studded brim of her décolletage, her enormous dark breasts, sustained by a vision of the world that deserved, in the judgment of the venerable ladies of the Sacred Heart, the steaming torments of the cauldrons of hell.

The mango had been a present from Carlotta, who had brought it secretly into the school after spending the weekend at her father's house. She took it out of her pocket at recess and held it before her friend, balancing it in the palm of her hand.

"It was a present from the members of the carnival's committee at lunch today," she said, smiling. "It's of a variety called Columbus's kidney; sweet like a sugar loaf and soft like butter. Keep it; it's my gift to you."

Merceditas accepted the mango with a laugh and they walked together toward the small grove of honeyberries that grew at the end of the school's patio. It was their favorite haunt, because the shade of the trees provided a temporary release from the heat and also because the nuns rarely patrolled that part of the garden. Carlotta was describing the details of the lunch to her, all of which had had to do with the carnival's theme.

"Silver candelabra and plenas, cod fritters and Venetian tablecloths. You would have enjoyed the combination if you'd been there to see it.

But what I really liked best was that the committee should have thought of that beautiful mango, Columbus's kidney, as an official gift. In the past, carnival queens were always presented with a jewel, be it a gold ring or a bracelet, on the day of their appointment."

Merceditas laughed again loudly, her head thrown back, thinking her friend was teasing her.

"It's called like that not in memory of Christopher Columbus's kidney, though, but of Juan Ponce de León's," Carlotta added. "He brought that variety of mango over from India, from a city called Columbus, and planted it himself on the island."

Merceditas looked at her friend and saw that, in spite of the historical blunder she had just made, she was speaking in earnest. "Then it's settled? You've accepted the appointment of carnival queen?" she asked.

"I'll be the first truly Creole queen in Santa Cruz, don't you think?" she said, rubbing her hand lightly over her dark cheeks. "Before, queens were always so pale and insipid. If Don Juan Ponce de León should have seen me he would have picked me. Spaniards always preferred swarthy girls."

Merceditas tried her best to imagine her friend decked out in silk ruff, crown, and farthingale, but to no avail. Carlotta was too plump, and she lacked all the necessary social graces. It was precisely because of that, and because of her merry, candid disposition, that she had picked her as her friend.

"It's just that I can't picture you dressed up like a queen."

Carlotta smiled reassuringly and put her hand affectionately on her friend's shoulder. "Cleopatra was plump and rowdy, and you have to admit, from the pictures of her we've seen in the *Treasure of Youth,* that she never had hair as nice as mine."

Merceditas looked at her from the corner of her eye. It was true; her friend had a beautiful mane of hair that she had always admired, and which she wore carefully combed in heavy mahogany tresses, in compliance with the school's regulations. "Many visitors will come to town for the feasts," Carlotta added enthusiastically, "and if in the past we were famous for our tobacco and our coffee, in the future we'll be known everywhere for our carnival." They walked on together in silence, until they got to the wire fence that marked the end of the school's property at the edge of the garden. On the other side of the fence they could see the Portugués's stony riverbed, glinting in the sun like an unpaved highway.

"Aren't you afraid Mother Artigas may not like the idea of your carnival having to do with Juan Ponce de León? You know how finicky she is about historical matters."

"Whoever wants the sky must learn to fly," Carlotta answered, shrugging her shoulders. "I have no choice but to take the risk. And in any case, if Mother Artigas dislikes the idea of the carnival, you can be sure she'll have other reasons."

They finally heard the school bell ring and they parted company, walking toward the study hall building. Merceditas had dropped the mango in her skirt pocket; she could feel it swing there against her leg, and enjoyed its perfume of roses like an anticipated banquet. When she arrived at her seat she took it out surreptitiously and hid it at the bottom of her desk.

Merceditas Cáceres and Carlotta Rodriguez had become good friends in a short time. In truth, one couldn't find two students more unlike each other in the whole school. Merceditas came from a landholding family who owned some of the most fertile sugarcane valleys on the south of the island, as well as the mill after which she had been named. The Las Mercedes Sugar Mill was nearly as large as Snow White Mills, the huge sugar complex of the western town of Guamaní. She had been brought up by English governesses until she entered the Sacred Heart as a boarder; she had few friends and had always led a lonely life, having permission to leave the school only on weekends, when she was driven up the mill's slope in her family's limousine.

She had many cousins and relatives and had hardly had any contact with the people of the town. Inside the mill's compound there were several sundry and utility stores, a drugstore, medical offices, a swimming pool, and tennis courts where her cousins played daily with one another. Merceditas's shyness was in part the result of her not being used to talking to strangers, but it was also the outcome of the Cáceres's unpopular image in Santa Cruz. They had refused to belong to the local casino and *paso fino* club, for example; and their huge fortune had led them to feel a certain mistrust, and in some cases even disdain, of the townspeople. The latter responded in kind, and would never invite the Cáceres to the political and social activities that went on in their homes, an exile that the Cáceres undoubtedly welcomed, since they would seldom bend down to dealing with local authorities at the municipal level for the problems of their sugar empire, resorting always to the central sources of power on the mainland. When they were accused of having no patriotic spirit and of being citizens of nowhere, the Cácereses would laugh wholeheartedly, throwing back their blond heads (of which they were inordinately proud, attributing them to a German ancestor) and claiming that, in fact, the accusation was correct, as they considered themselves to be citizens of the world, and the only good thing about Santa Cruz was the highway that led to the capital.

Because of these reasons, every Friday afternoon, when Merceditas left the Sacred Heart, she would lean curiously out the gray velvet-curtained windows of her family's limousine, observing the houses of the town attentively and wondering what life would be like inside. In spite of her great efforts to make friends with the classmates who she knew lived in these houses, she had had little luck. It had only been on meeting Carlotta that she had for the first time felt appreciated for her own self, without her family name being in the least important. Carlotta's conversation, always peppered with jokes and mischievous innuendos, both cheered and amused her, and she found it especially interesting when she spoke to her of the town.

Carlotta, for her part, had discovered in Merceditas a valuable ally. Her presence in school, unthinkable a few years before, had been the result of the new outlook the nuns had been forced to adopt when they discovered that the school's enrollment was only half full. It was an expensive academy, and the economic difficulties that even the most respectable families of the town had begun to encounter had forced them to begin to send their daughters to less exclusive establishments. The nuns had then altered their policy of admission, and for the last few years the daughters of the Acuñas, the De la Valles, and the Arzuagas had been obliged to share their top-rank education with the daughters of the Rodriguezes, the Torreses, and the Moraleses.

Among the latter Carlotta had always stood out for her friendliness, although the shade of her skin condemned her, even among the "new" girls, to a relative isolation. She was the first mulatto student to be admitted to the school in its half century of existence, and her recent admission had been talked about as something unheard of and radical even by the families of the "new." The surnames of the recent upcoming elite were still tottering insecurely in the social registers of the town, and this caused them to be undecided as to whether they should assume the canons of purity of blood that their peers, the old aristocratic families of Santa Cruz, had so zealously defended in the past. Thus they chose, in those cases that were unfortunately more obvious, to adopt a benevolent, distant attitude, which would establish the priority of the "mingled but not mixed."

It was true that Don Agapito Rodriguez's considerable assets had contributed greatly to the democratization of the admission requirements of the academy, so that now the venerable Ladies of the Sacred Heart would risk even the admittance of Carlotta Rodriguez to the school. Don Agapito was a small dry-goods merchant who had recently struck it rich with a chain of supermarkets that had modernized the shopping habits of the town. In his establishments one could now choose all kinds of fruits and vegetables, as well as dairy and meat products brought from faraway towns or imported from the mainland, so that all the corner vegetable and neighborhood meat stores had been forced to close down. He was a widower, and his daughter was the apple of his eye. All of this added to the nuns' good fortune at having her with them. He had persuaded the owners of the town's food markets to provide the convent's modest daily staples, the dried beef, tripe, and pig's knuckles with chick-peas they so enjoyed, at half price; a visit to the town mayor, his second cousin, produced considerable savings in their electric bill; a call to Don Tomás Rodriguez, chief fireman and his uncle, yielded the promise that a modern water heater would soon be installed at the convent, the cost of which Don Agapito was willing to foot.

The nuns were congratulating one another for their wise decision in admitting Carlotta to the academy when they noticed that an unexpected friendship had begun to bud between her and Merceditas Cáceres. They always strove to be together—in the garden at recess; in the classrooms and in the dining room; and they had had the good luck to have been assigned neighboring beds in the boarding-student dormitory. At first the nuns were concerned that Merceditas's family might disapprove of such an intimacy, but they soon realized their fears were unfounded. The Cácereses spent their lives commuting from the island to the mainland in their planes and yachts, and Merceditas's friends were of little concern to them. The girls' friendship, on the other hand, offered the nuns the opportunity to make Carlotta feel accepted and loved at the school, thus partially allaying her loneliness. For Don Agapito, his daughter's friendship with no less than Merceditas Cáceres was undoubtedly a blessing from heaven. The school parents had traditionally attributed a great deal of importance to the social relations that were established between the girls at the school, since they often served as a base for favorable future business transactions, and in some cases even for unexpected betrothals. (Don Agapito might perhaps have been thinking of Merceditas's many brothers and cousins, in the case of Carlotta's possible future visits to the Cáceres home.) The nuns believed, in short, that the generous Don Agapito very well merited the friendship that had sprung up between his daughter and Merceditas; as to the Cácereses, who never cared a fig for the welfare of the town, and much less for that of the school, they deserved fully whatever harmful social consequences the girls' rapport might bring.

Having vanquished the obstacles to their friendship, the girls spent the year in happy camaraderie, and were waiting for the day when they would graduate together from the Sacred Heart. Merceditas had confessed to Carlotta that it was very important for her to graduate with as many honors as possible, because a high academic index would mean a scholarship, which would permit her to continue her studies at a university on the mainland. Her parents had made it clear that they would pay for her education only as far as high school, since at that time a profession was considered superfluous in a girl of good family.

Merceditas had nightmares every time she considered the possibility of having to stay buried at the mill's compound, married to a second cousin and enslaved to household chores, spending her free time running back and forth after a stupid ball on the family's green clay tennis courts, surrounded by equally green cane fields. She thought of Mother Artigas's offer to help her acquire a grant on the mainland as her only ticket to freedom, and because of it she had put heart and soul into her studies all year.

Carlotta, for her part, had no intellectual ambitions, but she knew that graduating from the Sacred Heart could open many future doors for her in town, and she thus tried to do her best. She knew that knowledge had a practical value, and she hoped, with her newly acquired training in mathematics and science, to help her father in his campaign to modernize the town. She admired Merceditas greatly, her dauntless daring in whatever project she undertook; and she looked to her as her saving Nike. All through the year Merceditas had taken her under her wing, and no one at school had ever dared call her a disparaging name, which might remind her of her humble origins.

Carlotta's good-natured ways, on the other hand, would act on Merceditas like a balm. She amused her endlessly with stories of Santa Cruz. She would describe the sunbaked streets one by one, shaded by groves of honeyberries and centuries-old mahogany trees, although a subtle ironic tinge would always creep into her voice when she talked about the nineteenth-century mansions of the patrician families of the town. She liked to point out that these houses, with whitewashed façades heavily gessoed and hung with garlands, amphorae, and plaster cupids, reminded her of a row of wedding cakes just out of the oven and set on the sidewalk to cool. She also talked about the lives that went on behind their walls with a good-natured lilt of reproach, describing, without the merest hint of hate or resentment, how their inhabitants lived eternally in the half-light of respectability, hiding the fact that they were forced to live with much more modest means than those that the opulent walls of their mansions proclaimed to the world.

Thanks to Carlotta's stories Merceditas began to find out about the history of Santa Cruz. The old bourgeois families' proud stance before the economic ruin that the arrival of the troops from the north had provoked at the turn of the century seemed to her quixotic, but worthy of respect. The town's prosperity had hinged on the importance of its port, which had been praised by General Miles after his regiment of volunteers from Illinois had landed. It was blessed by a jetty and a deep bay, which had served as a stimulating rendezvous for commerce all during the nineteenth century, since it offered protection to the many vessels that sailed for Europe and North America, loaded with coffee, sugar, and tobacco.

The mountain range that surrounded the town to the north and to the west had been profusely planted with coffee and tobacco at the time, which the small landowners of the region would transport to the coast in mule trains, to be shipped abroad. Sugarcane, on the other hand, was grown in the lowlands, and it spread over the valley of Santa Cruz like a rippling green mane. Santa Cruzans were at that time a proud people, and they boasted that their coffee, tobacco, and sugar were famous all over the world for their excellent quality. They had, furthermore, made wise use of their bonanza, and with the revenues had built elegant theaters, plazas, loggias, a horse-racing track and a dog-racing track, as well as a splendid cathedral, whose towers could be seen gleaming arrogantly from far out at sea because they had been carved in silver.

All this began to change, and was still changing, with the arrival of the armies from the north. With the ruin of the tobacco and coffee plantations, the farmlands on the mountains were abandoned, and the trading firms that had dealt with them in town were forced to foreclose. Many of the criollo-owned sugar mills had then passed to form a part of the three or four super mills established on the island with the aid of foreign capital, as had been the case with Diamond Dust, the De la Valle family enterprise. Some of them, however, had managed to survive the crises thanks to their ingenuity, and such was the case of Las Mercedes Sugar Mill. More than twenty years before, the Cácereses had decided to build a rum distillery. At first it was no more than a rustic evaporating still, one of the many illegal contraptions that had sprung up by the hundreds in the back patios of the old mills of the valley. The Second World War had begun, and the veterans from Santa Cruz were returning home by the hundreds, armless and lame from its bloody battles, and looking for a magic balm that might make them forget their sorrows. It had been this sorry spectacle that had given the Cácereses the brilliant idea of naming their rum Don Quijote de la Mancha, as the islanders would immediately identify the beaten, half-starved gentleman on the label with the ravaged pride of their own country.

And it wasn't just amid the island's war veterans that Don Quijote's popularity became rampant; it also began to sell surprisingly well on the mainland. The inhabitants of the metropolis had acquired a taste for the exotic rum produced by their colonies, and they felt inordinately proud of it. Don Quijote became proof that they were becoming internationally sophisticated: from now on, France could well have its Ron Negrita, distilled in Martinique; and England its Tío Pepe, packed and bottled in Dover; without worrying them in the least. They had their own Don Quijote, who would conquer the world from the lanky heights of his scrawny steed.

With the profits from the fabulous sales of their rum, the Cácereses built their family compound in the vicinity of the mill, turning it into a modern village. The houses all had swimming pools that shone like emeralds under the noonday sun, as well as manicured tennis courts. The atmosphere was refreshingly informal, in contrast to the stuffy customs of the town, where women would never be allowed to go out in pants "tight as sausages," as the Spanish priest used to shriek from the cathedral's pulpit on Sundays. While the women of the town were often overweight and never did any exercise, alternating between the church and the kitchen, where they were the fairy godmothers of their families' pampered appetites, at Las Mercedes women wore white shorts and tennis shoes, played badminton, skeet, and tennis, and would make a daily ritual of tanning themselves half-naked next to their pools.

During this same period Santa Cruz became a skeleton town, and quietly folded upon itself the exuberant flesh it had previously exhibited to the world. The magnificent buildings of yore, the theaters with Greek porticoes, and the plazas decorated with fountains had fallen into disrepair, so that they stuck out in the noon heat like the mysterious bones of a dream, monuments of a past whose practical use could only be guessed at by the townspeople. Sliding like shades at the back of their palatial houses, however, the old aristocratic families still survived, concealing their hurt pride and poverty behind their ornately decorated balconies.

This picture of Santa Cruz that Carlotta painted was a revelation to Merceditas, who had lived until then a sheltered life in the midst of her family's greenbacked cane fields. As she listened to her sitting next to the Grotto of the Virgin of Lourdes, or during their strolls through the school's garden, she was surprised at her love for the town. Carlotta's interest in the old aristocratic families was mainly romantic in character. Like her father, she believed in progress and wanted to participate, once she had graduated from the Sacred Heart, in the town's political and civic development. Don Agapito was an active member of the board of directors of the municipal hospital, as well as of the state penitentiary, and he strove for progressive measures, such as importing the latest cancer-treating equipment with federal aid or adopting a more humane policy toward convicts. He was also manager of the Little League baseball team and an influential member of the chamber of commerce and of the Lion's Club, from whose boards he always encouraged the admission of new, energetically active members, very different from those aristocratic gentlemen who had been on the board till then and who lived as recluses in their own homes, dreaming of the glories of yore while the town went on dying around them.

Only once a year did Santa Cruz allow itself to return to the past, and it was at carnival time. As far back as anyone could remember, Juan Ponce de León's carnival had been the preeminent social event of the town. King Momo, conga dancers, demons, and ogres could change costumes but would always remain the same; to take part in the carnival as one of these popular figures needed no special voucher, no official investigation as to family and ancestors. When it came to the select company of Juan Ponce de León's retinue, however, it was a different matter. To qualify for the role of gentleman, with the right to wear a breastplate, plumed casque, and foil, one had inevitably to be an Acuña, a Portalatini, or an Arzuaga. In the specific case of the queen, the central figure of the celebrations, the requisite of social decorum was considered to be almost sacred. For this reason a committee of worthy citizens was elected every year, who took pride in selecting an adequate sovereign.

Once the court was assembled, after careful consideration of all the candidates and a disputed voting campaign, the old aristocratic families would throw themselves body and soul into the proceedings, ready to astound once again the inhabitants of the town with the pageantry of their timeworn riches. Each year they would pick out a theme from colonial times, as for example the buccaneers of Sir Francis Drake, who had once boldly roved the island's coasts; or the tragic, unfortunate visit

Rosario Ferré

of Sir George Clifford, Count of Cumberland, to the fortress of El Morro, where he had lost seven hundred men before stealing the organ of the cathedral and the bells of all the churches of San Juan; or, as in the case of Carlotta's court, which was to be selected for the feasts of 1955, the heroic exploits of Christopher Columbus.

Perched as a child on her family's modest balustered balcony, Carlotta had been present at many of these carnivals. From it she had often admired the slow, stately carriages as they rolled before her house, heaped with calla lilies and roses and powdered with gold dust, on which rode the members of Juan Ponce de León's court, the children of the Acuñas, the Arzuagas, and the De la Valles, pitilessly distant in their disdain for the world and wrapped in their diamond-studded mantles like immemorial insects that anteceded history and defied the ravages of time.

Mother Artigas was wandering up and down the study-hall aisle at sewing class, keeping watch of the rhythmic rise and fall of the girls' needles as they flew like tiny silver darts in their hands, when she suddenly came to a stop. She noticed an aroma of roses nearby and, joining her hands severely under her shoulder cape, she carefully scrutinized the faces around her. She noticed that Merceditas's cheeks had suddenly become flushed, and she walked slowly up to her.

"Would you be so kind as to open your desk top?" she asked with a smile, leaning attentively toward her, but taking care that the fringe of her veil wouldn't graze the girl's shoulder.

Merceditas felt tempted to look at Carlotta, but she controlled herself. She fixed her gaze on the heavy black beads of the rosary that hung from Mother Artigas's waist. She lifted the lid slowly, exposing the desk's contents: books, soap dish, folding glass, sharpened pencils, blue apron, white veil and black veil, neatly rolled next to each other. Mother Artigas reached into it with her hand, as though pursuing, with the sense of smell transferred to the tips of her fingers, the scent of the Columbus's kidney. Her sense of direction was accurate: she lifted the black veil and there it was, round and exuberant, giving off its secret perfume in all directions. She gave her a surprised look, a smile still playing on her lips.

"It was a present from Carlotta, Mother; the committee offered it to

213

her on a silver platter at the luncheon where she was elected carnival queen. If you'd like to taste it, I'll slice you a piece."

She trusted that Mother Artigas would be lenient with her. She knew there was a law against bringing fruits into study hall, but it wasn't a serious offense.

"You did wrong to accept such a gift," whispered the nun haughtily. "Now you'll have to live with it until graduation day." And, turning her back on Merceditas, she walked rapidly away.

Mother Artigas's beauty had a great deal to do with the authority she wielded at the academy at the time. She had one of those translucent faces in which the lack of cosmetics emphasized the features' perfect harmony, and her exquisite breeding and courteous ways gave proof of her privileged upbringing. Tall and limber, she would appear in hallways and classrooms when it was least expected, and the students would all rise immediately and curtsy before her. Her black canvas half-boots, carefully dusted by the order's sisters at dawn, and her black gauze veil scented daily with lavender, seemed to be everywhere at all times, as her shadow could be seen gliding through the house like a mournful willow's.

In contrast to most of the other nuns, Mother Artigas had been born on the island, and because of her native upbringing it was considered she could deal more effectively than her companions with whatever problems of discipline the students might have, since she could understand them better. The girls were, after all, just ordinary misses from well-to-do families; but once they graduated, their social status would become something very different, since as alumnae of the Sacred Heart they had the right to expect the highest respect and esteem of the town.

Most of Mother Artigas's companions had been born in far-away foreign cities such as Valparaiso, Cali, and Buenos Aires. Their sad, polite manners, as well as their nervously fluttering eyelids, betrayed the reasons that had brought them to Santa Cruz, where they had taken refuge behind the solid colonial walls of their convent, trying to forget their own worlds in a small, anonymous Caribbean town. Under their tucked wimples they hid endless bitter disillusionments, romantic as well as economic, and their personal dramas were probably a symptomatic sampling of the difficulties Latin American patrician families were going through at the time. The landed aristocracy's tragic fate seemed to be sealed by industrial development, military dictatorships, and the gradual disintegration of a Latin American national consciousness among the new well-to-do.

Imprisoned in their memories, these nuns shunned an everyday reality that they found increasingly disagreeable, and they did their best to forget, through prayer and meditation, that they were living in a mediocre town inhabited by a people whose customs seemed so difficult to understand. Their entrance to the convent had been a hazardous enough ordeal, having had to raise two thousand dollars, the dowry one was obliged to bring to the altar as a bride of the Sacred Heart at the time, with great personal sacrifices. Once the wedding had taken place, they aspired only to the peace and forgetfulness they felt was their due, submitting without complaint to the strict rules of the convent, which required the virtues of silence, anonymity, and indifference to the world.

In their eyes, the girls that swarmed daily into their classrooms like restless swallows had neither face nor name, but were rather hosts of souls. They knew that, at any minute, they'd be forced to abandon them, since in obedience to the iron regulations of the Mother House in Rome, nuns were not allowed to remain in the same convent for more than three years. For this reason they saw them flock into their classrooms not as girls born in a particular country or educated in a specific cultural tradition, but as the daughters of all and of none; and they willingly surrendered the thorny duties of discipline and ethical instruction to Mother Artigas.

There was an additional circumstance that had conferred on Mother Artigas the mantle of authority in the nuns' eyes. It had been thanks to the generosity of the Artigas family, who thirty years ago had donated their old colonial palace to the Mother House in Rome, that the convent had been founded in Santa Cruz in the first place and that the privileged daughters of the town's bourgeoisie could study today at the Sacred Heart. Mother Artigas had an untiring amount of energy, and under her baton the school hummed like a well-trained orchestra. At dawn she'd already be standing at the kitchen door, ordering the sisters to baste, broil, and roast, with economy and wisdom, the simple fares that would be consumed at the convent during the course of the day. She'd also taken over the complicated duties of laundering and ironing the sacred altar linens as well as the girls' bed linen, taking scrupulous care that no fragment of the sacred host should fall carelessly among them; she personally supervised the starching of the nuns' dozens of veils and habits, ordering them to be dipped in lye once a month to prevent lice and vermin from multiplying inordinately, and hung out to dry on the roof under the noonday sun, so that from afar the convent often resembled Theseus's ship, with black sails unfurled by Caribbean winds. In short, she took care of everybody and of everything, and she would claim with pride that she did it all because the house was so close to her own heart.

Mother Artigas had had no difficulties in paying the dowry of two thousand dollars that made it possible to enter the order. Her family had been, and still was, one of the most powerful in the country, related to the De la Valles on her mother's side, and her parents had moved to the capital a long time ago. She had received an exceptional papal dispensation when she had taken her vows that exempted her from the cruel law of resettling every three years in a different country. To compensate she had promised herself, at the moment of becoming the bride of the Lord, when the priest was about to crown her head with the resplendent veil of chastity, to abide unfalteringly by the rest of the convent rules, casting off all human affection from her soul and tending only to that future moment of absolute happiness when she would be admitted into His embrace. She felt so deeply grateful for the privilege of remaining on the island that she swore she'd never fall victim to fond attachments, tendernesses, or endearments toward her fellow human beings, which became treacherous pitfalls of the will.

For this reason she regarded all display of emotion, all devoted attachments that might spring up among the girls, or between the nuns and the girls (the convent's sisters didn't count because they were of humble origin, and thus even though they cooked, ironed, and laundered, they were invisible to Mother Artigas), as a sort of scandal. In her eyes affection, devotedness, or even friendship were all suspect emotions that attempted against that sole union, perfect and irreversible, which would one day take place between the disciples of the Sacred Heart and their future husband on earth.

Since Mother Artigas had been named Corrector of Discipline, she had implanted a strict system of vigilance in the school. In every class-room, in every green-shuttered hallway, in every dusty path of the school's garden down which the students ambled at recess, she had posted an eagle-eyed, vigilant nun, whose black veil clouded all laughter and turned the girls' amicable conversation into frightened whispers. Her idea of discipline would change drastically, however, whenever she met Mer-ceditas Cáceres, for whom she felt a special fondness. Merceditas had been a model student during her three and a half years at the school, and this made her inordinately tolerant and understanding toward her. Mother Artigas held high hopes for her, and she liked to supervise her studies personally. She had had an extensive education and had acquired more than one doctoral degree at foreign universities. She believed that women had an undeniable right to knowledge, having been unjustly barred from it by men for centuries, and the only obstacle that for a while had made her hesitate on her decision to enter the convent had been the clergy's traditional feminization of ignorance. She herself had at one time wanted to become a writer and had played with the idea of challenging the social and literary conventions of her world that condemned women to silence or, what was worse, to euphemistic, romantic verses, chock full of ruby bleeding hearts, cooing love affairs, and lace-flounced babies, but that hadn't the slightest notion of history, politics, or science. She had by now renounced her fantasy of a literary life, but had stuck to her guns in certain aspects of it even after entering the convent. She thus had always displayed the utmost disdain for the joyless writing of mystical nuns, whose ultimate role was submission, and she never encouraged the students to read a sacred book, be it the *Imitation of Christ* or *Lives of the Saints*.

Mother Artigas would spend hours with Merceditas poring over books and explaining to her the most difficult problems of calculus, philosophy, and linguistics. She always insisted to her that learning could be a higher goal than bearing children and that discipline was thus a necessary evil, because it taught people to forgo the comforts of the body and the plea-sures of the senses for the good of the spirit. At these moments she insisted that the Greeks had only been half right, and that they would have earned themselves a lot of sorrow if their approach to life had been to have a Spartan mind in an Athenian soul. She therefore insisted that, in her future writing at least (Mother Artigas hoped that one day Merceditas would become a writer), she never accept the dictates of male authority and that, be it in politics, science, or the arts, she always look to her own heart.

Mother Artigas, in short, believed that the only way women could dedicate themselves to the pursuit of knowledge was by forgoing human love and dedicating themselves to the divine order of things. She was an ardent soul, inspired by the zeal of her vocation, and she often talked to Merceditas about the spiritual advantages of deserving a destiny similar to that of the Princess of Clèves. Her tongue was soft as silk, and her protégée loved to listen to her when she talked of spiritual things, feeling from time to time the urge to follow in her footsteps. Mother Artigas talked to her then of the Sacred Heart's "burning flame, in which the believer must purify his soul, before arriving at the divine union with God," and she encouraged her to alternate her studies with frequent visits to the school's chapel, where there were always pious ceremonies going on. For Mother Artigas, religious indifference was the most dangerous sin, because it landed the larger part of humanity in hell. Merceditas tried to heed her counsel, and she made a conscious effort to take part in the frequent novenas, rosaries, and benedictions that went on daily at the chapel. She even began going to communion at seven o'clock in the morning every first Friday of the month, because the nuns had assured her that whoever managed to do so for nine months in a row was guaranteed salvation, but she found it more and more difficult to remember, and when she arrived at the fifth or sixth month she inevitably forgot about it, and found herself sound asleep in bed. This inexplicable weakness became an obsession with her, and when the situation had recurred half a dozen times she had to face the possibility that perhaps she was not meant to be saved. Kneeling next to the other students at her bench in the chapel, she would then listen desperately to their whispered prayers and fervid chants, letting herself become faint under the clouds of incense and the perfume of the lilies that thronged the altar, only to arrive at the conclusion, wiping her bloodless brow, that if salvation couldn't be earned by doing good deeds but only by praying, she didn't stand a chance. They could torture her knees all they wanted but not her mind, because she couldn't stand being bored.

In spite of Merceditas's sincere admiration for Mother Artigas, something in the nun had always made her keep her distance. Perhaps it was the perfect beauty of her face or her exquisite manners at dinnertime, but the nun had always made her feel a certain apprehension. Since Carlotta's arrival at the school a year before, moreover, Mother Artigas had shown herself more reticent in her expressions of affection, as though she resented the fact that Merceditas now had a close friend. For all of these reasons, during her three and a half years at the convent Merceditas had hovered like a moth around the nun's incandescent allure, feeling at times attracted and at times repelled by her presence.

Thus she wasn't really surprised at Mother Artigas's cold tone of reproach on the morning she discovered Carlotta's mango hidden in her desk. She kept quiet, and she did exactly as she was told. She laid the fruit at an angle at the end of the writing table, so that the drops of syrup that ran down its skin wouldn't stain the other objects that were kept there. At first Merceditas didn't quite understand the extent of her punishment and she reveled in the fruit's aroma, which seemed to her an unmerited reward. She would look at it from the corner of her eye as she wrote her assignments, read, or sewed, secretly enjoying the fact that the mango reminded her of her friend, and finding a funny resemblance between its heart-shaped, golden silhouette and Carlotta's burnished cheeks.

The fact that Carlotta Rodriguez was elected carnival queen didn't take anyone in Santa Cruz by surprise that year, with the exception of the nuns of the Sacred Heart. Don Agapito's influence had already spread to wider circles, and several of his friends had been elected committee members of Juan Ponce de León's feasts. Carlotta, on the other hand, had always dreamed of being carnival queen, and she jumped at the chance she was being offered. A few days after her appointment Don Agapito came to the convent and asked the nuns to give Carlotta permission to leave the school every afternoon from three to six, so she could attend to her carnival duties.

Once scepter and orb were held firmly in hand, Carlotta threw herself into the planning of the feasts. She met daily with her aides at the casino, from where she announced, as part of the updating of the celebration, that from then on the students of all public and private schools, and not only the children of the bourgeois families of Santa Cruz, could participate in the carnival ceremonies. Everything went well and a good number of boys and girls, many of them the children of Don Agapito's friends, had begun to turn up at the casino's door, asking to be admitted to this or that cortege, when Carlotta's enthusiasm for the celebrations began to make her feel the arrangements were inadequate, and that enough wasn't being done.

Set on giving the occasion an even greater luster and a truly international renown, she decreed that there be not just one but three parade floats for her retinue to ride in, which were to be built according to the exact measurements of Christopher Columbus's galleons, the *Pinta,* the *Niña,* and the *Santa María,* and which were to slide over a runner of blue silk that was to be laid down all along Ponce de León Avenue, bordering the harbors of the capital like a streak of ice next to a wind-tossed sea. She took it upon herself to supervise the opulent decoration of the costumes to be worn by her entourage, and she designed her own queenly robes herself, for which it would be necessary to melt several trunkfuls of coins worth a pirate's ransom. She ordered, on the other hand, to give the carnival a more popular appeal, that the orchestras play only guaracha and mambo, banishing the stiff cadences of the *danza* and the waltz to the depths of Lethe; and she commanded that the food that was to be served at the feasts should all be of Creole confection, perfumed with thyme, laurel leaf, and coriander, and braised in the ancient wisdom of kinki fritters gilded in lard. The coronation ceremony, which was to take place after the traditional two-orchestra ball, would not be celebrated within the revered hall of mirrors of the casino but in the middle of the town plaza, where Carlotta had ordered her throne be set up.

When Carlotta's plans became known, Don Agapito's enemies, the old aristocratic families of the town, began to complain that the carnival was turning into a grotesque affair and that it was no longer the elegant social event that it had been in the past. Their dignity wounded because their children's surnames would not be paged out loud at the casino's doors at the beginning of the ball, and horrified to think that they would have to parade down Ponce de León Avenue in their jeweled attire, easy prey to street hoodlums and an envious rabble, they began to take them out of the corteges and forbid them to participate in the celebrations.

When Carlotta realized that her courtiers were abandoning her and that the carnival would have to be canceled if not enough young people participated in it, she immediately took action. She had the walls of the town plastered with edicts that announced that, from that day on, not just the children from the Sacred Heart, from Saint Ignatius's, and from the French Lycée were invited to the carnival, but *all* the young people of the town, whether they could afford to go to school or not. The very next day a motley crowd of suspiciously bedraggled courtiers and duennas began to mob the casino's doors, gentlemen and ladies decked out in cardboard cuirasses, tin-foil crowns, and crepe-paper trains who had begun to pour out of the town's ramshackle slums, as well as from its impoverished middle-class suburbs, and they were all admitted into Carlotta's court.

At the convent Mother Artigas had finally succeeded in a campaign to expel Carlotta Rodriguez from the Sacred Heart as soon as possible. She argued that Carlotta's behavior in the carnival's planned activities was an insult not only to the school but to the social class to which she so desperately wished to belong and for which she was carefully being groomed. The debate had been a prolonged affair, which had taken place behind closed doors in the impregnable secrecy of the cloister. At first the nuns had refused to listen to Mother Artigas's arguments because they were concerned with the adverse economic consequences they would have to face if Don Agapito were to withdraw his generous subsidy to the school. They reminded Mother Artigas that the world had changed drastically in the last ten years, and they insisted that the school's requirements for admission be flexible enough to accept the fact that Santa Cruz's society was in a state of flux, so that today's nobodies might be tomorrow's dons. They mistakenly believed, furthermore, that Mother Artigas's scruples against Carlotta were based on moral grounds, and that she had been scandalized by the daring design of her queenly robes, which had been recently published in the town newspaper, and thus they had tried to humor her out of her old-fashioned prudery, pointing out the fact that today the students of the Sacred Heart all wore plunging necklines at parties, innocently baring breasts and displaying their legs under the sweeping, bell-like crinolines of Luisa Alfaro and Rosenda Matienzo, the town's most fashionable designers.

Mother Artigas's arguments for expelling Carlotta, however, were devastating and final. She pointed out to her companions that Don Agapito's behavior in the feasts' arrangements had left much to be desired, and that he was indulging his daughter in an uncalled-for Asiatic splendor, spending an extravagant amount of money on her wardrobe and on her orphaned court. As a result of such excesses she had heard that his business, a chain of local supermarkets called the Golden Galleon, would soon be declared bankrupt. The nuns discussed between themselves, in frightened whispers, the ominous implications of such a scandal, and concluded that Don Agapito's economic ruin could bring about a serious loss of the academy's credibility in banking circles, as well as its eventual disrepute. Faced with these possibilities, the nuns voted unanimously to expel Carlotta Rodriguez from school. This was to be done as prudently as possible, as soon as Don Agapito returned from a trip abroad of several weeks. Carlotta would be sent home for a few days, with the excuse that the recent feverish round of activities had made her look peaked, extending her absence until it became final for reasons of health.

It's probable that nothing extraordinary would have happened and that Carlotta's expulsion would have gone practically unnoticed if it hadn't been for the striking metamorphosis she underwent at the time. She had always abided by the convent's rules in dress and appearance, so that when she walked in the study hall with her face smeared with makeup for the first time, the nun who was patrolling the hallways thought it was a joke. She quietly called her aside and asked her if she wasn't rehearsing for her role as carnival queen somewhat prematurely, and ordered her to go to the bathroom to scrub her face.

Carlotta obeyed without complaint and returned to her desk with face sparkling clean. But meekness could become, in her case, a powerful weapon, as is often the case with gentle souls. As soon as she found herself alone the next day at recess, she took out a stick of mascara, a lipstick, and a tube of heavy pancake makeup, and applied them generously to her face. Her features, shaded by the thick layers of paint, acquired a grotesque aspect that, as Carlotta later told Merceditas, laughing, was in character with the savage nature of the mestizo women with whom Juan

Ponce de León probably fell in love. It was because she was their direct descendant that she painted her face with burned coal, corozo nut oil, and the juice of the achiote seed, to test the courage of those not yet respectful of the island's way of life. She had piled her hair on top of her head in a wild cathedral of curls and thus ambled absentmindedly among the students, adorned with bracelets and necklaces that jangled on her white organdy blouse with heretic dismay.

Wherever Carlotta went there was laughter and fingers pointing her way, so that the school was in a constant turmoil. The nuns tried everything in their power to put a stop to this, but to no avail. Carlotta proved equally indifferent to rebuffs and reprimands, and continued smearing her face with paint and adorning herself like a harlot. Since her father was still away, moreover, she couldn't be sent home to stay. It was at this point that Mother Artigas decided to intervene, forbidding everyone in the school from talking to Carlotta, under pain of expulsion.

Final exams were drawing near and Merceditas had begun to prepare herself in earnest. She needed to concentrate more than ever on her daily tasks in order to graduate with honors, but she found it difficult to accomplish. She was always keeping an eye on her friend, who would spend her days silently ambling down the school's corridors, naive and graceless as ever and with her face now disfigured by layers of horrid makeup, and it seemed to her Carlotta was trying to prove something she couldn't understand.

Although she didn't dare to defy Mother Artigas's prohibition by talking to her in public, Merceditas would always save her a space next to her at the dining-room table and the chapel bench, and did her best to prevent the other girls from pushing her out of the school games at recess. Carlotta behaved as though nothing extraordinary was going on. She kept silent whenever she was ill treated, and smiled good-naturedly at everyone, even when she was denied permission to go to the bathroom or to have a drink of water.

"I'd like to know why you're doing this, the point of the harebrained hairdo, of the stuff smeared on your face," Merceditas said to her one day when they were far enough away from the watchnun not to be overheard. "Why the gypsy bangles, the whore's love beads, the floozie rings?" She was angry at her friend, but she didn't dare mention the rumors of expulsion that were flying around the school. She hoped Carlotta hadn't heard them, because she couldn't believe they were true.

Her questions went unanswered, and her friend's silence was magnified by the screams of the girls playing volleyball nearby. A shadow of resentment crossed Carlotta's face, but she soon got over her dispirited mood.

"As soon as Father returns from his trip I'll be going home," she said gaily. "You have no idea how many things still have to be done before my coronation! But I promise I'll come back to see you graduate."

Merceditas pretended she hadn't heard her. She had always thought that if Carlotta was expelled she'd leave school, but now she knew she didn't have the courage. She just couldn't leave after so many years of struggle. After all, Carlotta seemed to be taking everything in stride and not letting the disgraceful events get her down.

"If you come see me graduate, I'll go see you crowned," she said to her gamely, but without looking into her eyes.

Merceditas began to realize the full implications of Mother Artigas's delayed sentence around that same time, three weeks after it had been enforced. The fruit, which at first had so delighted her, had begun to turn color, and had passed from an appetizing golden brown to a bloody purple. It no longer made her think of Carlotta's smiling cheeks, but of a painfully battered face. Sitting before it during her long hours of study, she couldn't help being aware of the slow changes that came over its skin, which became thick and opaque like a huge drop of blood. It was as though the whole palette of colors in the passage from life to death had spilled over the fruit, staining it with cruel misgivings.

The thought of the fruit began to follow her everywhere, like the cloud of insects that flew about it at noontime, when the heat became unbearable. She'd think of it at recess, at breakfast and dinner, but when she saw it most vividly was before going to sleep at night, when she lay down on her iron cot at the dormitory. She'd look then at the ghostly reflections of the canvas curtains separating her sleeping alcove from that of Carlotta's, swinging heavily in the moonlit breeze; she'd look at the white pewter washbowl and at the water jug standing on the night table; she'd look at the black tips of the lookout's boots posted behind the breathing curtains, which reminded her of a snout in ambush, and she could hear, in the still of the night, the mango's slowly beating heart.

At that time Merceditas also began to notice a strange odor whenever she walked into a classroom or when she stood in one of the school's winding corridors waiting to be summoned by the nuns. It surprised her that she was holding her breath at breakfast, before the cup of fragrant hot chocolate the sisters served her every morning; when she knelt on her bench at the back of the chapel; even when she was taking a shower. It was an uneven smell, and it reached her at unexpected moments, when she was least thinking about it. Carlotta had noticed it, too, and had asked Merceditas if she knew where it came from, but she hadn't been able to answer. They had agreed, however, that it seemed to become stronger whenever a nun was nearby, as if the smell had a mysterious association with the morbid exuberance of their veils.

It was Carlotta's cheap perfume that brought Merceditas out of the dangerous melancholic state she was in, on the day Don Agapito was supposed to come to pick her up at the school. She stopped reading and looked at her friend in surprise. It was strictly forbidden to change seats at study-hall time, but Carlotta behaved as if rules had ceased to exist. Made up and scented like a street tart, she sat at the desk next to hers and, instead of whispering, began to talk in a normal tone of voice. The lookout's furious glance and the neighboring students' mutterings left her unmoved.

"Are you coming to say good-bye? Father's downstairs waiting in the car, and everything's ready. I just have to go up to my room to get my suitcase. If you like, you can help me bring it down."

Her voice was steady but her cheeks were trembling slightly under the heavy coat of makeup.

"All right; I'll go with you," answered Merceditas as she put away her book and swiftly lowered the lid of her desk, to prevent her friend from noticing its tomblike aspect. She went out to the corridor and Carlotta stayed behind a few minutes, to say good-bye to several of her classmates. She peered out sadly through the green-louvered windows at the court-yard, and wondered what Carlotta would do now that she wouldn't finish high school. She told herself that perhaps it wouldn't make much difference, and that knowing Carlotta, she'd probably find something in which to make herself useful in no time at all. Her friend lived in a world in which action was what mattered, action that eased other people's sufferings in particular; while she lived in a world of thought. All week she had dreaded the moment of saying good-bye, but now that it had come she felt almost relieved, convinced that her departure was for the better. She felt sad, and she knew she probably wouldn't see Carlotta again for a long time, but she welcomed the thought of having peace reign once more at the school, so she could go back to studying. Above all, she'd be free from the ominous feeling she'd had all week, that something terrible was going to happen to her.

They went up the spiral staircase together and quietly entered the senior dormitory on the third floor. Carlotta took her suitcase out from under the bed and emptied her drawers into it, stuffing in everything as fast as possible. She talked constantly about trivial matters, and her voice had a defiant ring to it, as though willfully breaking the silence that enshrouded the room. Carlotta's voice had a strange effect on Merceditas, who had been used to talking in whispers and walking on the dormitory floorboards always on tiptoe. She looked at what surrounded her as though seeing it for the first time: the heavy canvas curtains, now drawn back toward the walls to ventilate the room, revealed to her how near her own bed had been to her friend's, and hers to those of the other boarders. The night table, the water basin and the jug, the crucifix and the chamber pot, repeated again and again the length of the room as if reflected in a double mirror, made her feel everything was happening in a dream.

Talking and laughing at the same time, they picked up the suitcase between them and began the long trek to the school's main entrance on the first floor. Taking each other by the arm, they flew down the spiral stairs and, a few minutes later, were crossing the green-louvered dormitories of second and third year on the second floor. Once on ground level, they passed the laundry rooms and Merceditas saw the sisters bending over their ironing boards and cement sinks full of suds, pressing and scrubbing altar cloths and bedsheets; they passed the chapel and she saw several of her classmates kneeling in their benches amid clouds of incense, monotonously repeating the same chants and prayers. She saw classrooms, corridors, cloisters, classmates all fly by as from a great distance. Carlotta walked calmly beside her, as though she had managed to rise above everything. She went on talking animatedly to Merceditas, and reminded her of the date when the carnival's feasts would begin. She had never mentioned the true reason for her departure, and she insisted she was grateful for the opportunity to devote herself entirely to her coronation duties.

They were walking now more rapidly, crossing through the galleries that opened onto the main classrooms, when Merceditas gave a sigh of relief. She hadn't even considered how she was going to feel after Carlotta had left and she would be without a single friend at the school, but she didn't want to think about that now. Her sole concern was that they hadn't met anyone hiding behind the classroom doors or lying in wait behind the corridor's shuttered windows to fling insults at her as she went by. The girls were all bent over their books or listening intently to their teachers, and they didn't even turn around to look at them. She had almost begun to believe her forebodings were wrong and that Carlotta would finally be permitted to leave in peace, and she already saw herself saying good-bye to her at the school's entrance hall, when the smell reached her again. She stopped in her tracks and put her hand on Carlotta's arm. They saw them at the same time, standing together in a half circle and crouching under their somber veils, obstructing the way to the door.

Mother Artigas stepped forward and disengaged herself from the other nuns. Her feet slid softly over the slate-tiled floor, and as she did so her gauze veil billowed around her like an overcast cloud. Her face, framed by her wimple's snowy curves, seemed to Merceditas more beautiful than ever, as though she were looking out at her through a skylight. She was smiling, but her smile was an icy wound on her face.

Merceditas let go of Carlotta's suitcase and warned her to put it slowly on the ground. It was then that she noticed Mother Artigas's long Spanish scissors, whose sparkling steel blades she had confused in the hallway's opaque light with those of the crucifix she wore on her chest; and that she saw the second nun, half-hidden behind Mother Artigas's headdress, take a firm step toward Carlotta, holding in her hands a white porcelain basin. Everything that came later seemed to Merceditas to happen in a dream.

She saw Carlotta's silky curls begin to fall, still warm and perfumed, on the floor, and that Carlotta wouldn't budge; she saw Mother Artigas's alabaster-white hands and arms, bare up to the elbows for the first time, clipping her friend's head until she was sheared like a sheep, and still Carlotta wouldn't budge; she saw her take the sponge the acolyte handed to her and dip it in the purplish foam of the basin, which had a pungent smell, and she still wouldn't budge; she saw her wipe her face with it slowly, almost tenderly, until the heroic features that Carlotta had drawn over her own began to fade, erasing her lips and eyebrows, the eyelashes she had so painfully glued to her lids one by one, her poppy-red cheeks and her passion-flower eyes, and still she wouldn't budge.

Struck dumb like a statue, Merceditas listened to what Mother Artigas was saying; to the stream of curses that flew out of her mouth in whipping flurries, lashing her friend with a veritable maelstrom of insults. She was screaming the dirtiest swear words she had ever heard in her life, such as "Just who do you think you are, you filthy nigger, you're not good enough to be one of the convent's cooks and you want to be carnival queen, stuck up on your throne like a mud-smeared blackamoor, like the glorified idol of the rabble's most vulgar dreams! Cursed be the day you first set foot in our school! Damn the very hour when they brought you here to be educated, dishonoring as you have done the holy image of our Sacred Heart!"

As she spoke, Mother Artigas tore at Carlotta's uniform, ripping it apart with her nails while she rained slaps and cuffs at her bent head. Carlotta, who in her panic had kept the suitcase clutched in her hand, let go of it at last, and lifted her arms to protect herself from the shower of blows. The case fell open, spilling its contents all over the floor. Merceditas stared at the jumble of clothes, shoes, and books thrown at her feet and finally understood everything. She approached Mother Artigas slowly and stopped her next blow in midair. Mother Artigas turned toward her in surprise, not so much because she had intervened but because she had dared lay a hand on her.

"That's enough, Mother," she heard herself say.

Mother Artigas took two steps backward and looked at Merceditas with all the hate she was capable of. Carlotta stood between them, her head trounced like a billard ball and her blouse slashed in such a way that her bruised flesh showed through everyplace. She was crying silently, like a huge beaten creature. Merceditas drew near to her and slid an arm over her shoulders.

"You know what I'm thinking?" she said with a smile. "I appreciate your good intentions, but it really wasn't necessary. You didn't have to take my punishment home with you, because now we know for sure where the smell was coming from." And bending down, she searched in the huddle of clothes on the floor and came up with a stinking, ulcerated object, which dripped a mournful, tarlike liquid on all its sides.

"Here it is, Mother," she said, curtsying before Mother Artigas for the last time. "Here's your Sacred Heart. It's my gift to you."

PERMISSIONS